# PARDON FALLS

## PHOENIX BOOK 2

## KIMBERLY PACKARD

abalos
publishing

Abalos Publishing
P.O. Box 333
Colleyville, TX  76034

Book cover designed by okay creations.
The text in this book is set in Baskerville.
Library of Congress Cataloging-in-Publication Data
Available Upon Request

ISBN-13 Print: 978-0-9992015-2-7

ISBN-13 Ebook: 978-0-9992015-3-4

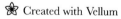 Created with Vellum

# ALSO BY KIMBERLY PACKARD

*For my Parents*
*They saw the author in me and nurtured her*

# 1

Even though she'd been paddling across this calm part of the Rio Grande to Mexico for the past several weeks, Amanda Martin waited, holding her breath, listening for sounds other than the tinkling of the river.

The nose of the canoe collided with the shore, and she checked the depth of the river with her paddle, convincing herself the murky water wouldn't fill her rain boots.

She pulled the boat into tall, bamboo-like weeds to camouflage it, the blades of leaves grasping her bare shoulders like the fingers of the dead. Despite the triple digit heat, goosebumps erupted on her arms.

Amanda emerged and waded through sandy gravel lining the floor of the small canyon. The permanent shadow of the walls made her feel like she was ensconced in a womb, birthing her from the relative safety of far south Texas to the cartel-ruled northern Mexico. Unlike her actual birth and childhood, she was *not* the dutiful daughter who followed her parents' rules without question.

In this life, she was an orphan.

Forced on her journey alone.

Sunlight and heat welcomed her into Mexico. A man stood next to an old pickup, puffing on a cigarette. They exchanged no words; she pulled a faded, worn map from the back pocket of her shorts, pointed at a lone town sitting south of a field of black *X's* and handed him several crumpled *pesos*.

He nodded and tossed the stub of his cigarette.

She hopped in the back of his truck, the sun-scorched metal scalding the back of her legs as she settled between an old woman with cataract-glazed eyes and a young couple, the girl clutching her pregnant belly and breathing through her mouth. Her eyes darted around the packed truck bed, looking to make contact with anyone who seemed perplexed by an American woman sneaking into an area where most people fled, but the lack of acknowledgment made her feel like a ghost.

"The haystack is getting smaller, Josh," Amanda murmured to the rumpled map in her hands before tilting her face to the sun.

The gentle rocking of the old junker relaxed her as the tires dipped and rose on the rutted out dirt road like a ship meeting the waves at sea. Down, left, up. Right, up, down.

Sleep was a luxury she could no longer afford, but with the heat, the rocking, the exhaustion, her eyelids made the impulse buy.

The pickup lurched to a stop, jolting her awake. The young couple climbed over her. Everyone scooted around, spreading out and claiming more space before the driver shot forward again.

They went further south. Away from the river, the landscape quickly dried out under the harsh sun. Meager farms fought the encroaching desert. A snaggletoothed windmill stood sentry over an abandoned farmhouse. Buzzards circled off in the desert and a few on the ground fought over a lump of clothes. Amanda tried to rip her gaze away from the savage scenery, but they were frozen, watching as scavengers devoured the last of someone's brother, sister, father, child.

*Would my family find me in a similar state?*

She shuddered.

The truck rumbled by a grove of graves. Crude crosses constructed with sticks and string, the last testaments of someone's demise at the hand of the man who was the unofficial ruler of this part of Mexico.

She'd slipped in and out of this territory many times. Each successful trip home was one step closer to getting caught. It was a risk worth taking to clear her name, and make Josh face the consequences for the crimes he'd framed her for.

A knock on the back glass of the truck jolted her upright.

"*Gringa*, I pick you up. One hour, okay?" The driver leaned out his open window.

She didn't know his name and he didn't know hers. In an area ruled by drug cartels, anonymity sheltered everyone.

"*Muchas gracias.*" Amanda hopped down, her sweaty feet sliding inside her rubber boots. Tennis shoes would've been so much more practical.

*With my luck I'd pick up one of those flesh-eating bacteria and waste away before finding Josh's sorry ass.*

The town was small. Population seemed to be even smaller.

Three young boys ran past her, a soccer ball bouncing between them and a skinny dog yelping in delight. It was easy to find her first stop. The gray-green bricks of the town's Catholic Church stood out against the rust-brown landscape.

Outside in the town, she was vulnerable, but crossing the threshold of the church she felt the safety of a lost child found by another mother. The panic was still there, but at a lower volume that allowed her to think.

The air inside was markedly cooler, but a warm embrace wrapped around her as soon as she crossed herself. Incense tickled her nose. A soft rustling echoed through the cathedral.

The priest must be preparing for Mass.

She dropped *pesos* in the offering box, the clanging ricocheting off the walls. Kneeling in front of the candles, Amanda cleared her mind of all thoughts except the memory.

Josh had been avoiding her, and this time she'd catch him cheating. His office was empty. The heavy wooden desk sat devoid of its usual stacks of files and papers, except for a lone manila folder.

She flipped it open and her eyes grazed the boarding pass to El

Paso. She squinted, wishing she had a few moments to flip through the rest of the folder before her boyfriend appeared in his doorway, and began his escape from the SEC.

Her memory skipped ahead, to the image of Liz lying dead on the floor. But, her eyes never escaped that visual, as if it were a mental flogging for her part in Josh's crimes, assaulting her.

A year after parking outside a private investigator's office in El Paso, Amanda returned to that night so often, scanning her brain for another detail from her last night in Chicago that would lead her to her ex.

She hadn't expected it to take so long to find him. Hadn't expected to use the last of her stolen money to sneak *into* Mexico. Hadn't expected thorns to pierce her heart every time she thought of David, the man she'd fallen in love with during a two-month stop in the small town of Phoenix, Texas.

Like the Biblical Jonah, she could only run from the whale for so long. David had thrown her overboard so it was time to face her true purpose.

Turning both Josh and herself in.

Amanda brushed the tears from her cheeks before bowing her head, her lips moved along with her silent prayer.

*Please God, forgive me of my sins. Grant me strength to continue this mission. Give me wisdom and guidance to find him. Show me patience as I try to right all of my wrongs. I don't deserve your protection, but please watch over me. And, David …*

She gnawed on her lower lip. There was so much more she wanted to say, but words would weaken what was in her heart. She mumbled through her prayer a second time, but the feeling of someone staring at her pierced her shoulder blades and her eyes flew open.

"Amen," she gasped, crossing herself and hurrying down the aisle and out of the church. Amanda headed for her second stop; the town bar.

The few Spanish phrases she'd learned proved useful, but it was difficult to pick up more than a couple of words in each conversation. For all she knew, Josh could've been found weeks ago, if her language skills were stronger.

"*Hola, como esta?*" she called to a man wiping down the bar. "*Habla Ingles?*"

The man glared his answer.

*Damn, why can't this just be easy?*

She pulled the picture of Josh from her pocket. It was getting soft around the edges and the paper was wavy from near-constant sweat. She cleared her throat, going over the words in her head before embarrassing herself. "*Estoy buscando a este hombre.*" Amanda slid the picture across the bar, but the man turned his back on her and busied himself with something that didn't involve talking to an American woman with bad pronunciation.

She tapped her finger on the bar, loud enough to remind him she was there but also to tick off a minute. "*Señor, por favor, él es mi novio,*" she said, picking her way through the words. She didn't know how to say 'scum-sucking ex-boyfriend' in Spanish, so she just settled on his previous title.

The bartender walked away and didn't return.

Amanda fumbled through the same exchange with a group of men clustered around a mechanic's shop.

These men actually took the time to listen to her and look at the picture, but their shaking heads indicated that she'd likely put another black *X* over this town.

A blast of cool air from a rotating fan greeted her when she entered the *supermercado*. She paused at the open door of a cooler, holding her long hair off her neck, letting the sweat dry in chilling relief. A welcomed shiver rocked her body and she grabbed a bottle of mineral water and stood in line with a few *pesos* in hand.

A pretty young woman smiled shyly at her under long dark lashes when it was her turn to check out.

"*Hola, como esta?*" Amanda asked.

"*Bien,*" the girl answered. "*Y tu?*"

*Hot, thirsty, frustrated, exhausted. Lonely.*

She unveiled one of her well-practiced-win-them-over smiles normally saved for grouchy investors or cynical media. "*Bien.*" She pulled the picture of Josh out and held it out to her. "*Mi novio. ¿Él está aquí?*"

The young woman froze and sucked in a sharp breath before her gaze began flitting around the small market.

"You know him. *Por favor.*" Her voice fell to a whisper. "*Ayuadame.*"

The woman dropped change in Amanda's hands and leaned forward. "You must not ask about him. Not here, not anywhere." Her English was heavily accented.

She grabbed the girl's wrist, refusing to let go of the only lead for Josh. "Is he here? Have you seen him? Where can I find him?"

"He works for *Señor* Vargas. You will not find."

Her heart sped up. Josh was real, alive, close.

*Mine.*

"No, please you don't understand. I *have* to find him," Amanda's throat burned with desperate sobs. "Where can I find Vargas? Please anything."

The girl's skin went cold in her grasp. "Go. Now." She jerked her wrist back and her eyes darted toward a woman approaching the checkout.

The cashier ended the conversation, but Amanda refused to move.

An older woman nudged her out of the way and carried on her transaction.

More questions stacked up on her tongue, waiting for a weak spot in the wall the girl constructed between them, but a tap on her shoulder made her jump.

"You were not waiting." Her driver stood before her, puffing on a fresh cigarette. "You do not want to be here after dark, *gringa.*"

The back of the truck was empty during her early evening ride back. Amanda stretched her legs; her feet grew cold in the boots even though the heat of the day lingered.

The name Vargas wasn't new to Amanda, and it was the only lead that connected Josh with El Paso. As one of her ex's private clients, she knew nothing about him other than he was a VIP investor. Fear and elation curled around each other and settled in her stomach. The cashier's reaction should steer her away, but *finally*, after weeks of marking *X's* over Mexican villages, she circled the town she just visited with weary satisfaction.

*Here. He's here.*

She relished her victory with two stabs and a slash of her pen, adding a smiley face in the circle.

The sun hung low by the time her ride bumped along the dirt road back at the river. Her chauffeur leaned out of the window when she jumped out.

"I'll be back in two days," he called.

"I'll be here. *Muchas gracias.*" Amanda couldn't hide her excitement, as much as she tried to lower her voice and slow her words, her body betrayed her. It was high on hope, a drug she hadn't had a hit of in a very long time.

The girl might not have wanted to talk to her today, but she knew the power of pleasant persistence. She hadn't traveled this far and lose everything—including David—to let Josh slip through her fingers again.

He was hers.

It didn't matter who stood between them. They'd either get out of her way or get knocked down.

She jogged back through the dark canyon, shadows so thick that she reached out in front of her to avoid running head first into a rock.

On the other side, the gray twilight of evening settled over the calm river like a cool blanket. Her canoe waited where she'd left it. A quick check to make sure nothing with fangs, pinchers or poison stowed away, and Amanda pushed off the bank to paddle the fifteen strokes directly across the river.

Eager to be back on U.S. soil with enough light to secure the boat in her Bronco, she hopped out a moment too soon and water rushed into her boots. Her shoulders tensed, she could feel tiny bacteria invading her pores. "Crap," she mumbled, inhaling deeply to calm her nerves.

With a hold on the canoe, she tugged it up the shore. At the sound of a click, she held her breath and paused, squinting into the near darkness.

The only sound she heard was the lapping of the river. She took two more steps.

Three other clicks assaulted the air and bright lights battered her eyes.

"U.S. Border Patrol. Put your hands up."

The bow landed on her foot, causing a tidal wave of river water to splash her leg. Amanda shielded her eyes to try to see beyond the blinding light, but the command echoed.

"Both hands up. Now."

"Shit."

## 2

Amanda laid her head on the table but jerked upright as soon as her forehead hit the cold metal. How long had they had her in this room? Her butt tingled from the awkward angle of the uncomfortable chair and her toes were icicles inside her damp rain boots.

This had to be some sort of police brutality.

White-painted cinderblock walls stared back at her, neither foretelling her fate nor the time. She expected them to sweat answers out of her, but in south Texas, they employed air conditioning as the weapon of choice.

Agent Burns, the man who'd barked orders at her and the younger men in his wake, walked into the room with two steaming Styrofoam cups and a folder tucked under his arm. "Thought you might like something to warm you up." He set the cups on the table before taking the chair across from her. Burns scowled as he flipped open the folder to an empty page, seeming to take on the role of good cop and bad cop simultaneously. "See this piece of paper here?" he drawled, a pen poised in his right hand and his left stabbing down at the blank page. "This is how much information you've given us about yourself in the six hours since we brought you in."

Amanda crossed her arms and leaned back against the gray metal chair, commanding her body to suppress shivers from the cold. "It's appropriate, considering you've told me nothing about why I'm here."

"Miss ..." His face hardened. "You see, right there we have a problem because you refuse to tell me your name. Miss whoever-the-hell-you-are, *you* are in no position to take an attitude with me."

"I'm not some criminal you can scare into compliance." She shot up from the chair. Blood drained from her brain to fill the veins in her butt, clouding her vision with stars. "Unless I'm being charged, I'm going home."

"Well, I'm glad to know who you're not." Burns didn't lift his eyes. "But if you don't sit your ass down it won't matter what your name is, you'll just be an inmate number."

Amanda fell to her chair as her heart took the plunge on the first hill of a roller coaster, pulling G's as it sped up around a curve.

The agent was right.

Sitting in a stark interrogation room loomed on her horizon like a jagged mountain, far enough away that it was always out of reach, but close enough to cast a shadow. Despite who she was before, who she became since and who she was today, in the end she would just be known as a number.

Sneaking in and out of Mexico was the least of her crimes, but it would be the one to get her caught. Images of a gunman in Chicago and the dead bodies of her colleagues flickered behind Burns' head, like another story trying to bleed into this one.

The steam from the stale coffee in front of her wafted to her nose, but it smelled more like the acrid smell of burned flesh. In just a little more than a year, Amanda had lost everything.

Her career, her family, even her new life in Phoenix and the love of a really good man. Losing her freedom while trying to find the person who caused the contagion of harm seemed fitting.

"I see that got your attention."

"Do you interrogate everyone who canoes down the Rio Grande?"

"We saw you come across it. It's illegal to enter this country outside of a checkpoint."

"You found nothing in my canoe, right? Or, my car. It's not what you think," she said.

"And, you carried no valid ID. Put yourself in *my* seat and tell me what you see."

Amanda took a long drink of her coffee, hoping the warmth of the bitter liquid would prevent her from outwardly blanching. Her purse, with her fake ID tucked inside, stayed home during her journeys into Mexico. If she were caught by the cartels, it'd be better for no one to know of her demise. Getting caught by the good guys had never figured into her equation.

Burns leaned back and laced his fingers at the back of his head. His dark green eyes narrowed to study her. She could see his assessment of her in his face; a fair-skinned young woman, who despite her cheap tank top, worn cut-off jeans, and rubber rain boots carried herself like she was in control of a boardroom. Amanda didn't fit his image of a strung-out junky crossing into Mexico for discount drugs. There was more to her story, and by the gleam in his eyes, he was eager to crack open the book.

"My name's Mandy," she said. "I answered your question. Can I go, please?"

His pen moved across the page and Burns looked up from under his dark brow. "Not quite. Now tell me why you were coming across the river rather than down it."

"I needed to use the bathroom and the weeds on the south shore offered more privacy than on the Texas side."

The officer expelled an I-don't-get-paid-enough-for-this sigh, sat his pen down and stared her down. "Now, little lady, you and I both know that's bullshit." His face grew red and he stabbed the air with his pen. "You asked if you were under arrest, the answer is *not yet*, but I can damn sure make that happen." He slapped the folder shut and his chair screeched as it scooted back against the linoleum floor.

The whole room shook as he slammed the door behind him. Once he was out of the room, the strength in her shoulders melted and her forehead fell to the table in a *clunk*.

"Good job, Martin," she whispered as she gently beat her forehead on the metal. "One step forward, one landing-on-your-butt-in-jail backwards."

Six hours.

That was how long they had her. Her landlord and boss, Elridge Calchera, would be sufficiently freaked out by now. And, had likely called Hank.

*Hank will turn fifty shades of red when he finds out.*

The thought of her private investigator's reprimand launched another wave of head thumping. Intoxicated by impatience, Amanda had ignored Hank Snare's repeated requests to leave the case to him. With each day that ticked by, she could feel Josh slipping further away, taking her resolve with him.

She couldn't lose her determination. Finding Josh was her only companion in life. Without it, all she had left was loneliness, fear and loss.

Amanda sat up with a start as the heavy door flung open, blinking at the harsh fluorescent light glaring down at her.

Burns filled the doorway, scowling, but relief relaxed the tense muscles around his eyes.

Rubbing her eyes and stretching her arms in front of her did little to shake awake her groggy brain cells. The cinderblocks gave no indication how long she'd slept, but it wasn't enough.

"Well, *Mandy*," the officer said, putting extra emphasis on her name as if he didn't believe it was real. "This is your lucky day. Your uncle came to vouch for you."

She opened her mouth to ask who, but a yawn interfered, giving El a moment to peek around Burns' broad shoulders. His white hair glowed like a halo against his weather-worn face and light brown eyes. Dressed in his uniform of a New York Dolls concert T-shirt older than she was, faded jeans with dusty boots and a tattered cowboy hat, he managed to straddle the fence between the hippies and cowboys that made up the meager population of Pardon Falls, Texas.

"Uncle El," she smiled at her boss and private investigator's brother-in-law. "I bet you were worried sick."

Burns stepped aside. "Despite what my gut is telling me, you're free to go."

"Oh, well that's good news," Amanda said, cutting her eyes to El. She scooped up her half empty cup of bad coffee. "Mind if I take this to go?"

The Border Patrol agent led them down the hall toward a glass door. Daylight streamed in and she guessed that he was coming to the end of his shift, meaning whatever lies El had fed him, he'd greedily consumed.

*Maybe that's what's churning in his gut, settling for the easy answer rather than the right one.* Amanda knew that feeling. She settled for it time after time when something felt wrong during her relationship with Josh Williams.

*The bitter aftertaste never fades.*

"Young lady, you can save us all a bunch of time and trouble if you'll just tell us the truth," Burns lectured as walked them out. His voice was slower and heavier than earlier in the evening. Definitely coming to the end of his shift.

She turned to the man to her left and cocked an eyebrow, but said nothing. El walked on, his long wiry frame moved easily despite the bow of his legs.

"Oh you know how young ladies are these days," her *'uncle's'* gravelly voice bounced off the walls. "So stubborn and headstrong, refusing to play the victim. Mandy didn't want admit to doing something as stupid as leaving her purse in her unlocked car and having it stolen."

"Well, she needs to report it and get a replacement ID," he said as he pushed the door open.

"Yes, sir," she said, smiling perhaps a bit too brightly as she brushed past him to her freedom. "I'll do that today." She followed El three steps into the parking lot before Burns spoke again.

"Oh, Miss Snare," he called.

Amanda wasted no time turning to face him, even though the name belonged to her private investigator, not her. The look on Burns' face displayed his disappointment at not catching her and El in a lie.

"Yes, Agent Burns?"

"Keep your head down. Someone else may not be quite as forgiving and understanding as *me*."

Even though he had to squint to look at her in the rising sun, she read what his eyes were telling her. *Next time I catch you, I won't be throwing you back in with the other fish.*

Amanda nodded and caught up with her boss as he waited by his old truck. "Snare?" she murmured under her breath as El pulled a cigar out of his shirt pocket.

"We both know that Hank would've dropped you as a client if he didn't think of you like a daughter. You're a pain in the ass, but we keep you around for the entertainment value. Is government-bucks coffee really that good?"

She shrugged and leaned against the tailgate next to him. "Fingerprints."

"Good girl. Mind if I have a few puffs before we get on the road, Chicago?"

El was one of the few people who knew her true identity. His nickname of her hometown made her feel somewhat closer to the city she loved, the city she hasn't been to in over a year since she'd escaped a vengeful investor's wrath at her part of securities fraud that robbed him and many other clients of their savings.

The nickname also reminded her of Liz, and the little boy growing up without a mother because of her. Amanda had taken a big risk in being honest with him, but at the same time it was refreshing to not lie.

"Does Hank know?" she asked.

"If he did do you think I'd be here alone?"

"How did you know?"

He exhaled, the white cigar smoke lingering in the air before dissipating. "When my darling *niece* didn't come home last night, I called the sheriff to see if there had been any wrecks or abandoned cars reported. He said he caught wind of some Border Patrol agents thinking they busted a drug mule down at the river." El paused to draw another lungful of smoke. "Did you think you can really sneak across the border in my old beat up canoe without me noticing? Hell, I figured that thing would have sunk on your first go with it."

She shuffled, toeing at a rock with her rubber boots. She'd been eyeing the upturned canoe perched on a couple of sawhorses at the back of El's house since she'd moved into the casita behind him. Snatching it and launching it across to Mexico was a knee-jerk reaction to boredom. After that first quick trip across the Rio Grande, she'd made contacts and built up her confidence, convincing herself that this was the only way to find Josh without anyone else getting hurt. "If you knew, why didn't you try to stop me?"

"Because I'd rather have you half-heartedly sneak behind my back than put a lot of effort into it. I showed up here asking if my canoe-enthusiast, dingbat of a niece was around." Smoke huffed out of his lungs as he laughed. "Hell, I think they were ready to get rid of you anyway."

They stood silently, watching the sun finish its ascent into the deep blue Texas sky.

"I think I found him, El," Amanda's voice floated out like one of his plumes of cigar smoke. "A girl at a store there said he's working for Vargas. I'm close. Really close."

He tossed the cigar and snubbed it with the toe of his boots before turning to face her. "Chicago, I get what you're doing. But there *is* a reason Hank sent you here. You're lucky the folks with the big guns last night were the good guys. Next time might not be the case." He turned to the driver's side of the truck.

Amanda drummed her fingers on the top of the tailgate.

The past year of her life was nothing more than purgatory.

She couldn't go forward to jail for her part in securities fraud, nor could she go backwards to Phoenix; to David, to a place where she'd finally felt at home before she'd turned the whole town against her with a misguided murder accusation of one of their own.

Amanda hated herself for publicly calling Shiloh a murderer.

"I'm tired, El," she called to his back. "I'm so tired of waiting for something to happen."

He turned slightly and squinted at her. "An attitude like that and you won't have to wait much longer. Get in. Just because you spent the night in lockup doesn't mean you get out of working this afternoon."

*Work*. There was no way she could focus on pouring drinks and talking to customers at El's bar. She needed to strategize, plan, prepare.

What would it take to get Josh?

A translator, for sure. Maybe she needed to bring a backpack, plan to spend a few days there rather than have to meet her curfew.

*Money*. Whatever her next move, it would cost money. Something she didn't have much of.

Amanda stared out the passenger window like a petulant child as El pulled out of the parking spot. A rusty red Ford truck appeared on horizon to the right.

Just the sight of it sent her back, back to before she ruined lives, before she felt the pull to solve a murder, back to a night when she got lost in a run and followed a handsome stranger home.

He turned, moving away from the truck.

Amanda twirled around in the seat, ignoring the seatbelt cutting into her throat. She wasn't ready to let go of the mirage of David's truck. She wasn't ready to look at the road ahead of her.

She wasn't ready to let go of this past.

# 3

The mirror wasn't as kind to Josh Williams as it once was. He leaned close, examining the roadmap of the last year etched on his face. The crow's feet told of blinking away desert dust. Wrinkles on his forehead whispered worry about working for a drug cartel. A deep tan against his blond hair, the only feature he was proud of, boasted the cruelty of the Mexican sun.

He slathered more perfumed moisturizer on his cheeks, wincing at the powerful jasmine scent. The men in Mexico weren't so worried about their skin, and the cheap, chemical-perfumed goop from the women's aisle at the *supermercado* produced whispers behind his back. He didn't care. These were necessary steps to stave off aging until he returned to the U.S. and his dermatologist.

*If I ever get back.*

Josh wiped off excess cream with a tissue as his final month in Chicago haunted him. It'd been pure luck when he'd started banging a pretty young attorney from the local office of the SEC.

"You're not as bad as they say you are," she'd said one night, just two weeks before it'd all gone down.

They'd been curled up in bed and she got post-coital chattiness. It'd taken two more nights, including one evening with an expensive bottle of champagne and caviar, before he'd gotten the whole picture.

Another team in the agency had investigated his father's firm for securities fraud; they'd narrowed their focus on three people, Keith Cooper, Amanda Martin and him.

The breakfast bell reverberating through the compound broke his thoughts. Instead of joining the other tenants on his employer's *hacienda*, he crossed his room in three steps and fell into an over-stuffed leather chair.

Josh recalled Keith's panic when he'd shared the news. "What the hell did you do?" Keith had screamed at him in an empty Chicago baseball field, his anger captured in puffs of white frost from his breath. "You and your dick caused all this."

"You should thank my dick for uncovering this or we'd be preparing ourselves for the federal pen," Josh said. Maybe it was because he'd had time to process the news, or he had his escape plan in place, but he was glad he didn't get as riled up.

Keith paced for a few minutes, calming with each stride. "You're right. How much time do we have?"

"Less than two weeks."

"Does Amanda know?"

"She's clueless, as usual."

"Good, let's keep it that way," Keith said. "The less she knows, the less likely she'll be able to bargain with prosecutors. What next?"

"Well, depending on if you want to go to jail or not, I'd say we need to get out of the country. I've got something in the works for me, but it's best we part ways."

The man nodded. "I've been moving money off-shore just in case. We've got some time to get a little bit out of our stock options before they freeze them. You need to stop using your credit cards, get as much cash as possible. Don't tell me where you're going. When we part ways, don't try to reach out to me."

A second bell sounded outside his window.

The meaning was clear; his employer had done a head count and realized someone was missing.

Josh exhaled and ran his hands through his shoulder-length hair.

He'd had only one haircut since his arrival and the man had buzzed it, even though he'd given him exact instructions to work around his hair's wave. After that, he'd just let it grow. He'd cut it when, *if*, he got back to the States.

His subtle plan for escape was still in its infancy, but so far no one, including his employer seemed to be the wiser. So much money flowed in from Vargas' men that skimming a bit off here and there, and pocketing it could be explained as a simple rounding error.

Josh hoped, as his meager savings built, so would Vargas' trust in him. It'd only take a few trips into town alone for him to make contact with someone who could drive him to the border. A quick swim across the river and he'd be back in the States.

His mind vacillated between believing he could pull it off and thinking he was crazy for even considering it. It'd worked once in Chicago, but that didn't mean that lightning would strike twice. If it did, he might get burned this time.

He replayed his final days in Chicago so many times that it felt like an old VHS tape starting to wear out with parts missing, and his mind fast forwarding through others.

When Josh had called Vargas, he'd expected to pay for an over-priced fake passport and a too-expensive plane ticket to a tropical part of Mexico, where he would sip margaritas by the ocean while the SEC thing blew over.

He'd barely had time to take in the city of El Paso after his plane landed before the van had pulled over and a black hood covered his head without an explanation from his escorts.

No ocean breeze waited for him.

"Thank God I didn't bring Amanda into this," he said to his shoes. Even though he'd cheated, manipulated and lied to her, he still felt something for her.

Not love, at least not in the way she'd wanted. His final gift to her was a stack of cash he hoped she'd stashed in her purse, and a call to her friend, reporter Roland Burrows, with the tip that the SEC was about to indict her.

*At least she wasn't in that building when the psycho attacked. Maybe she's on some tropical island sipping cocktails.*

Josh laughed at the irony.

A knock on his door ended the movie in his head. "*Señor* Williams." A teenage boy entered. "*Señor* Vargas asked me to check on you."

"Sorry, Pedro. I got a late start," he said, tightening his shoelaces to reinforce his tardiness. "I need to run back into town today. Any chance I could get a ride?"

Gaining trust was like building a stock portfolio. Josh would need to make some calculated investments that would pay off in the long-term, to prepare for a riskier investment with what he hoped would yield a one-time return.

His freedom.

The boy blinked a few times, as if trying to decide which words to use.

"I'm not sure if that is possible today, *Señor*. *Señor* Vargas asked to meet with you after breakfast," Pedro paused and looked down at his feet. "I can run to town to pick up what you need."

Josh closed the door behind him, sighing. He'd traded one prison for another.

## 4

The ghost of David's truck haunted her the entire drive back to her car.

"Get some sleep, Chicago," El shouted out his window. "You're south of pleasant without it."

Amanda took a deep breath, hoping the extra oxygen would rejuvenate her. "Rental turnover today, I have to help Willa clean."

He gave her a long stare with brown eyes that held the faintest hint of oncoming cataracts. His lips twitched, eager to form words but not willing to let them go. "I worry about you, Mandy." He broke eye contact to look out over the rolling sandy bank of the Rio Grande. "You nearly get arrested, you're working yourself to the bone. Is it worth it?"

It was a question she'd asked herself so many times, telling herself over and over that it was all going to be worth it.

The question on someone else's lips splintered her resolve. Amanda shouldn't have run that day, when her friends were killed and office on fire. She should've stayed in Chicago to face whatever charges filed against her.

Was she on a fool's errand? Was she simply arm wrestling fate and starting to lose?

She squared her shoulders and straightened her back, lifting her head to give herself that much needed jolt of I-can-do-this. Her resolve was splintered, not broken. "It's the most important thing I've ever done."

El's head bobbed a slow nod. "Well." He popped open his door. "Least I can do is take the canoe back for you. Get moving, so you can get a nap in before you have to come in."

Heat poured out of her Bronco. She lowered the ragtop hoping that moving hot air would dry the sweat sliding down her temple, but the desert sun scorned down on her.

The drive along the Rio Grande to Pardon Falls was her favorite. Breathtaking cliffs rose up with vertigo-inducing drops into the river. Cacti dotted the roadside, rewarding those who survived this hostile environment with flowers of orange, blue, red and yellow. They were coming to the end of the spring tourist season. A few more weeks and summer would bear down with bouts of rain breaking the monotony of triple-digit heat and wide blue skies.

When Hank had first insisted Amanda move to Pardon Falls, she wondered how she'd survive the heat. She'd suffered through several Chicago heat waves, but it was different in the south Texas desert. It enveloped a person, latched on in early June and wrapped its searing fingers around her neck, threatening to suffocate until winter scared it away.

South of town, she pulled off the highway and followed a dirt road up to the top of a ridge. The adobe rental house was the local monstrosity. Built to serve as the roughing-it home of a wealthy oil baron several years ago, it'd ended up with an ex-wife who rented it out to vacationers.

Willa's dusty sedan sat parallel to the front of the house, the back bumper inches from the garage wall. The dashboard clock mocked Amanda for being a half hour late.

"About damn time you showed up." The woman shoved a pail of dirty water in her direction.

"Sorry, Willa." Amanda pulled her hair up in a bun. "If I told you why, you'd think I was lying."

Willa hitched her hand on her hip and glared. She fell to the hippie side of the Pardon Falls population. Her long hair was matted into dreadlocks, a gold ring snuggled one nostril. Although she was only a couple years older than Amanda, lines across her forehead tattled on too much sun and not enough sunscreen.

"We have three hours to get this whole house ready. If I have to call in extra help, it comes from your pocket."

"I'll clean all the bathrooms."

Willa dropped the empty pail and threw her arms around Amanda's neck. "Thank you! This is why I love you." She laughed, her earlier scorn gone. "Because the bathrooms are disgusting."

She grabbed her cleaning kit from the back of Willa's car and set off to work. Cleaning was not only extra income, but free therapy as well. Some days she needed an abundance of both.

The plastic gloves stung when Amanda snapped them into place, but her whole body relaxed, as if sinking into a therapist's couch. She swept, scrubbed and shined, barely processing the dirt and grime. She wanted to think about Josh, to punish him through the dirty bathroom, but David kept getting in her way.

When she first left Phoenix she'd dialed his number so many times that punching the numbers served as the connection she needed. Amanda didn't dare save his number in her cellphone.

Doing that would rob her of that ritual. But she never hit send. She couldn't. What would she say to him?

*I'm so sorry I left. It was for the best. You didn't expect me to stick around after the whole Shiloh thing, did you?*

She rocked back on her heels and surveyed the tile floor in the first of the four bathrooms. No dirt, no bugs, no hair. A crime scene investigator would be impressed.

Willa was on the other side of the house, singing along to Madonna. Her friend's voice rivaled the Material Girl's, but it would stay hidden away in this dusty little corner of Texas.

The second bathroom was going to take more work. A lot more.

Amanda stepped into the soiled room. Mud streaked the shower doors. At least, she *hoped* it was mud. Murky lines smudged across the mirror.

She opened the lid to the toilet and stumbled back out of the room, gasping for air as if she'd been submerged.

This was the perfect room for Josh.

A couple of hours south on a bumpy road and she'd be back in that town, talking to that cashier. The girl knew more. Amanda could draw it out of her. There *had* to be something the girl needed, wanted.

She focused on her favorite fantasy to distract herself. A chagrined Josh, his head hung so low she could only make eye contact with his blond waves. Hands locked behind his back. She even sometimes imagined his feet shackled, but that was a bit extreme.

*A girl can dream.*

The realization of the fantasy came with a steep price, her own arrest.

Amanda flushed away the first layer of grime and set to scrubbing the deeper stains, those that coated her heart with regret. If she'd never fallen for Josh's charms, would she have still gotten caught up in his fraud? Or would she have been one of the innocent shot that day? Would she have been eulogized as a nice girl who fell under Josh's thrall like so many other women?

So many times she was a breath away from breaking up because of his infidelity, but she'd feared who she would have been without Josh.

Now she knew.

Without Josh, Amanda wouldn't have ruined so many lives in Phoenix; those like Dugan who'd blindly walked into a crumbling stock market, or like Shiloh who didn't ask to be publicly humiliated.

Or, David ...

Amanda looked up at the ceiling. The noxious fumes made her eyes water, but she refused to let them turn into tears.

It always circled back to David.

She needed to break herself of the habit of dialing his number.

*Tomorrow. I'll start tomorrow.*

She studied the soiled paper towels in her hands. Without Josh, she wouldn't have gone from being a public relations executive to scrubbing toilets. More stinging pierced her eyes.

"It's almost breathable in here." Willa appeared in the doorway behind her. "Come on, let's take a break and see what goodies they left in the kitchen."

As if by suggestion alone, her stomach grumbled. She followed her friend through the expansive house, glancing out the huge windows. A wispy haze hung over the top of the mountains. Scattered puffy clouds cast shadows over the desert floor, cooling the cacti and trees for just a brief moment before floating away.

The town of Pardon Falls sat on a parallel mesa. If she squinted, she could make out El's bar. The turquoise adobe building looked like a piece of the fallen sky.

"It never gets old," Amanda sighed.

"Why do you think I'm still here?" Willa spoke into the refrigerator. "So we have cheap beer and Fig Newtons."

"No wonder the bathroom was destroyed." She perched herself on the counter and chewed on a cookie.

"You left me hanging long enough," her friend said through a mouthful. "Sorry I snapped. I was worried."

She let her mouth drop open and released a theatric gasp. "You like me?"

Willa laughed and threw a dirty dishtowel at her. "Any other person, I'd assume you were sleeping one off, but since you won't even drink free, bad beer... Want to talk about it?"

Amanda popped another Fig Newton in her mouth to avoid a quick answer. Her friend never asked many questions, and she never volunteered much information.

Everyone had a story in Pardon Falls. Some were more interesting than others, but like politics and religion, it was generally avoided in polite company.

"Remember that guy I was looking for? The one I thought was in Mexico?" She waited for Willa's nod before continuing. "I think I found him, but since I didn't go through official means to visit Mexico, I got busted coming back in last night. Spent the evening with Border Patrol before El saved me."

A high-pitched yelp escaped the woman's lips and her eyes crinkled shut. "You're kidding? You just earned some serious street cred,
my friend."

Amanda begged her face to smile and her lungs to join in the
laugh, but the stony muscles disobeyed.

"There's more, isn't there?" Willa asked once her laughter
passed.

"There's always more," she answered, gazing back at the mountains. "Do you mind if I run outside? I need to make a quick call."

"Sure, best cell service in town. I was going to make a couple of
calls before I left, too."

Her phone hid in her glove box, turned off and rarely used.
Living in Pardon Falls was like living in the 1980s. There were only
a few spots that had reliable cell phone coverage. It wasn't
uncommon to see a local pulled over on the side of the road on the
phone, taking advantage of precious signal bars.

Amanda's hands shook when the little black device woke up.
The tone of the buttons was deafening in the silence of the desert.
She made it halfway through David's number and erased it. What
would she say?

*I'm sorry.* The best two words she could start with.

*Forgive me.* She meant it with every ounce of her being.

*I need you.* Her heart stuttered at the thought of seeing
him again.

She closed her eyes and took three deep breaths. "I can do this.
People make calls all the time. It's like ordering a pizza."

The numbers appeared on the screen easily this time. Her
thumb only hesitated over the send button for a moment before the
word "Calling" appeared. With the phone to her ear, she held her
breath.

"The number you have dialed has been disconnected or is no
longer in service. Please check the number and try again."

"What?" Amanda asked the phone, but the message only
repeated itself. She dialed again. She'd probably just messed up,
but... then the same message.

She held the phone over her head, but the number of bars never moved. Her fingers had been dialing this number weekly since she'd left; it was a number she had committed to heart in Phoenix.

A number she knew almost as well as David's face.

She dug through her glove box for an old reporter's notebook and flipped through the pages. An automated voice told her David's home number was disconnected, too.

Panic swelled in her chest. He couldn't be gone.

It took three tries to call the Phoenix Police Department. Her fingers trembled so violently she had to back up and start over a few times. A cry shot up her throat, but she swallowed it down.

"Phoenix Police Department, how can I direct your call?"

She could see the 9-1-1 operator sitting there with a magazine in her hands.

"Captain." The word came out in a watery whisper. Amanda cleared her throat and started over. "Captain David Stephens, please."

The woman paused so long, she looked at the phone to make sure she hadn't lost the connection. "Hello?" she asked.

"He no longer works here." A cold, steel edge came over the woman's voice.

Pain and disbelief danced together, but let denial cut in. *No.* The word repeated in her head. Was it coming out of her mouth, too?

"Do you know – do you know where I can find him?"

"He's gone. Left town and didn't tell anyone where to find him."

The phone dropped out of Amanda's hand and her knees hit the hard dirt.

She was alone.

Utterly, completely alone.

Dialing David's number had kept her together; it made her feel, despite everything that'd happened between them, he was still hers.

Dialing that number was her lifeline to hope, to the fact he was the one good thing in her life.

With it gone, she could feel herself being carried out to sea. The current was swift and a storm loomed on the horizon.

# 5

Despite Pedro's announcement that Vargas wanted to see him, the man avoided eye contact with Josh during breakfast, making him endure the meal completely alone. It wasn't until after the *huevos rancheros*, after lingering over thick coffee with cigarettes, after Vargas whispered to one of his captains and disappeared into the house. The dishes were cleared, and Josh was lead to the large, wrap-around front porch and told to wait.

His loafers smacked the wood. A hot breeze dried an errant bead of sweat that dripped down his neck. Laughter broke through the silence as a group of kids sprinted to the center of the sprawling dirt courtyard, tossing a soccer ball high into the air.

Children from both sides laughed and cheered, except for one little girl. Concentration knitted her young brow and her small legs moved twice as fast to keep up with the older children. As Vargas' oldest child, she shared his golden brown hair and furious intensity. The few times Josh saw the girl, she stoically held her face steady and refused to unleash a laugh or a smile.

With no end to his waiting in sight, he sank into one of plush outdoor chairs and tried to focus on the game in front of him rather than the chess moves he'd have to play when Vargas arrived.

Soft Spanish and the click of a door pulled his attention behind him. The windows were open to Vargas' personal parlor, allowing a glimpse into a room that typically stayed closed to everyone but those deep within the inner circle.

A light curtain danced in the wind as he turned. Vargas entered alone, closed the door behind him and kneeled. Walking forward on his knees, he crossed the parlor and stopped at a small table set up as a shrine.

The curtain flickered across his sight, but Josh could see his boss lighting candles with the ghastly image of a skeletal woman in a white dress. At the center of the shrine sat a statue of the same figure. A crown topped her head, dead roses decayed at her feet.

Josh could even make out what looked like human bones scattered about. *Santa Muerta*. The unofficial patron saint of the drug cartels. He'd heard rumors of those who prayed to her, but he'd assumed they were simply ghost stories for children and scared Americans.

Vargas sat in reverent silence with his head bowed. His lips moved in a rapid-fire, soundless prayer. He finished and reached for the shrine, plucking a knife from the feet of *Santa Muerta*. Without flinching, he dragged the blade across his palm and blood dripped at the statue's feet.

Josh's hands went cold as a look of total ecstasy crossed Vargas's face.

He moved off the shaded porch to stand in the sun, hoping to both warm himself up and get as far away from the darkness as possible. He wouldn't call himself religious, but the ritual made him believe in evil.

Vargas' daughter landed hard on her knee. The other children immediately froze. Did they know she was untouchable, but yet in their childhood innocence forgot that they weren't supposed to trip up the daughter of the local cartel leader?

"Catalina?" Vargas shouted as he ran through the front door, still wrapping a bandage around his hand.

The child and the man met at Josh's side. The stoic little girl, with the same stony eyes as her father, let a single tear slip from her right eye. Blood ran down her shin.

"*Papa*." The girl sniffled, her arms twitched at her side, as if holding back her natural inclination to reach for her father.

He thumbed the tear away. "What's the rule, my child?" His words were sharp.

"No tears, *Papa*."

Vargas kissed his daughter's forehead before kneeling in the dirt, his beige linen suit rustling in the wind as he wiped the girl's knee clean. If it weren't for Vargas' men forming a circle around them, Josh would've felt like a voyeur.

"Sorry to have kept you waiting, Josh," Vargas said between soothing Spanish to his daughter.

"It's ok, *señor*. Is she okay?" Like her father, she had the same stunning green eyes glowing against her golden skin.

"You know children, what hurts at this moment will be nothing but a memory the next," he paused to tousle her hair before straightening her ponytail. Catalina still held tight to her father. "I was just reviewing the latest report and noticed some discrepancies I hoped you could clear up."

Josh's heart thumped twice and the girl looked up at him, her eyes searing as they scanned his body. "Oh?"

Vargas spoke over his shoulder to one of his men, who turned and jogged back to the house. "It's Manuel's reports."

"What about them?"

Catalina's eyes narrowed.

Could she hear his heart pounding?

"They seem to be markedly low. Much more than normal fluctuations. Are you sure that's what he turned in?"

Before he could answer, the man came back from the house with a box of Band-Aids in his hand, and Manuel following behind.

A lower level worker, Manuel's nervous eyes jockeyed between Josh, Vargas and the other men who closed in around him.

He hadn't targeted this man on purpose, Manuel just had the most variation in his past reports, leading Josh to the conclusion he could skim a little off and Vargas would think it was business as usual.

"Are you sure the numbers are right?" Vargas didn't look at him, instead rummaging through the box of bandages.

Numbers never let him down. Numbers never fought at night, or ignored him. Numbers never promised to go to his baseball game, only to leave a hole in the stands. And, numbers didn't have an illegitimate daughter to leave their entire family fortune.

Josh had nothing but faith in numbers. "They're right."

Vargas nodded as he peeled open the wrapper. "Very well. Take his left hand."

The man closest to Manuel grabbed his hand and yanked it high over his head while another drew a large knife. Even though the order was given in English, Manuel knew exactly what it'd meant, his Spanish words pleading.

The children that'd been jumping and laughing while waiting for their fallen comrade to rejoin them froze. Even the gentle wind that had been blowing died as soon as the command had left Vargas' lips.

"Not in front of the children," he cooed as he secured the bandage on his daughter's knee and sent her off to play after a kiss.

Two men dragged the crying Manuel around the house and the children resumed their game.

Moments after they'd disappeared, an agonizing scream pierced Josh's ears.

The children paused for only a moment, before the ball went back into play.

A man was maimed because of his lie. Somehow that felt much more personal than the embezzling he'd committed in Chicago. Sure, people died and were injured as a result of his actions. His cloak of denial was becoming threadbare, and what had just happened to Manuel found one of the many holes.

"Now, on to other matters," Vargas said after the world around them resumed. "Shall we go inside where it's cool?"

The man led Josh down a long, dark hallway to his office and closed the door behind them.

They only recently had begun meeting alone, without a body-guard or a captain. The conversations were friendly and focused more on U.S. politics or literature than Josh's work at the compound, but they usually came in the evening, after work was done and tequila flowed, never in the middle of a workday.

"Josh, come, sit with me," Vargas directed. Unlike many of the people there, he could say his name with the hard J instead of the H of the Spanish language. His boss revealed during one of their late night visits that he was an American citizen, born and raised in Arizona. After college, he'd moved to Mexico to be closer to his father, which included joining the family business. He'd risen through the ranks and was given a territory of his own to manage. But, Vargas was getting antsy.

Ambitious.

*Malignant.*

"My apologies for not bringing up the discrepancies to you before today," Josh said. "He'd had variations before, and I wanted to watch it to make sure it wasn't anything more than the usual fluctuations. It won't happen again, sir."

Vargas swatted his apology away like an annoying fly. "Your accommodations are comfortable, are they not?"

"Oh, absolutely. You're very generous for allowing me to stay here for so long. I hope I'm not becoming a burden." He took a risk bringing up his status like he did. Burdens weren't politely asked to leave in Vargas' world; they simply ceased being a burden.

"Quite the opposite. You prove to be more valuable every day."

Relief and disappointment pumped from his heart. Relief that his life was spared for now, disappointment that disengaging from the man's hold would prove difficult.

"Your new privilege of joining the captains on the trips into town, do you enjoy it?" Vargas leaned back in his chair and drummed his fingers on a manila folder on his desk.

Something was in that folder.

The cartel leader didn't ask idle questions. Somewhere along the way, Josh slipped up.

A bell tinkled in the distance, signaling it was time for *siesta*. The laughter of the children died as a woman shouted instructions. Neither man's focus drifted, no eyes blinked, and no breath was exhaled.

"Very much." He spoke slowly, hoping for cues that his answer satisfied his employer. "But, would it kill the grocery store owner to stock some unscented moisturizer?"

Vargas laughed and Josh exhaled. "I know, my friend, I know. When I first moved here, I sent away for many comforts of home. But, you'll see soon enough this becomes home and you settle into the comfort afforded you here."

His heart shrank two sizes. His brain registered its new definition of home, but his diminished heart refused to accept it.

"I'm glad you appreciate what I've given you," the man continued. "I was presented with a conundrum that concerned me greatly. It's regarding your security."

*Breathe. Normally, just breathe.*

Vargas flipped open the folder and handed Josh several pictures. The first was a woman in cut-offs and a tank top wearing dark green rubber boots. Her brown hair flowed down her back. Even with the sunglasses perched on her nose and darker hair, he knew her instantly.

In the next picture she spoke with a group of Mexican men, a shot that gave him a view of her backside as well; a backside he'd rather enjoyed.

The final picture showed her in the same *supermercado* he visited, speaking with the pretty cashier he always flirted with.

*What the hell is Amanda doing here?*

Josh clamped down on his jaw, hoping the only movement of his face was his eyes scanning the images. His heart pounded once, twice, then slowed as the edge of his vision grew fuzzy.

"Do you know this young woman?"

His head began the lie with a shake before his mouth opened. "Should I?" he swallowed, moistening his throat.

Vargas reached across the table and plucked the pictures from his hand, shuffling through them before tossing them back. "Seems this young woman was in town recently, inquiring about you. Said you were her boyfriend." He nodded toward the pictures. "Take another look. This is important."

Josh grabbed the three pieces of paper, but rather than flip through, he focused on the one of her alone, nearly facing the camera with her arms folded across her chest. She'd always been beautiful, that was part of the reason he'd hired her. Even standing there in her ridiculous green rubber boots with cut-off denim shorts, something within him stirred. Not desire, as much as he expected, but fear.

Fear for her, but mostly fear for himself.

"*Señor*, as you may be aware, I was somewhat... popular, back home." He refused to look at his ex-girlfriend more. "She might be that girl from the coat closet at The Pump Room, right before I left Chicago. I guess I pumped her better than I thought." Josh tried his best frat-boy scoff, but held his eyes steady on his employer.

Vargas was looking deep into his soul for the truth. After what felt like several long minutes of staring each other down, the blinked and sat up straight. "Part of our arrangement was no loose ends from Chicago, no?"

*There was definitely nothing loose about her end.*

Josh cleared his throat and matched Vargas's posture. "This is not a loose end, sir."

"How can you be sure?"

"Why are you so worried about this woman? From the looks of it, the greatest threat she poses is to herself. Do you think someone will talk?"

Vargas smiled.

Adrenalin rushed through Josh's blood at the sight of his employer's teeth, igniting his need to flee the man's presence.

"You're right. My people are loyal and cautious, and from what I can ascertain, this woman left town and crossed the border back into Texas." Vargas paused to pull a cigarette from a pack on his desk, lighting it in a drawn out inhale. "Until I mitigate this threat, you should stay close to home. Both for your safety and to ensure my business success."

His throat tightened, forcing his spine to stiffen. He was gaining valuable ground within the ranks. In his estimation, it'd only take a few more weeks before he was able to travel into town alone, and then Josh would simply disappear. What would this setback cost him?

"Don't worry, Josh. You are safe here, no one will get to you, I can assure you that." Vargas yawned and stretched before snubbing out his cigarette. "Now, if you'll excuse me, I have work to attend to. You should enjoy a *siesta*, Josh."

He climbed the steps back to his room and sat at the edge of his bed, studying the pictures of his ex-girlfriend. What body part would he lose if Vargas found out he'd lied to him? Why was Amanda looking for him now, after more than a year?

Was she trying to get him killed? Get them both killed? He hadn't practiced the lie about her identity, so he hoped his improvised performance was believable.

After passing through them for several more minutes, he wadded up the pictures and threw them at his door.

"Dammit, Amanda," he mumbled as he ran his hands over his face. "Why the hell couldn't you wait until I got out of here?"

## 6

Hangovers lingered longer in the desert. The dry air amplified the dehydration, filling David Stephens' mouth with so much cotton no amount of water quenched the endless thirst. Even from behind dark sunglasses, his pupils squeezed tight to let in the minimal light from the cruel sun. "Can you stop? I need to take a leak." He scanned the pancake-flat ground outside the government-issued truck.

The desert floor swelled to a towering rock formation only to deflate back to the stark earth before rising again to a mountain like ocean waves coming in to shore.

With the help of Lloyd Carson's lead foot, the flowing beige topography made David's head swim. "We'll be at the field office in twenty minutes," he answered.

"Can't wait that long." A thick mesquite bush rose up in the distance providing perfect cover for why David really needed to get out of the truck. "Stop here."

His partner slammed on the brakes and David's stomach shifted. The guy knew only two speeds. Fast and stop.

He offered to drive when he and Lloyd were out on patrol, but the younger man always pulled rank and grabbed the keys.

Gravel crunched under the tires. The truck swerved off the road and a cloud of dust billowed in the side view mirror. David stumbled as he escaped the roller coaster ride, his hand gripping the hot metal doorframe of the truck.

"Careful there, old man," Lloyd shouted through the cracked window.

Just ten years his senior, David hated the man he was forced to partner with as a rookie member of the U.S. Border Patrol.

He hated himself more for the mistakes that had put him there.

The coarse hair of his beard scraped against the back of his hand as he swiped away any hints of nausea. It was only mid-morning and the heat rose from the ground in watery waves, giving the illusion the truck was submerged in a ghostly river.

"Shit, I can't do this anymore. It's not worth it." David hoped saying those words aloud changed what he was thinking. It was worth the burning stomach to spend a brief, few hours forgetting that the last year had actually happened.

It was worth the blinding headaches to remember the exact shade of Mandy's golden brown hair and her intoxicating smile. It was worth the hangovers to pretend that night with Shiloh never happened.

Drinking was the only way he could forget what he did to Shiloh and remember Mandy. Remember Mandy so when he saw her, he could arrest her and reclaim his life in Phoenix.

Lloyd's shaggy blond head nodded as he spoke into his phone. His twenty-something superior was a cross between Texas cowboy and California surfer, a kid who shirked responsibility one minute, only to pull a power trip the next.

"All right, I'll pass that along. And sure, I'll see if I can convince Old Man Stephens to come out tonight." He dropped the phone in his lap as David closed the truck door.

"Who was that?" His voice sounded raspy in his ears.

"Walker. Called to say some guy dropped by the office looking for you. Told him you were out this way with me. A group of us are going across the river, meet some ladies. Wanna join us?"

Sweat chilled David through his Border Patrol green shirt and he zipped the truck's air conditioning to high even though Lloyd had lowered the windows. He took a swig of a warm Gatorade, the sugary liquid curdled in his stomach, forcing him to swallow back another rising tide of acid. "Who was looking for me?"

Lloyd pulled onto the road without looking behind him, reaching the speed limit in just a few seconds. "So tonight," he said, ignoring David's question. "Walker knows a place where the *señoritas* are *muy bonita* and cheap. You in?"

"Lloyd." His voice took the annoyed tone of an older brother. "Who's looking for me?"

The younger man's spirited, yet menacing blue eyes studied him from the driver's seat. A sharp turn approached, but he handled it with ease; his right hand barely gripping the top of the steering wheel and his left draped out the open window.

David would have admonished Lloyd for taking his eyes off the road at such high speeds, but the young man had grown up in the area and knew the highways as intimately as a lover's body.

"How long we been working together, Stephens?"

"Will you just answer the question? Who was in Presidio?"

"When were you going to tell me? I thought we were teammates or something."

*What is he pouting about now?*

He went back to studying the passing landscape. The hazy layer cake of the Sierra de Carmen mountain range blocked his view too far into Mexico, but it was there, just past a tired, meandering river that divided two countries and two completely different worlds.

On this side sat a raw beauty that drew thousands of tourists each year, on the other side was a world where young girls were sold into slavery, cartels ruled with an iron fist, and possibly where Mandy was, a thought that forced him to spend each night hating himself—and her—with a bottle of tequila.

No one in his new life knew what had driven him from Phoenix, Texas. After she'd left, investigators and media had filled his small hometown. It'd taken less time than he thought for fingers to start pointing in his direction.

*How much did he know? Why didn't he report her fake driver's license to the chief? How could she slip out of town on the day that the authorities found her?*

His picture and name had been all over the news just a year ago. And while David doubted Lloyd had read anything more riveting than the back of a cereal box, some of the other guys must've stumbled across it.

"I can't believe I've been riding around here with one of the best quarterbacks in Longhorn history, and you never once told me you played."

He held his back straight, hoping that Lloyd wouldn't notice his shoulders sink in relief. His secret, his greatest embarrassment, remained locked away in his past. For a little while longer, at least. "It never came up." His college years seemed like they belonged to someone else; a man who didn't let a pretty face blind him to the fact that the woman he was in love with was a liar.

"Man, I remember watching you against Alabama. The most beautiful spiral right when that defensive lineman nailed you. One of the greatest moments in college football history if you ask me."

"Yeah, that hit cost me my career." David mindlessly rubbed his right knee at his other painful end. The surgery to repair his ruined knee was less than successful, and fifteen years later, he still ran with a heavy knee brace.

"So you gotta come out tonight. You're a celebrity; the boys will want to hear all about it. Hell, I'm nearly famous, too, just for riding around with you."

"How about this." He shifted his gaze to the open road ahead of them. "You tell me who was asking for me and I'll come out tonight." As soon as David offered the bargain, he tried to come up with ways to back out. He had no desire to get drunk in public, but he also had no intention to stay sober that night. Besides, finding dates, which he knew damn well meant prostitutes, only deepened his nausea.

"What?" Lloyd spared him a glance and swerved, forcing him to brace even though he was belted in. "Oh yeah, that's right, nearly forgot. I don't know, some guy. Costello. Something like that."

*Costello.*

David ran the names through his brain, waiting for it to hitch to a memory but it simply came back empty-handed. "I don't know a Costello. Did Walker say anything else? What the guy needed from me?"

His partner took a left turn on two wheels, heading the truck back to the north toward the field office. Lloyd's phone buzzed and he reached to retrieve it from his lap, reading a text message while navigating the two-lane road. "Yeah, actually he did. Said the guy's got a lead on finding some broad. Amanda." Like the layers of sand that made up the Chihuahuan Desert, the top layer of Lloyd's voice shifted unveiling a threat just below the surface. "Who is she? Some girl who stole your heart and your money?"

He bit back the curse at the sound of Mandy's name falling from another man's lips. Deep down, he'd know Alex Kostas, the SEC agent who'd showed up in his hometown a year earlier looking for Mandy, would come around again.

Just as David was driven to find her to right his own reputation, he was up against the man who had the federal government at his back. Sure, he imagined clamping handcuffs on her wrists while reciting her Miranda Rights, but Mandy's name from his partner's mouth felt wrong.

Like a curse, igniting his need to protect her.

"You do not get to say her name," David growled. So low that maybe the warning drifted out Lloyd's open window without penetrating his ears.

Lloyd locked down hard on the breaks.

David's torso strained against the seatbelt and his sunglasses flew off his face, bouncing off the windshield. The acid he'd swallowed shot up his throat.

When the truck rocked back on its rear tires, Lloyd turned to face him. He was no longer the laid-back Californian or swaggering Texan. His eyes were as hard as the packed earth as he stared in vicious curiosity. "What else are you not telling me, Stephens?"

## 7

D avid would have hell to pay the next time he saw Lloyd, but he didn't care. After clocking out, he hurried into the locker room and changed his uniform for worn jeans and a t-shirt.

Lloyd chatted up the new receptionist and didn't see him sneak out the side door.

Once on the road, he turned his cell phone off and headed back to Presidio for an early dinner and his usual evening entertainment; drinking and stewing.

Alex Kostas was nearby and armed with a lead on Mandy, but he was eager to get home. After spending the better part of the last year looking for her, what was one more day? What was one more day of trying to convince himself he hated her rather than loved her?

Forty-five minutes later, he pulled his truck into his favorite Tex-Mex restaurant. Cars crowded the small, packed-dirt parking lot as bodies streamed into the front door. David nodded to a few Border Patrol agents as he entered, but chose a table by himself in the back. Training had taught him to always sit facing the door. He faced the wall. A stray bullet to the back of his head wouldn't be the worst thing that could happen.

The steaming *chile relleno* sat impaled on his fork as his jaw dropped at the sound of the voice next to him.

"Hey man, it's been a while. How you doing?" Alex Kostas held out his hand, but David answered by closing his lips around his fork. The dark-haired man moved his outstretched hand to pull out the empty chair across from him. "You look good. How's the Border Patrol treating you?"

There were many people to blame for why David had left Phoenix. He could dole it out if it were his mom's famous cherry pie. Half of it rested on his plate, oozing thick red sauce.

A sliver of the blame went to Shiloh Garcia, mostly crust from the decade-old murder of her best friend and the long-harbored crush she had on him. A bigger piece was for Clint Brown, a lifelong instigator who wasn't happy unless someone else was miserable.

Then some belonged to Mandy, the hottest part of the pie, steam rising off the plate. But the rest... the crumbs that falls apart into a large gooey mess the minute it was put on a plate... *that* part David gave to the man sitting across from him.

"How did you find me?" he asked, washing down his *relleno* with a long gulp of sweet tea. He studied the former SEC agent.

When they'd first met, Alex had a sort of false confidence and carried extra weight in his face and neck, and his curly hair was unruly. He'd slimmed down, his hair was cut short and, he sat with her shoulders squared, holding steady eye contact with David.

Alex flagged down a waitress and ordered a grilled chicken breast and a light beer.

David salivated at the name of his favorite beer. He wasn't going to drink, not in public where he could lose control and apologize profusely to the apparition of Shiloh and call out for the ghost of Mandy.

"Oh that was pretty easy," the man replied when the waitress brought his beer.

David's gaze followed a droplet of condensation as it trickled down the side of the glass. He could almost taste the cold smoky flavor.

"After tracking Amanda halfway across the country, you weren't much of a challenge. The chief in Phoenix told me you took a job here and the guys at the Border Patrol office told me what time your shift ended. Running into you here, though, was pure luck." Alex paused to take a long gulp of his beer, his Adam's apple bobbing as he drained a good part of the bottle. "Damn, it's hot here."

He filled his mouth with another bite of the *relleno*, hoping it would fool his taste buds into thinking it was beer. *Just one. One beer won't get me drunk. Plenty of guys have a beer with a friend.* Then again, this was *not* a friend, and he carried a burden that would buckle most men.

His momma would admonish him for eating while Alex waited for his own food to arrive, but she wasn't here and he wasn't about to let the only meal he'd had all day get cold. "Why are you here?"

The waitress sat Alex's plate in front of him and the man lowered his head in a quick, silent prayer.

David looked down at his hands, mimicking the gesture but grappling to find something to be thankful for.

"I'm glad you asked that, man." The former SEC agent cut into his chicken. "I've got a book deal, you see. A real stroke of luck, a publisher sought me out and suggested I write a memoir on the case. How I uncovered the fraud, everything that happened in Chicago, Amanda ending up in Phoenix, solving the case there before running again. He said it has bestseller written all over it."

He winced at Mandy's name. Although, in his mind Amanda Martin and Mandy Jackson were two completely different women. He wanted to keep them separate for a little while longer, to hold on to the woman he fell in love with, but they were on a collision course.

"There are two reasons I'm here," Alex continued. "One is to interview you, learn who Mandy Jackson was."

"Is."

"And, the other reason is for the last part of the book, the part when I apprehend Amanda. My publisher thought it would launch sales if I were to find her before the book comes out."

"Why do you need me for that? You found her in Phoenix just fine on your own."

The man drained the last of his beer and signaled to the waitress for another.

"Make that two," David interjected. He was going to need a drink if this conversation continued.

"I don't need you for *that*. I know exactly where she is." Alex leaned to one hip, reaching into his back pocket and pulling out a scrap of paper.

He ignored the sheet, instead focusing on the fresh beer just delivered by the waitress. The glass didn't touch the table before he plucked it out of her hand and took a long drink, gulping down mouthful after mouthful until he'd drained it all.

His companion's eyes darted around the restaurant, his bouncing knee jostled the table. It was obvious that he'd been hoping for a different reaction. "It's an address," Alex said.

"I can see that."

"Amanda's been spotted there. It's the best lead we have on her whereabouts."

"If that's the case, why are *you* sitting here giving me indigestion? Why don't you just get her and sell your book?"

Alex reclined in his chair and let one arm drape over the back. "I know it may be hard to believe, but underneath this tough guy persona is a romantic."

"The tough guy persona is harder to believe."

His lips puckered at David's insult. "I get that you're bitter. She left you and your life fell apart because of it. You were an innocent bystander. I'm on your side, Stephens. Really, I am."

David glanced at his half-eaten *relleno*, his stomach suddenly calling it quits.

Alex leaned forward and lowered his voice. "I know you don't like to think of yourself as the victim, but you are. We can find her together."

The table shook as he slammed his empty glass on the table. He didn't need this man to remind him of everything he'd lost. It stared at him every day when he put on his Border Patrol uniform and mocked him when he came home to a foreign, empty trailer. David clenched his fist, wanting to break his knuckles against the guy's cheek, but what would it do besides get him arrested. "We? Kostas, you can take that book deal and shove it–" His voice came out louder than expected and the men at the table next to them halted their conversation and stared. He lowered his voice. "What do you think you'll get from bringing us together? A star-crossed love story?"

"No, I–"

"I bet that would be a real touching chapter in your book," David snapped.

"That's not what–"

"You're willing to make two people hurt for what, a few bucks?"

"You don't under–"

"Have you stopped to consider that maybe instead of looking for a reunion that I'm looking for an arrest?" Powered by anger at Mandy's lies and betrayal, his words echoed around the restaurant, once again dulling the din of conversation. He leaned back in his chair as both he and Alex heaved to catch their breaths, like fighters going back to their corners.

Despite admitting his true feelings toward Mandy, his nostrils filled with the scent of her shampoo, apples with a touch of vanilla. He rubbed his palms on his thighs, but instead of feeling course denim they felt the softness of her skin. His tongue flicked away a remnant of his dinner, but instead of tasting the spice of the *chile*, he savored the sweetness of her lips. "Do me a favor." The chair scraped against the floor as David pushed back from the table. "If you find her, don't tell her you saw me." He dug money out of his wallet to pay for his meal. He pulled out a twenty so he could escape Alex.

And, his own emotions.

"Shiloh said hi, by the way."

"What did you just say?" He only turned his head slightly.

"Shiloh said hi. I stopped by to see her before heading down here. She wanted me to ask you when you were coming home."

David focused on a spot on the dirty concrete floor. Desert dust settled into permanent crevices, forming a minuscule model of the outside landscape.

He walked out of the restaurant and crossed the dirt parking lot for the small general store. This was going to be a hell of a night and he needed to make sure he had enough liquor to make it through.

## 8

Amanda listened to the automated message telling her David was gone for the hundredth time. She sat on the couch of her *casita*, staring out the window until an ache reminded her to blink. The message ended and her thumb moved from the *end* button to press *call*. No longer was dialing his number an important part of the connection, now she hurried to hear that she'd lost him forever.

But what did she lose? David had broken up with her a year ago. She'd left Phoenix, left him, with a quick goodbye note.

Fate had given her a new life, a chance to start over and she ruined it. Like trusting and loving Josh had ruined her life in Chicago.

Was David's disconnected number Fate's way of reminding her of her mission?

"The number you have dialed ..."

Amanda ended the call and closed her eyes.

*One more. Just one more message and I'll take a shower.*

"The number ..."

She heaved herself off the couch and ambled into the bathroom. Steam filled the room and Amanda stripped off the clothes she'd been wearing for the last twenty-four hours. The hot shower cleaned her body but did nothing for her soul.

It was cold, numb. Detached.

She braided her long wet hair and dressed quickly. Didn't want to continue her streak of being late for work. "Thank God I work in the dark," she said to the circles under her eyes.

The parking lot of El Capitan was empty. Insects buzzed in the creosote bushes. White clouds stacked up like an approaching tsunami on the western horizon. The rainy season was waiting for the starting gun to come barreling down on Pardon Falls.

El's whistling tune pinged around the walls. It would still be a bit before happy hour, giving them time to talk without guilty whispers.

"Hello, dear niece. Did you get some of that much-needed beauty sleep?" He rounded a corner carrying a case of beer.

Amanda took it and followed him to the bar. She nibbled on her lower lip as her boss opened the cooler and began pulling bottles from the box. "I'm living on caffeine and concealer."

El paused and looked up from under his bushy gray eyebrows.

"Don't worry," she added. "I got this."

He shook his head and went back to stocking bottles. "It should be a quiet night. Not much going on in the park and the campgrounds are pretty empty."

Her gaze focused on dust motes floating in on a ray of sun. El's voice faded away as she watched the suspended specks swirl and fall, swirl and fall. Amanda swayed, as if she too were riding on a current of air, weightless as she rose and dense as she fell.

"Chicago, you going to stand there all day holding an empty box?"

His voice snapped her back to her body. She looked down at her hands, the box still felt heavy, but he was no longer beside her. How long had she been in her trance?

"You sure you're okay, Mandy?"

Amanda swallowed. "Sorry, lost in thought."

"I can handle the bar tonight."

"No, I'll be fine, I promise." She tried to add a shimmer of alertness to her voice. There was no way she could spend the evening

home alone with nothing to do but hit redial on David's old, disconnected number.

The clock on the wall inched closer to five; it'd only be a few
minutes before the first of the regulars showed up.

She crossed the bar to gaze out the high windows. "Three
hundred and sixty," she whispered to the sun.

Three hundred and sixty days of her life devoted to finding Josh
and bringing him to justice for his crimes.

Crimes that he'd left her to deal with.

More time than he was worth, but it was the only way for her to
right all the wrongs of the money he stole and the lives lost because
of him.

The shift of air behind her as the door opened drew her back to
the present. She forced a smile and greeted one of the regular
patrons as she settled in behind the bar for the evening.

As predicted, it was a quiet night with low conversations spoken
to a country and *Tejano* soundtrack with bouts of rock music thrown
in for variety.

With only regulars in the bar, Amanda relaxed into an ease as
comfortable as old yoga pants and a threadbare sweatshirt.

Satisfied that everyone had a drink, she excused herself to the
bathroom and locked herself in a stall. Like a junky needing a hit,
she pressed the redial button for David's number.

"The number you have dialed ..."

She took a deep breath and rested the back of her head against
the graffiti-covered wall. Amanda waited until the automated
message finished and exhaled. The needling sadness energized her.
It reminded her that life was not about returning to the past, it was
about marching toward the future.

Her life was about finding Josh, not pining for what she lost
with David.

Fearing the next hit would lead to an overdose, she stuffed her
cell phone into her back pocket and walked back to the bar.

A man stood with his back to her, tall with dark curly hair
trimmed neatly and cargo pants with a fleece jacket. He dressed as

if he was trying to blend into two different worlds, but instead looking like he didn't belong to either.

"Hi, what can I get you?" Amanda tried to sound welcoming, but her voice squeaked instead.

"Just a light beer, please." He was handsome in a boyish way. Soft cheeks covered with a five o'clock shadow, flanked a prominent Greek nose.

He took a long sip, eyeing her over the rim with such intensity she wished she had other customers, a keg to change, broken glass, a telemarketer; anything that could break her away from his gaze.

"First time camping in the park?" Nerves tightened their grip on her voice.

The man put his glass down and stared at her for a second. "Park? Oh yeah, that's right, no, I mean yes first time here, but no, I'm not here for camping." He fumbled over his words like a nervous, geeky teenager asking the homecoming queen to prom. "Actually, I'm here for..." he paused, unzipped a pocket on the leg of his cargo pants and pulled out some sheets of paper. "I'm here looking for someone. Have you seen her?"

He pushed the paper toward her, but somehow she knew what was on it before her she saw it.

Her corporate headshot stared up at her. Perfect blonde hair, impeccable makeup glossed over creamy skin and that red blazer. God, she loved that red suit.

Looking at that picture, Amanda felt like Jeckyl and Hyde. The question was, which one was the monster?

The woman staring up from the scarred wood, or the woman with the cold flash of fear coursing through her veins.

"Can't say that I have," she said. "Who is she? She missing?"

The man took another drink, drawing out his answer so long that the tiniest flush of perspiration dotted her forehead.

Did he see her? Under the long brown hair, stringy with split ends, uneven self-trimmed bangs, and tanned skin with a smattering of freckles, did he see the old her lurking just below the surface?

"She goes by a couple of names. Amanda Martin is her legal

name, but she lived under the alias Mandy Jackson for a while. She was an accomplice in a white collar crime."

Her heart threatened to run away, to get as far away from this man holding her past in his hands, but her brain reminded her to breathe, think. *Relax.*

This was no harder than a difficult media interview. She'd glided through those with ease numerous times. Then again, she *was* a little out of practice. Amanda nodded and furrowed her brow. "Wow, tough stuff. So does that make you a cop or FBI?"

"Oh sorry, introductions. Alex Kostas, private investigator, but I worked for the SEC. I was actually the analyst that uncovered the whole thing."

She blinked twice. Somehow it felt poetic that this gangly nervous kid was the one who'd undone Josh's Jenga game of fraud, embezzlement and lies.

"You said she's an accomplice, right? What about the others?" If he'd found her, perhaps he knew where Josh was. Would it be worth telling him the truth? Maybe they could work out a deal; she'd freely turn herself in if he could also arrest Josh.

Alex drained the last of his beer. "Nah, they're likely out of the country by now. She's our strongest lead."

"Another beer?" Amanda reached for the glass at his nod and refilled the pint. "What makes you think she's down this way?"

Before the PI could answer, El pulled out the barstool next to him. "Pretty girl." He picked up the picture. Even though her boss kept his gaze steady on the paper, she could still feel his stare. "Looking for her?"

"Yeah, you seen her around here?"

He dropped the picture and pulled a cigar out of his breast pocket. "Not in a while." He paused to light the cigar. "She came around about a year ago, looking for some guy."

Alex turned and gave El the same look, one that made her think he was picking apart every tick, breath and blink to catch him in a lie. "You sure it was her?"

He nodded as he drew in a drag of the cigar. "Hard to miss a girl like that down here. Stuck out like a sore thumb. She was looking for a way into Mexico. You might want to move your search a little further south."

Alex's headed bobbed.

She couldn't tell if he was absorbing El's lie wholeheartedly or was about to throw it back in their faces.

Finally, the scooped up the picture and dug his wallet out of his back pocket. "Well, thank you for your time." Alex slid some bills across the bar at Amanda with his business card on top. He turned to walk away but stopped and looked over his shoulder. "I've spent some time with her parents. They really miss her. For the record, I don't think she's a bad person. She just trusted the wrong guy."

She held her breath until the door leading out of El's bar slammed shut and she heard the hum of a car engine in the parking lot.

She and El exhaled simultaneously.

"He didn't buy it," she said.

"Not a single word." He pulled two shot glasses from under the bar and filled them each with whisky.

Amanda shook so much that more of the liquor dribbled down the back of her hand than what went down her throat. A cold draft brushed by her, the kind usually associated with the paranormal, but the ghost was her past, creeping up on her and jumping out of dark corners when she least expected it.

"Chicago, your cover's blown. The next time you see that man, he won't be alone."

# 9

The remainder of the evening at El's bar felt like a funeral. They rarely spoke, and when they did, it was in hushed, somber tones. Amanda's eyes burned with unspent tears and her stomach vacillated between nausea and hunger. The only thing they needed was a casserole and a casket.

"We'll keep you holed up until we're sure he's gone," her boss said. "And, Willa can change your hair color. Ever thought about being a red head?"

"Maybe we're wrong. Maybe he doesn't think that's me." He tilted his head and gave her an *ah-honey-bless-your-heart* look.

It *was* wishful thinking that Alex didn't realize the face in the picture was the same that'd served him a beer, despite the longer, darker hair and bangs draped over her forehead. She'd always considered herself pretty in a plain sort of way; she could stand out if she tried, or fade into the background if necessary.

The former SEC agent knew her face, whether she had blonde, brown, red or no hair; he'd know her anywhere. It was obvious this was his mission. To find that face and bring it back to Chicago.

And, she knew what it was like to be driven by a mission. "Or maybe you should go stay with Hank for a few days," El continued.

"You'd stand out less in a bigger city and he'll know what to do." Amanda stretched her arms overhead. Exhaustion settled over shoulders like a heavy blanket. The past two days slammed into her like a train and all she could think about was crawling under her covers and never coming out. "Mind if I call it an evening? I'll be able to think better after a good night's sleep."

He nodded. "Just come on down the road when you're ready for coffee. G'night Chicago."

The sky was dark and the stars shone on the horizon as she drove the few miles home. A new moon out here was a stargazer's delight, making the night sky truly multi-dimensional.

She crawled into bed, waiting for sleep to reach up and pull her under, but instead of being dragged into its blissful undertow, she rocked on restless waves.

Josh was so close she could almost smell his expensive cologne and see his overly-bleached teeth. What if she shared her leads with Alex? Could she convince him to hold off taking her back to Chicago and instead help her find her ex?

Then again, he said he was a private investigator, maybe his job wasn't to take her into custody. He'd mentioned her parents. Could they have hired him to find her?

Amanda rubbed her chest at the thought of her family. Every time they crept into her mind she'd find herself unable to breathe and her heart thundering with the raw energy of a herd of thoroughbreds. It was better to pretend she was alone, that there was no one left in her life rather than deal with the pain of missing her family.

A coyote yelped, his call answered by other pack members. Who would answer when she cried out for help?

She kicked off the covers and stumbled into the kitchen. She might as well start her caffeine consumption for the next day. With a full cup of coffee, Amanda nestled in on the step of her front porch. The floating steam whirled in gray-blue tones against the black backdrop of the night.

It was poetic that the same day she'd found Josh, she also

learned that her connection to David was forever gone. It was a balance. Give and take.

What role did Alex play? Was he the embodiment of her life in Chicago? He'd admitted to uncovering Josh's fraud, he'd spoken with her family and just like her past, he'd shown up unannounced eager to hold her back from the future.

She pushed herself off the porch, walking until she was at the fringe of the light pool. Total darkness was only a few feet away. A black abyss that in the safety of the sun, was her driveway. Just because she couldn't see her next step didn't mean monsters lurked there.

Amanda peered over her shoulder. Her little adobe *casita* had been her home for nearly a year. This little outpost of far south Texas was her haven. The man down the driveway was her guardian angel, giving her a home and a job.

Realization tugged at her stomach. She'd gotten complacent.

She'd made this mistake in Phoenix. Distracted by David, by a forgotten murder. Rather than look for Josh, she'd broken a man's heart and publicly shamed an innocent woman.

The signs were so obvious they were practically written in flashing neon. Josh. David. Alex. Everything was pointing south. To Mexico and finding Josh. It was time for her to go all-in.

Suddenly, the stars were crisper. The hazy cloud of indecision dissipated leaving behind the very clear vision of the future. Her bed beckoned, telling her now she could sleep, singing to her the sweet lullaby of renewed focus.

When Amanda awoke the next morning, light poured into her bedroom and a mourning dove cooed outside. *This* was going to be the last morning she woke up in her *casita*. The last time to wait for the slow water heater to awaken for her shower. As much as it pained her to think, it would be her last day in Pardon Falls, too. A town named after a mythical waterfall that appeared during flash floods, said to wash away sin.

She was tired of waiting for the flood.

It was time to set out to make it rain.

Over the past year, her belongings had outgrown the old backpack she'd gotten on her way to Texas from Chicago. She held tight to it anyway. One day she'd once again have to pare her life down to what it could hold.

A pair of shorts, underwear, a couple of tank tops, socks and her toothbrush was all she managed to shove into it. Everything else would likely be divvied up between the locals. Willa might end up with the dress she wore on her first date with David, or maybe she'd call dibs on worn-soft jeans.

The first time Amanda ran, it was an automatic action. Primal. The second time, it'd still had the raw edge of emotion, of having to get away before she messed things up worse, but also it had the orderliness of a fire drill. Now she felt like a pro. Starting her life over was coming naturally.

Many people reveled in the newness of a beginning, but not Amanda. Endings were sacred to her. She stood at the doorway of her bedroom, memorizing how the sun streamed in through the window, the star-shaped pattern on the comforter and how the top drawer of the bureau was just a little bit warped and didn't push in all the way. The faded couch in the living room watched as she passed through for the final time. It's companion, a tile-top dining table, sighed under the weight of a potted cactus.

When she got to the front door, she didn't glance over her shoulder for one final look. Instead, Amanda sat the keys on the counter and walked out. She drove her Bronco past El's home, out onto the highway and out of Pardon Falls.

One thing she'd has learned about leaving; it was so much easier without a goodbye.

## 10

J osh wasn't surprised that the knock at his door was a pretty young woman. The knocking was softer, quicker. Hesitant.

"A gift from *Señor* Vargas," she said before entering his room and kissing him.

His gut shouted that this was a bad idea. No matter how hard he tried to enjoy the first taste of a woman in a year, he didn't want her to be there.

"*Lo siento.*" He pulled his lips from hers. "It's not you. I'm just really tired. Maybe another time?"

The girl blinked and a frown marred her pretty face. Her thick hair hung in loose waves around one shoulder, offering a glimpse of her delicate neck and the modest gold chain with a cross disappearing beneath her neckline.

He'd admired that neck before, gazed at the spot where the bottom of the cross pointed to her most holy of secrets. "You work at the market in town, don't you?"

She nodded, but refused to make eye contact.

"What's your name?"

"Maribel." Her accent made her name sound both seductive

and sweet, a name that could fall from a father's lips as easily as a lover's.

"That's a pretty name. Do you live on the *hacienda*?"

"No, I live in town," she stared past Josh's shoulders, as if seeing the gate to her freedom through his closed French doors. "This is my first time to visit."

"I'm not sure what you were told, but we don't have to do anything." Josh lead her away from the door and sat on the edge of his bed. "We can just talk. It can be our secret."

"Thank you." Her voice had a youthful timbre, but the words had the weariness of someone more than twice her age. She joined him on the bed and folded her hands together, as if in prayer.

Several more minutes passed with Maribel gazing at her hands and Josh staring at his feet. How much time should he allow before letting her go?

Would Vargas or one of his captains examine her for a post-coital flush? Or, worse? Was he doing more harm than good by not allowing her to fulfill her duty?

"How old are you, Maribel?"

"Nineteen."

He nodded. Legal enough to keep him from committing another crime, but toeing the moral line. "Will they know if we don't?" Josh whispered.

A soft whimper escaped her throat as she nodded.

"Dammit." He exhaled and ran his hands through his hair.

Never in his life did he think that by *not* having sex with someone he could hurt her. Of all the women for him to grow a conscience with, it had to be the one girl that could pay the steepest price.

A year ago, Josh would've laughed about taking one for the team. In Chicago, he wouldn't have questioned if a beautiful young woman showed up at his doorstep, proclaiming to be a gift. He would've accepted her with open arms, eager to unwrap her.

Josh took her hand in his.

*Can I perform under this pressure?*

"Maribel." He gave her hand a squeeze. "I want you to know, if either of us had a choice –'" His voice cracked so he cleared his throat.

Before he could speak again, her mouth was on his and he pulled her onto his lap. It only took a moment for muscle memory to set in.

He undressed her, finding his appetite. He was careful, afraid he would break her like a China doll. When they were done, he held her tight, protecting her from whatever waited outside his door, but also hoping she could save him.

"I must go." Maribel pushed from the bed.

Josh realized her trepidation with not completing her job. "Maribel. Why are you here?"

"I'm your gift." She dressed quickly and with the modesty of a cashier at a *supermercado*, not with the exhibitionism of a prostitute.

"I know this was your first time."

Maribel faced him, her tears formed deep trenches on her cheeks. The girl's shoulders fell and her eyes focused on the blood on the sheets. "I'm so sorry, *señor*. I made a mess."

"I'll take care of it. Why you?"

"My papa." Her words were nearly lost in the rustling outside his door. "He owed *Señor* Vargas money." She trembled as she buttoned her shirt.

"Manuel," Josh whispered, but in the stillness of the room it reverberated like a shout. It hadn't stopped with the loss of the man's hand. "Your father is Manuel."

Maribel finished dressing and hurried to his door.

Rather than comfort her, or give her hope that despite what was being forced upon her, life wouldn't really be that cruel, he stared at his hands as she left his room. As he suspected, two sets of steps retreated down the tile hallway.

He waited until he could no longer hear the footsteps and bolted for his bathroom, curling himself around the porcelain toilet as his stomach convulsed on the revulsion from taking the man's money, his hand and, now, his daughter's innocence.

A fine sheen of sweat broke out on his naked body from the heaving and Josh clung to the toilet and vanity as he righted himself.

Kneeling, he lifted the lid from the toilet tank. The numbness in his fingers made the lid feel twice as heavy.

It was still there.

Josh changed his sheets in the dark, stuffing the soiled ones in a hamper by his door for the maid. The *hacienda* was silent and the desert was dark with the sky void of a moon. Armed men stood sentry at the compound walls. If he listened hard enough, he could hear their occasional footsteps.

The room was warm and his stomach still curdled at the sound of Manuel's earlier screams and Maribel's anxiety. The ceiling fan whizzed over his head, not enough to stir the air around his naked body. Guilt whirled in his gut. He pounded his fists the mattress.

Sending Maribel to his room was a clear message.

*I am officially screwed.*

## 11

In no hurry for the hardest goodbye, Amanda took the scenic route to El Paso, using the winding road along the river to straighten out her thoughts. She turned her phone off and tossed it in her glove box. It'd be useless during most of her drive, but she didn't want it coming alive as she got closer to the city, reminding her of leaving El behind without so much as a hug or a thank you. Every time she tried to practice her farewell speech to Hank, David crept into her mind.

Her Bronco chugged up a vertigo-inducing hill, but she barely registered the beauty of the desert. Instead her mind replayed her time with David.

Their evenings spent running through the streets of Phoenix, no destination in mind, just enjoying the feel of being next to each other. Tender kisses, moments of feeling at home, that with David she found her true self, even if she did cover herself with the cloak of Mandy Jackson.

What would he say if he were to ever meet Mandy Martin? Or, worse, what would he think of Amanda Martin? Her stomach roiled with remorse

She pulled into the shopping strip that housed Hank's office. She'd broken one of his cardinal rules during her entire drive.

*Don't just glance in your rearview mirror, watch to see if anyone follows you.*

Amanda couldn't even remember if she'd looked up once during her drive.

Parking in the same spot she had a year earlier, she gazed at the blacked-out door of Hank Snare's private investigation office. When she'd left Phoenix after Horace Foster's fiery confession that he'd murdered Katie Shelton and led her to believe it'd been Shiloh, she'd driven through the night to El Paso. Embarrassment over her very public accusation and fear from her near-death experience had fueled her escape and reignited her mission to find Josh and bring him to justice.

It was well after midnight when she'd pulled into El Paso. With nowhere to go, she'd parked at the derelict shopping center and waited.

Hank had woken her the next morning, hiding any surprise he must've had over finding a young woman sleeping in his parking lot.

Exhausted and rattled, she'd sat down and told him *everything*. About her family in Chicago. About her career at Jefferson Williams Investments and how the founder's gorgeous son had seduced her.

She'd told him about the last time she'd seen Josh, the boarding pass in a folder and the name of his client, Rafael Vargas. She'd told him about the gunman in her office, and how he'd killed her best friend under the assumption Liz was her.

She'd stopped at telling him about Phoenix. The pain she'd caused was too raw to rehash it. But, over time, she'd filled in the gaps of her life, and mistakes, in Phoenix.

Somewhere along the way, Hank had stopped handing her a monthly retainer bill, but Amanda hadn't stop paying him. It became a game. She'd hide an envelope filled with cash somewhere in his office, and he'd try to return it to her. She guessed El not charging her rent to live in his *casita* was a form of repayment.

Even though it was early afternoon, the parking lot only held a handful of cars. She looked around and waited for any movement, silently ticking off a full minute before turning off the car and heading inside.

Hank Snare sat at his metal desk. His white-blond crew cut greeted her as he bent over a legal pad, his hand visibly shaking as he scribbled notes.

Amanda paused just inside the door to study him. In the year since she'd known him, his color had taken on a gray pallor and his uniform of a button-down shirt and chinos grew looser. She'd never said anything to El, but it was an unspoken concern that sat between them.

Hank was sick.

He still carried himself like the ex-mercenary he was, but the big bear of a man seemed deflated, like a helium balloon with a slow, bleeding leak. Sometimes he'd soar with energy, but most of the time he'd float by listlessly.

She worried that he'd hurt himself during the investigation. That was part of the catalyst for her trips into Mexico, to take some of the pressure off him.

"You're late," Hank said, keeping his eyes on the paper in front of him.

Amanda plopped down in the forest green pleather chair. "I guess that means you knew I was coming."

"El said to turn your cell phone on before you head home."

She looked down at the metal desktop. Aside from the legal pad, the desktop was tidy. Not a piece of paper out of place, or a pen being unused. It was a perfect companion to the steely man sitting across from her. "I'm not going home."

He looked up at her. "Do you care to elaborate?"

"I'm going into Mexico, to follow up on a lead." Like wading into the ocean, she hesitated, making sure that her feet were firmly planted before continuing. "I found him, Hank. There's a girl at the supermarket there. She knows where he is."

"Would this be the same lead that resulted in you getting picked up by Border Patrol and held overnight?" His face remained impassive, but his gray-blue eyes sharpened.

Amanda cursed under her breath. "Oh, you know about that."

"Yes, Amanda, I know about that." Hank put the pen down and leaned on his forearms. "What makes you so sure this is an actual lead? It could be a trap."

What *did* make her think this was a lead? A feeling she got while in the church? Or the pull she felt in the pit of her stomach, like a compass needle pointing in the right direction?

Maybe she just wanted it to be a break. Proof that she wasn't going crazy, that Josh really did still exist and all she'd sacrificed wasn't for nothing. "I don't know. But what I do know is either I go to Mexico now or Josh goes free."

He stared at her for a long time. "What else is there?"

"A man came by El's bar last night. A man from Chicago, looking for me." She couldn't meet his gaze, so instead focused on the laminated map of Texas on the wall behind him. Her eyes traced the path from Phoenix to Pardon Falls. If it were a map of the U.S., she would've started with Chicago.

All places she'd called home. All places she could never return to.

"El told him I'd come and gone a year ago, but he didn't buy it. He'll be back and I'll be arrested. They aren't even looking for Josh."

Hank pushed himself out of his chair and crossed to the coffee pot in the kitchenette. The lure of coffee called to her, but Amanda stayed put. She needed her words to soak in.

"No," he said. "It's too dangerous. You don't know the land, you barely speak the language."

"You can't stop me." She sprang to her feet. "I'm going. It's what I have to do."

"What you *have* to do is let me do the job you hired me for."

"So you want me to sit tight and let this guy arrest me? Then what? Hank, you're too sick to do this alone." The words escaped her mouth before she could stop them.

The coffeepot trembled in his hand, causing the dark liquid to ripple as it poured into his cup.

"I'm sorry, I didn't mean—" But she *did* mean it. He couldn't do it alone. She had a better chance of making it back to Mexico, back to the town and the supermarket where the girl was. *She* had a better chance of convincing someone to take her to Josh, to bargain with Vargas and get her ex back to the U.S.

She also had a better chance of not making it at all. That didn't really matter, because to the people she loved, she was already dead.

Amanda put her hand on Hank's forearm, and the muscles tightened under her palm, but she refused to flinch. "Alex knows El and I lied to him. It's unfair to all the people who died if I just wait for him to come back and arrest me. You have to trust me on this."

He pushed past her and paced the length of his office. "And you're just going to have to trust me when I say no. Give me a few days to gather some resources and we can do this together."

She opened her mouth to argue, but Hank cut her off.

"I'm not *asking*, kiddo. I'm telling you. Please, go back to Pardon Falls. El and the folks there can circle the wagons around you. I sent you there for a reason, to keep you safe."

She crossed her arms and took a deep breath. He was right, she needed him. And she hated that. "Will you make me a promise?"

He gave her a steely stare that acknowledged her bargaining power. A slight step above an annoying gnat.

"If something happens to me, promise me you'll find Josh, that you'll get him back here and that someone will arrest him. I'll go home if you can do that for me."

Hank nodded only once, but he'd hold that promise as dear as any vow. "I'll walk you out."

He pushed opened the black-out front door, walked through it first and looked both ways before opening it wider for her.

She hugged Hank with the ferocity of someone saying goodbye. Her fingers fell into the space between bones. Hank had lost a lot of weight in the last few months.

His body tensed at the first touch of her embrace, but then he softened and eventually returned her hug.

"Thank you," Amanda whispered in his ear. "I don't know if you realize how much you've done for me."

"It's what you hired me for. Get out of here, kiddo. In the meantime, find a new hobby and stay off the Rio Grande, my lovely *daughter*."

She had her keys in her hand, but couldn't force herself to open her car door, to get inside and leave him. She hadn't told him good-bye, but yet everything about their exchange felt like it.

She stared at Hank's door, contemplating going back in and saying it anyway. Or, maybe she could just slip into Mexico.

If Hank was right and it *was* a trap, then she'd saved him from falling into it with her. Or, if *she* were right and Alex was waiting for her back in Pardon Falls, then she side-stepped the inevitable long enough to at least try to find Josh.

Going back didn't feel right. The road ahead had many paths, and none of them were U-turns.

Hank would be furious, but she had to do it.

With her reinforced plan firmly in place, she unlocked her door. Her mind whirled plans and next steps, to-dos and checklists.

She paid no attention to the approaching footsteps until a hand grasped her arm and yanked.

# 12

The staring contest with the toilet was entering its fourth hour. Numbness from sitting on the cold tile floor moved from Josh's butt to his feet. His brain was fully alert, processing Vargas' message with Maribel, running through the steps for his escape and wondering what his boss would order cut off if he found out what was hiding inside the tank.

Inside was his salvation.

And, his curse.

He tried to ignore the irony that his future was in the toilet, but the gleaming white porcelain mocked him.

Wrapped tightly and untampered with was the baggie full of mixed *pesos*. He wanted more before he left, but time was money. He didn't have much of either.

Josh just had to lift off the lid, rescue the money and leave.

There had to be holes in Vargas' security. He was one man. How hard would it be to slip out the gates and into the night? He'd done it once when he'd left Chicago. It'd been far easier than expected. Like going to the store for milk.

Maybe he could convince Maribel to meet him. They could run

away together, save each other from the paths laid before them by Vargas.

Who was he kidding? After years of sharing Amanda's bed, Josh didn't give it more than a passing thought to take her with him. Why was he considering running away with a woman he'd spent one night with? Not even a full night, just a couple of hours.

He banged his head against the white tiled wall.

Vargas' subliminal message was right.

Josh was royally screwed.

The rhythmic *thumping* of his head was interrupted by beating at his door.

"Josh? May I interrupt you?" Vargas spoke as he opened the door a crack. The man didn't believe in door locks, especially when it came to *other* people's quarters.

He jumped to his feet and flushed the toilet, hoping to convey that there was only one reason for sitting in the bathroom. "Absolutely, *señor*. What can I do for you?" He dried his hands on a towel.

Vargas stood at the closed French doors, peering down at the children playing below. The air inside his room was stifling, but Josh had been afraid to open the doors for relief, afraid that somehow one of the men would spy him sitting in his bathroom staring at a toilet.

"Your world changes the moment you become a father, Josh." His boss moved the sheer curtain. "Have you ever thought of having children?"

The evening with Maribel flashed through his mind. Was his child growing inside her? It wouldn't surprise him if Vargas had planned her visit to ensure conception, another means of entrapping him. "Truthfully, sir, I've thought more about preventing it."

The kids played a game of tag. Running and cheering; and laughing and playing.

Josh reached back into his memories for a similar moment. Had he ever just run and laughed? He was born into a world of money and power, but with it came expectations. He would sit quietly at dinner. He'd engage the adults in meaningful conversation. When the adults had tired of the intelligent little boy, he'd go to bed with no argument.

"I didn't have the best paternal role model," he mumbled.

"Sometimes it takes absence for one to fully understand presence," Vargas turned to him, his green eyes sharp. "Come, let's walk."

When they left his room, Josh noticed the two guards nearby. One was tall, his hair balding, but long in the back and pulled into a low ponytail. Pockmarked skin and a thin mustache confirmed this man was smart to choose life as one of Vargas' goons over being a male model.

The other was shorter, stockier with white knuckles gripping his rifle so tight as if daring someone to take it away from him. The skittish guard walked in front of them, the man who Josh guessed to be the real enforcer followed behind. In the recent months, Vargas dropped the guards when he visited Josh. The reappearance of these two—well, one-and-a-half—made Josh worry that Maribel had been akin to his last meal. The final cigarette before the firing squad.

The cartel leader walked down the stairs, and led them down a hallway past his personal study and through the center atrium. They walked through a long kitchen and emerged into a back courtyard. Vargas pointed to a building to his right and Josh followed a step behind, using the moment to examine this side of the compound.

Like the front entrance, this one was barren with reddish dirt. Next to the house, a small vegetable garden struggled under the hot sun. A football field's length away sat a back gate. Behind them was a stable converted into a garage. Some of the stalls were empty, but a few were equipped with Vargas' black Jeeps and vans, and even his own personal white Mercedes.

"The moment Catalina came into the world, I understood my purpose." He spoke after lighting a cigarette, the smoke punctuating his words. "To secure her future, and the future of her brothers." He stopped ten feet from the building.

Josh cut his eyes to the structure, straining to see inside the dirty windows. A few shadows moved inside.

"And, that leads me to your purpose, Josh."

He whipped around at the sound of his name.

Vargas took a few more steps toward the building, pausing on the second wood step and motioning for him to join him. The boss took another long drag on his cigarette, reducing it by half before discarding it in the dirt. "When you reached out to me for help getting out of Chicago, I was hesitant to get involved with American politics. It was a big risk to take, but I prayed to The Saint for guidance, and She told me when the time comes, you would return the favor."

The hair on the back of Josh's neck stood, despite the hot sun.

Vargas climbed the remaining steps and opened the door. Cool air rushed out of the darkness, but that wasn't what made him shiver. It was the thought of Vargas kneeling at the bony statue of *Santa Muerta* with Josh's name on his lips.

"We're not that different," the man continued, his tone fraternal, friendly, like two friends sharing a beer and chicken wings instead of cartel boss and his captive. "We both grew up with absent fathers, both who chose money over their children. You had the good fortune of your father giving you his name. But me, my father treated my mother like a whore, sending her money, keeping us dependent on him."

He'd heard rumors of Vargas' father, that he ran the western Mexican drug syndicate or that he was a general in a Columbian cartel. It depended on who was gossiping, but the one consistency among the stories was that the son was a brash young man with a vendetta against his father. The old man had given him a territory and small army, hoping that it would appease him.

The old man was wrong.

Josh followed Vargas into the doorway of building, but they didn't cross the threshold. Three men in white hazmat suits clambered about the room. An intricate chemistry set lined two long benches. It didn't take long for the smell to hit him. Like walking into a cat sanctuary with a never-cleaned litter box. Tears blurred his vision at the smell of ammonia.

He'd never seen a meth lab before, but somehow the knowledge felt ingrained.

"In business, you'd call this a product-line expansion," he said. "The market is becoming flooded with the milder recreational drugs. And, as you know from business school, you have to create a product so profound that your customers keep coming back for more."

"You're cooking meth a stone's throw from your home?" He whispered. It was less accusatory, more surprised. "Isn't that dangerous?"

"Perhaps, but I have the finest chemists, we've taken every precaution. You have nothing to worry about with this new operation."

"Rafael, why did you show me this?" He rarely called his boss by his first name, but seeing that lab and knowing if a chemist sneezed or got the shakes they'd all be blown to pieces seemed as good a time as any to drop the formalities.

"As my chief financial officer, you should be aware of business advances, no? But it's more than that." Vargas clasped his hands behind his back and circled him.

The two enforcers moved closer in. He was, quite literally, trapped.

"This is your destiny. This is why The Saint sent you to me."

Panic pulsed from his heart, and his fingers tingled with numbness.

Vargas continued his orbit. The man's eyes were wild and glistening with tears. With each step he seemed to grow taller, broader.

"I don't... understand." Words were slow to form as thoughts pinged around his head. Was he expected to join Vargas' army? Did this mean he'd forgotten about Amanda?

Could he escape tonight? Had Vargas been testing his new product?

"My half-brothers are imbeciles. They're soft, spoiled, complacent. Yet, my father has chosen them as his heirs, leaving me to this exile. Imagine their surprise when they realize the forgotten son has surpassed them. Do you understand?"

He understood perfectly. When Josh had found his father's updated will, he'd discovered a silent party waited in the wings for his father's death. An illegitimate half-sister. It hadn't taken much work to uncover his had sister spent time in and out of trouble for drugs, hot checks and even suspicion of prostitution.

There was no way he was going to let the money he earned for his father go up her nose. So, he'd started stealing; from his father, their clients, his colleagues. From his sister.

"I still don't..."

Vargas draped an arm over his shoulders and lifted his eyes above the door.

Josh followed his gaze, losing control of a shudder that rocked his body at the sight of a portrait of *Santa Muerta* standing guard.

"I need support, from the others in our trade. I need to know if my father and brothers push back, they will be there, on our side." The man pulled open the door, the bright sunlight burst into the room. "Your purpose, is to meet with these men as my emissary, explain to them my business plan and convince them when, if, a war breaks out to side with me, us."

"Why me, Rafael? Why would any of these men listen to me? Shouldn't it be someone else?"

"Valid questions, my friend. I choose you because your loyalty is with me alone." He took two steps out to the porch of the lab, pausing to light another cigarette before he continued downward. "And, if your loyalty is displaced, *Santa Muerta* will accept your sacrifice with gratitude."

A cloud of dirt whipped up in the wind and Vargas vanished, taking with him Josh's hope.

# 13

It was a strange feeling. Looking into the eyes of the person Amanda wanted to see most in the world, yet at the same time wishing it wasn't really him.

Her heart sped up. She tried to slow her breathing, but her chest heaved, as if her lungs were eager to draw in his woodsy scent. Instead another smell assaulted her nose.

*Alcohol?*

"David?" She forced his name through her tightening throat. Her free hand reached up and cupped his bearded cheek. "Oh my God, it really is you."

He shook free and reached into his back pocket. The sun glinted off the handcuffs and he whirled her around, the warm metal clamping around one wrist.

"What are you doing?" she hissed over her shoulder. "David, what the– can we talk? Please."

"Mandy Jack– " He cleared his throat and closed the other cuff around her free wrist. "Amanda Martin, you have the right to remain silent..." The handcuffs clinked to punctuate his sentence.

"Seriously? You're doing this?" Amanda struggled, jerking her wrists away.

"I've waited over a year for this," David whispered in her ear as he gripped her bound wrists.

She craned her neck to get a better look at him. His close-crop haircut had grown out just a bit, and flecks of gray stood out at his temple. The beard looked to be at least several days old, sitting somewhere between neglect and meant for it to be there. His gray T-shirt was creased, as if he'd slept in it.

"You have exactly two seconds to release her, or your brain will be scattered across the parking lot." Hank's voice was low and steady. A click echoed the command.

David relaxed his grip, but Amanda didn't move. She couldn't if she'd tried. He was the flame and she was a moth. Now that she was near him it would be impossible to get away. But she had to move away, despite the need to remain close.

"Hank, he's okay. He's David Stephens, a friend of mine."

"A *friend* handcuffs you in a parking lot? Sounds like you need better friends," he said. "This is what I was talking about, Amanda."

She looked down at her feet.

"Stephens, uncuff her. Inside, both of you, now."

David walked beside her, and no matter how hard she stared, he kept his gaze straight ahead.

Her body wrestled with whiplash. Josh, David, Alex, El, Hank, *David*. It was all too much. Too much resentment, regret, heartbreak.

Once the door closed behind them, Hank put his gun on the desk and pointed at the matching chairs.

Amanda fell into one, less out of obedience and more because she wasn't convinced her knees would hold her upright.

David stood by the entrance, his arms crossed in defiance.

"Amanda, would you care to fill me in on what that was?" The P.I. matched David's stance.

They were both making her feel like a scolded child.

"I bumped into an old friend." She glanced up at David, but he kept his eyes on Hank. Her spiraling emotions hit a new low. Anger joined the grief, the guilt.

Why had he chosen this moment to show up? How long had he watched her?

"This is the kind of behavior that will prove deadly across the border," Hank said.

"She's not going anywhere but with me," David said.

"Under what jurisdiction?"

"What does it matter?"

"It matters, because unless you can produce an arrest warrant, I'm not letting her go anywhere with you."

"Will you both shut up," Amanda growled, pushing off the chair and pacing the small office. Her feet planted her in front of David.

He continued to look over her head, but she saw his eyes tug downward, as if a battle waged inside of him. Like part of him wanted to make eye contact, but the other half feared he'd turn to stone if he did.

*Was I really that bad to him?* A Medusa in his eyes?

She cleared her throat. "Look, I deserve to be locked up. I get that. And when the time comes, I won't fight you, but not now."

His jaw tightened and his gaze dropped just a bit lower.

"Trust me," Amanda whispered.

His eyes crashed into hers. "Trust *you*? You mean like how you trusted me last year when I knew you lied about your identity?"

Her heart stung. He was right. It wasn't that she hadn't trusted him when he'd asked her to, she hadn't trusted herself. Hadn't believed she was capable of telling David something that would make him reject her. Unable to look at him, she studied Hank's face, silently pleading for guidance. "How did you find me?" Her voice quivered in her ears.

David took a deep breath. "There's an investigator from Chicago."

"Alex sent you." She'd meant it as a question, but it felt more like an admission. Had the former SEC agent recruited David to work with him?

David shifted. "How do you know him?"

"He came into the bar where I work last night looking for me. How long have you been working with him?"

Before her former lover could answer, the glass door swung open. Alex paused in the open doorway, the blinding sunlight from the parking lot backlighting him.

"Why am I not surprised to see you here?" Alex said to David before looking past him. "Hi, Amanda, it's nice to formally meet you." Confidence buoyed his voice and an obviously self-satisfied smile tugged at one corner of his mouth.

She opened her mouth to answer, but her attention was drawn away from Alex's face to a dark shadow that rolled into view behind him. A black Jeep parked parallel to the door, the windows heavily tinted. A single gunshot pierced the silence of the office.

Alex's body tensed, his eyes widened, then he crumpled face first. In the space where his body was, a gun stared from a barely-lowered window.

"Down," David yelled, tackling her.

The world slowed. She fell what seemed forever before the ground slammed into her and David's big body covered hers.

More gunfire screamed through the office. Glass rained down in a storm of bullets.

Hank shouted, but the words were lost in the cacophony of pops.

A shudder radiated from her body and David turned his head, putting his mouth to her ear. "You're okay, you're okay," he said.

Like a lover's embrace, it was hard to tell where he ended and she began.

Amanda wanted to scream. Maybe she did. Her sneakers pushed against the floor, feet begging to take her far away, and her hands pushed against his shoulders, but his weight was so dense that she feared he was dead, too.

"Wait."

His voice calmed her mind, but her body still fought to escape.

In a pause in the volley, she could finally make out Hank's words. "Amanda, can you hear me kiddo?"

David shifted, giving her a chance to look toward her friend and private investigator. Hank leaned against the side of his desk, one leg pulled up against his chest, the other straight along the floor. A growing red circle stained the thigh of his pants. His gun rested in his lap.

*No.*

Amanda's heart fell into her stomach. She pushed even harder against David but he wouldn't budge.

"Hank!" His name burned in her throat. "Oh my God, you're hurt."

"This? Nah, just a scratch. I've had worse." His voice strained under the weight of his words. "Stephens, military or law enforcement?"

David paused, his chest pushed into hers as he took a deep breath. "Law."

Hank tossed his keys to them. "Go straight back and through that door. Black F-150 out back and there's a 9 millimeter under the front seat. Full mag in it. In about ten seconds they're going to come in here, I'll draw them to the front while you get Amanda out the back."

The words were quick, but the meaning was clear.

Hank was going to sacrifice himself.

The man she'd come to think of as more than a friend, more than someone she'd hired to find Josh. Hank was like a father to her. She wasn't prepared to leave him. She wasn't prepared to lose him.

*I'm not prepared...*

"No, Hank, no." This time when she struggled against David, he lifted off of her. "You're coming with us."

"I'll just slow you down, kiddo. Go with Stephens, lay low and stay safe. I'll wait here for the cops and let the paramedics patch me up." He took a deep breath. A slamming car door drew their attention to the front of the office. "On three. One, two."

If he said three, she never heard it.

Hank sprang up on his good leg, aiming through the shattered glass.

David popped up and dragged her with him.

Glass crunched under her feet and she slid through the spilled contents of the coffee pot. Amanda kept trying to pivot back to help

Hank, but David kept blocking her, pushing her forward toward the back door.

"Mandy if you stop they'll shoot us," he ordered. "Go."

They pushed through the door. The bright sunlight blinded her.

David grabbed her hand and unlocked Hank's truck, shoving her inside before climbing in. "Stay down." He threw the truck in *reverse* and back into *drive* without slowing down to shift gears.

The truck bounded over a sidewalk and over the curb. Three speeding police cars fish-tailed into the large, front parking lot.

She tried to reassure herself that help had already arrived and Hank would be fine.

It wasn't until David merged onto the interstate that she remembered to breathe.

## 14

manda stopped counting aloud thirty minutes outside of El Paso. But, it didn't stop the jumble of numbers flowing through her head.

*Seven. Ten. Four. Three. Nine. Eight.*

Fear and shock made her forget even basic counting.

Once her mumbling of numbers ceased, they drove in silence on the interstate. She stared at David until his eyes drifted in her direction, then she whipped her head to look out the passenger window.

Under David's command, Hank's truck far exceeded the speed limit, making time rush by like the blurring landscape outside.

Her mind couldn't find a clear path through the numbers to reach the questions. Had David really been looking for her? *Two.* Had Vargas' people found her? *Six.* What did this have to do with the lead on Josh?

Amanda cringed at the last question, fearing she already knew the answer. *One.*

"It had to be a robbery. They must've been aiming for the pawn shop next door, right?" She posed the question to the blur of desert sands and the whirring landscape outside her window.

The passing cacti told her she was only fooling herself.

Silence answered her.

"Were you really going to arrest me?"

David leaned forward, as if it would propel the truck faster. The dark beard covering his cheeks was only an illusion of softness, like moss covering a stone. Beneath, she could see his jaw tense and release, as if he was chewing on his tongue to prevent it from giving her the truth.

Like a boiling pot, rage bubbled up her body, heating her cheeks and pushing the fear to the side. Fury filled every pore, clouding her vision with hot tears, threatening to spill over the top. Her stomach roiled, digesting resentment instead of the precious nourishment she needed to think clearly.

After a year of wanting to see David, she wasn't ready to accept that she had to sacrifice Hank. Or, Josh.

Amanda slammed her open palm on the dashboard. "Dammit, David, answer me." The slap filled the still-silent truck. Her hand stung, satisfying her body's need to feel something. "There was a plan. If you would've just left it alone, none of this would've happened."

His eyes swung to the rearview mirror and he downshifted, slowing before pulling onto the dirt shoulder. "You want answers? What about *me*, Mandy? You said goodbye in *a note*. A note in which you claimed to love me, but you obviously didn't trust me. And, today. Who was Hank? He didn't seem shocked by the shooting? What are you tangled up in?" Brown eyes that'd once looked at her with adoration narrowed.

The David and Amanda sitting in Hank's truck were not the same couple who'd danced a night away at Riley's in Phoenix. Outside the haven of that small town, they no longer had the luxury to love each other.

David had been a distraction once, but not again. Not when Josh was so close. Not when the clarity of her purpose was indisputable. Not when she was finally at peace with her future, no matter how short-lived it might be.

"Take me back." Amanda's voice betrayed the strength of her conviction by coming out barely a whisper. She cleared her throat and tried again, but only slightly louder. "We have to go back." Her legs became restless, bouncing around the floor of the truck, pulling her away from her ex. "Turn around. Now."

"No. You heard him. I had to get you out of there."

"Fine." She pushed open the door and broke into a sprint toward the setting sun. Eighteen-wheelers flew by, the wind tunnel in their wakes tugged at her, threatening to whisk her into oblivion.

David grabbed her by the waist and spun her around. "Where do you think you're going?" He crossed his arms and widened his stance the moment he released her.

"El Paso." Amanda mirrored his stance and narrowed her eyes.

"For what? Hank isn't there anymore."

"You don't know that."

"You're right, I don't." He loosened his posture and took a step toward her. His eyes softened, suddenly he was her David again and she was his Mandy. "What I do know is he drew them to the front so we could get out the back." He took another step in her direction, his arm twitched as if it wanted to reach for her but a force-field held it down. "He was shot." His Adam's apple bobbed as he swallowed. "Baby, he sacrificed himself so I could get you out of there."

Her brain froze, the chill rushing down her limbs.

David reached to comfort her, but Amanda recoiled, fearing his slightest touch would break her.

"No," she whispered. "You saw them, the police were almost there. Take me back."

"I'm sorry, Mandy, but I can't do that."

She ran from him as fast as her body could move. Her ankles struggled to keep her upright as she stepped on loose rocks. She felt like a salmon swimming upstream against a river of cars and trucks. No matter how hard she ran, El Paso–and Hank–stayed just as far away.

Amanda jogged to a stop, watching the oncoming traffic. She glanced over her shoulder, in the day's dying light she watched David take slow steps in her direction, his head down but eyes looked up over his brow.

She turned back to the west. The cars drove like a school of fish, all following the same defined path, nothing affecting their journey eastward.

A black Jeep cut across two lanes of traffic and her instincts told her exactly what it was.

*Shark.*

David's head followed the vehicle as it passed by their parked truck, unable to get across a convoy of eighteen-wheelers to move into the far right lane. "Come on," he shouted over the din of the highway. "Run."

He ran behind her, his hand on the small of her back, pushing her along. They parted at the back of the truck. "Get in and get on the floor," he yelled. "Don't look up until I say so."

A half-mile ahead, the dark outline of the Jeep moved onto the shoulder. White lights illuminated as it reversed.

Amanda curled into the floor and felt the pull of the truck as David accelerated.

He jerked to the left and she watched his feet work the pedals and his hand shift gears like a race car driver on the track.

Another jerk to the left. Horns blared at them from behind. Two pops filled the air.

He moved the gearshift into its final place and, after a minute, the speed of the truck steadied. "Okay, I think we're safe," he said. "For now, at least."

She climbed into the seat and fastened her seatbelt. Deep breaths did nothing to calm her racing heart.

"We'll stop at my place. You'll be safe there. Anyway, we need to have a long talk," David paused to change lanes and pass a slow moving horse trailer. "What the hell I'm getting myself into?"

## 15

The small trailer park was dark and empty of cars when David pulled in. He parked Hank's truck in front of the first trailer.

An antenna rose from the top of the single wide, reminding Amanda of an insect rather than someone's prefabricated home.

"Home sweet home," David mumbled as he killed the engine.

Amanda glanced around before following him up the wooden porch. Some of the other trailer homes had plastic furniture and barbecue grills in front, but not his. Only the black truck parked in the driveway gave any indication someone lived there.

The aluminum door rattled as it bounced off the siding. She followed him inside and found him rummaging through the fridge.

"Want a beer?"

"Sure."

The humble coziness she loved of his ranch-style house in Phoenix was tossed aside for stark neglect. A particleboard shelf bulged under the weight of an old TV facing a faded tweed couch. Dirty, stiff brown carpet crunched under her feet, driving her to the even dirtier and torn linoleum in the kitchen.

Her nose twitched at the bitter whiff of stale air, as if he rarely visited this place. The smell was so unlike the scent that filled her memory when she thought of David; warm, woodsy with just a touch of salt to remind her of their evening runs.

"So this is yours?"

He met her eyes for the first time since arriving. "Yeah, not as nice as your boyfriend's penthouse." David handed her a beer before pushing past her and collapsing into a chair.

Amanda bit her tongue when he propped his dusty boots up on the edge of the kitchen table. "That's not what I meant." She took a seat across from him, angling her body away from his feet.

He pulled the bottle off his lips. As much as she wanted to study his face, her eyes focused on herself. Rings of pink encircled both wrists. Faint, more emotional than physical. Even though the cuffs had been on her for only minutes, the skin felt as raw as her heart.

He waited a year for her. To arrest her.

To make her face the punishment she deserved. If anyone was owed the honor of arresting her, it was David. Amanda would gladly offer her wrists to him, but not until she found Josh.

"Well," he said after another loud smacking sip of his beer.

"So is this the part where you tell me that anything I say will be used against me?" She took a long drink of her beer, hoping to drown the bitterness rising up her throat.

David laughed before draining the bottle. "We didn't get that far, so your *secrets* are safe. Hungry?" The emphasis he put on the word 'secrets' wasn't lost on her.

He pushed up from the chair and pulled open a few cabinets before tossing a box of saltines on the table. "Sorry, today was grocery day but I ran into an ex-girlfriend, got sidetracked."

The acid from his words scorched her heart. They each took several more drinks, their eyes working overtime to avoid each other. Amanda finally let her gaze wander to him anyway. His face was cold, hard, thinner despite the beard.

"You've lost weight." Her voice was soft.

"Could say the same about you," he said.

She rubbed her wrists as she struggled for words. Conversation had always flowed easily between them, but now she felt like she was sitting across from a stranger.

*I am, aren't I?*

She couldn't relate to *this* David.

"How are you?" she asked.

"Aside from getting shot at and chased, I'm peachy."

Amanda pursed her lips and narrowed her eyes. "Don't be that way. You know what I mean. How have you been?"

"Oh, you mean before today. Well, let's see, over the past year I was grilled by the SEC and FBI, lost my job, lost my friends, made my momma cry, moved from the only place I've ever called home. Oh, and my dog died. I've been pretty much living every country song written."

"You didn't have a dog."

David finished the rest of his beer in a single gulp and gave her a wry smile. "I threw that in there for sympathy. Want another beer?"

She couldn't stop the small laugh. He was still there, her David, beneath all the hurt she'd caused him.

He slammed a half full bottle of tequila and two shot glasses on the table between them followed by their refreshed beers. "Now that we got the pleasantries out of the way." David leaned forward on his elbows. "Who's Hank? And who's after you?"

Suddenly cold, Amanda pulled her long-sleeved shirt closed tighter, letting the front double up like a suit of armor.

How much could she tell him?

"Okay, I'll answer your questions but I have some of my own. How did you know to find me there?" she countered. "Were you working with Alex?"

He reached for the bottle of tequila, poured the two shots and tossed his back. "I just caught up with Alex. He found me, gave me that address and said you have been seen there." He paused to down a second shot. "I went to prove Alex wrong," he mumbled as he studied his empty shot glass. "Your turn." David nodded toward Amanda's untouched tequila.

"Hank Snare, private investigator." She coughed before taking a sip of beer. "I hired him to help me find Josh Williams." She downed the tequila.

David laughed when squeezed her eyes shut, the liquor leaving a trail of burning as it slid down her throat. "And Williams doesn't want to be found, so he sent people to kill you?"

"Josh doesn't care about anyone other than himself." Amanda scratched at her wrists, as if her skin was telling her to not say too much. "I almost didn't believe it was you."

Another light laugh escaped his lips. He poured two more shots, this time she sipped hers, allowing the liquor to punish her tongue.

"I could say the same thing." His voice was soft and the words tumbled into each other. "I still don't."

A car pulled into the trailer park.

Amanda held her breath. In her mind's eye she could see a black Jeep pull in. Stop at David's trailer. A single window rolled down and bullets would soon assail the aluminum siding.

Instead, the tires crunched on the rocky road as it drove past his home.

"We're safe here." His words pulled her out of the imagined attack.

Did he still know her well enough to read her thoughts as they flashed across her face? Or, did the same scenario play out in his mind?

She cleared her throat, trying to soothe the tequila afterburn. "Were you really going to arrest me?"

David poured another shot. "Yup." He held the bottle over her empty glass but she shook her head.

"Why?"

"You broke the law." Even though his voice was as flat as the Texas plains, there was something hidden just beneath the surface.

"I'm trying to fix that." She folded her arms over her chest.

"How? By getting other people killed?" He popped up, ignoring the clattering chair that bounced off the floor. He paced while he took another long drink. "You said Williams only thinks of himself. Sounds like the two of you were made for each other."

Amanda's chair fell this time as she blocked his pacing. "That's unfair." Her words were sharp and low. "I was coerced. I didn't do anything wrong. Not intentionally."

"Unfair? You want to talk to me about unfair? *Unfair* is lying about who you are, Amanda."

Her full name on his lips stung more than when his handcuffs bit into her wrists.

"*Unfair* is not trusting someone when they have never betrayed you." He took a step toward her, his face flushing red. "Unfair is leaving me to clean up your mess." His beer and tequila breath burned her nose. "Unfair is–" David's voice broke and he turned his back on her.

"What?"

He didn't answer her, instead drained his beer.

"Unfair is what, David?" Fear and curiosity curdled in her stomach. Amanda could hear a phone buzzing. Not hers, it was in her purse, left behind in the mayhem at Hank's office. It must have been his, a number she didn't have, a cord he'd cut.

Or maybe it was just the air vibrating with their tension. She wasn't sure. Was Josh was really that close? Was Hank was really dead? Was David really standing there in front of her?

"Unfair is seeing you and not hating you as much as I want." He spoke over his shoulder. "I need to get out of here. Take my bed. Don't open the door for anyone." David reached for Hank's keys on the counter.

Amanda ran around the table, blocking the door to keep him from leaving. Her heart screamed to let him go, but she ignored it. "Please don't go."

A sad smile crossed his lips as he stared up at the peeling paint on the ceiling. He shook his head. "Unfair is not getting to say that to you before you ran, Mandy."

## 16

He should've grabbed the tequila.

That wasn't his first mistake of the day, but it was the one he regretted most.

He drove Hank's truck up the highway, turning off at an unmarked dirt road. It ended at a small beach on the banks of the Rio Grande where David swung the vehicle into a tight U-turn, the back end facing the river.

A deep blue bruise mottled the western sky. The final remnant of the sun before everything went black.

He looked at his phone. A voicemail from Fallon stared back. He owed her a call. *That* was the other mistake. Standing her up. Or, was it when he'd asked her out?

If David was being honest with himself, his mistakes had started when he'd pursued the new girl in town, one with a thin past but an unforgettable smile. He hadn't seen that smile yet. Not the one that made Mandy look like she was made of light, that made her hazel eyes glow like the stars dotting the sky overhead.

Why had he approached her in the parking lot? He should've called Fallon. Told her that he had visual on a fugitive. Let the FBI take her. Would that have prevented Alex from being killed? And, Hank? It was hard to know, but it would have avoided him drudging up old feelings.

Old love.

Old hate.

Old regret.

What now?

She'd said she had a lead on her ex, but was that to keep him from arresting her?

David almost wished she'd be gone when he got home. She ran before. Twice, from Chicago and again from Phoenix. From him.

*Maybe she'll do it again. Old habits...*

He lay back in the bed of the borrowed pickup and studied the stars. The sky above him was clear, but a thunderstorm churned in the distance, streaking the horizon in lightning.

His phone dinged with a text message. Fallon. She was starting to worry. He needed to call her. But, what would he say?

*Sorry I stood you up. I ran into an old girlfriend, handcuffed her and then we ran for our lives after getting shot at. I brought her back to my place, and we had some drinks and reminisced on old times ...*

He and Fallon weren't technically dating, but she'd dump him after that. Probably punch him, too.

It'd been a nice coincidence when he'd run into Fallon Weatherby at a bust. Friends and classmates in college, she'd aced every test in law and criminology. Then again, she came from a long line of Texas lawmen. It was more than in her blood. It was her genetic makeup. Which meant she was *more* than a human lie detector. She was a human bullshit detector.

After Mandy had left Phoenix, he been sure she'd call him. Even though she'd only been there for a couple of months, her absence had felt like the loss of a limb.

Every time his phone rang, David had expected it to be her. Only after he'd been fired, after that disastrous night with Shiloh, *after* he'd left town that he changed his number.

That was the only way to start healing. With a prosthetic.

His chest vibrated again with an incoming call. The third from Fallon. If he didn't answer she'd start triangulating his location.

"Fallon," he said as a way of hello. "Hey, I'm so sorry."

"Oh, thank God." Her natural Texas accent was gone, her voice was drawn tight. "I was about to send out a search party."

David opened his mouth to see what response would come out, but instead only a heavy sigh escaped his lips. What was he thinking, that he could move on?

Mandy was more than the one who got away. She was the one who got inside his head and messed everything up.

"I thought we had—but maybe it wasn't tonight—or, was I supposed to meet you out?" The confusion in her voice unsettled him. She was a woman who was *always* sure.

He could tell her the truth. Tell her, up until yesterday, he'd gone a whole week without living in the past, but then the past had found him. Trapped him.

"No, this is totally my fault. Someone showed up from out of town, from back home." David swallowed the knot forming in his throat.

He hated lying more than he hated liars. As long as he walked the tightrope of truth he could look her in the eye the next time he saw her.

"Oh." It was a small sound, but one that conveyed much. Hurt. Anger. Disbelief. Embarrassment.

He sat up and looked out over the river. The silvery moon snaked across the water as it ran past him, rushing for the Gulf of Mexico. "Fallon, this is not about you, nor have I changed my mind about taking you out. I just got blindsided by this friend who needed my help, and I couldn't say no."

She paused for so long that he glanced at his phone to make sure they didn't lose the connection. Was she running everything he said through an internal filter? Checking it for holes or soft spots?

"You had me worried." Her tone was staying-out-past-curfew scolding.

"I should've called."

"You're damn right." Just like that, her accent was back, meaning he was off the hook or on the chopping block. Either way Fallon was inching her way back to normal. "So, what are you going to do to make it up?"

*I could hand you a fugitive and her ex-boyfriend.*

To a girl in law enforcement, that was much sweeter than flowers.

But could he?

Just because he was close to arresting Mandy himself didn't mean he could sit by and watch someone else take her away. David couldn't do that to her. The look of betrayal would haunt him for the rest of his life. "I could volunteer to hold the target for you at the shooting range."

Fallon had a laugh as big as his home state. Infectious and sincere, it set everyone immediately at ease; cops and criminals alike. "Don't tempt me, Stephens."

"Look, I really am sorry, today just got away from me. Can I call you tomorrow? I'll know more about my friend's situation and we can go from there."

"I hope everything's okay."

David hoped so too. "It will be. Call you tomorrow." He hung up and watched the water flow away.

For each minute that ticked by, he felt further and further away from the past. Yet *the past* sat in his trailer.

What had stopped him from telling Fallon about Mandy? Did he still love her?

That was obvious. A piece of him would always. But did he *believe* her?

Did he believe she was looking for her ex to turn him in?

What if she was simply meeting up with him?

He hopped out of the back of the truck and went closer to the water, the loamy sand slowing him as he trudged forward.

The river moved swiftly. Water must've been released from the reservoir hundreds of miles upstream. A simple act by an engineer that would be felt all the way down the river.

Mandy was a dam, holding him back, keeping him pooled in one place for her use. There were cracks in that dam. He could try to patch them and stay close to her.

Or, he could break the whole thing wide open.

## 17

Vargas used black vans for all of his dirty work. The white cars, his own Mercedes sedan, a Cadillac SUV and a rugged, yet pristine Jeep were reserved strictly for public persona. From what Josh had seen, the boss never touched one of the black vans. His Captains were in control of that fleet.

He'd arrived in a black van more than a year ago.

A rare northerly wind breezed through the compound in the early evening.

Vargas was missing from dinner that evening, as were many of his captains. Was the drug lord was putting plans in place to wage war on his father? Or, in his parlor, mumbling Josh's name as he knelt in prayer to *Santa Muerta*?

Wherever he was, it seemed as those remaining were forbidden to speak. Even the children were subdued and the usual clanging from the kitchen staff was muted. The tightness in the air affected his appetite and he pushed his food around the plate for twenty minutes before excusing himself.

He retired to his room, where he read the same page of a book three times. His agitated mind wouldn't let him focus on food for thought either. Tonight could be the perfect night to escape.

No Vargas. No captains. Josh could just walk away.

Disappear into the night.

With his back against the balcony railing, he played through the various moves as if he was studying a chessboard. He'd move one piece in his mind, then imagine which piece Vargas would countermove. Another piece, another move, another countermove.

The hum of an oncoming vehicle drew his attention to the window.

From the second floor, he could see pinpricks of headlights bouncing across the dirt road on the northern horizon. Josh scrambled to the light switch to darken his room. The car charged toward the *hacienda*, and a herd of men came from around the main building toward the massive gates.

Moments later, shouts and whistles erupted as a van and Jeep neared the compound. He scanned the courtyard for any signs of Vargas. The man in white was nowhere to be found.

This must be very dirty work.

Rocks crunched as the vehicles pulled through the gates and turned left toward a small stucco tool shed set apart from the main house. They stopped and all the doors opened. The men had guns slung over their shoulders. Josh recognized the van driver as the man who'd driven him across the border.

The back door of the van opened and the men formed a tighter circle. Two reached in and pulled out the cargo.

He leaned over the balcony railing, straining to see through the crowd. When they started walking he saw two of them half-dragging a hooded man to the shed. Men being brought to the *hacienda* with hoods over their heads were as common as grocery and tequila deliveries. He'd heard rumors of sunrise executions, that Vargas treated these slayings as sacrifices to *Santa Muerta*. That was too gruesome for him to have any interest in witnessing.

Josh remembered that hood and the stifling heat inside it from his own breath. The dizzying darkness had made him feel like he was in a vacuum. Nausea had lapped at him like oceans waves.

He was in Mexico because of that hood.

Tiny clues from Vargas and Pedro had helped him fill in that they were more than a two-hour drive south of Texas.

"You poor son of a bitch," Josh whispered.

A few moments later, the men emerged from the shed, laughing and speaking in rapid Spanish. The drivers moved their vehicles around to the back of the property where all the cars were kept, and the other men walked to the area where the workers lived. Plumes of white smoke from their cigarettes followed their retreating figures behind the house.

He was about to get back to the chess game in his mind when Vargas glided from the main house toward the shed. "Why is he going over there alone?" Josh asked himself.

With his near seclusion on the *hacienda,* he spoke to himself more and more, mostly out of loneliness. He even spoke to himself in German from time to time, practicing his mother's tongue should he ever see her again.

"Where are the guards?" Josh waited while Vargas slipped inside.

After several minutes, the drug lord exited the shed and his apparition disappeared behind the house. With no moon to light the courtyard, he had to rely on sound to determine if the guards made their nightly patrol of the perimeter. Only the wind blew through the compound.

"Screw it."

It was time to test one of his moves.

He took a moment to tie his hair back in a rubber band he stole from a stack of papers and gently opened his door.

The guard stationed across his room appeared to be dozing off. Josh was allowed to roam the property alone, but Vargas had insisted the guard was for his own protection.

When Josh arrived, a young, strong man was stationed outside his door. As he'd gained Vargas's trust, the boss had replaced the man with an older one, which signaled he was no longer considered a flight risk.

"Enrique," Josh whispered, gently shaking the old man's shoulder. There was no reason to sneak off. "I'm going to take a walk. *Un paseo*. Okay?"

His guard smacked his toothless gums and nodded. The one time he'd seen Enrique awake, the man's eyes were frosted over with cataracts and he wasn't fully convinced his hearing was intact. He must be someone's great-uncle or grandfather.

The hallway was dim and cool with fans circling overhead. Many of the rooms on the hall belonged to Vargas' inner circle and extended family. His immediate family lived on the third floor and used a private stairwell to come and go. Josh had seen his wife and children on a few occasions but saw his *compadres* on the second floor often enough to know their names.

He skipped down the wide staircase and out the front door. Normally, a few of the older kids threw dice on the front porch after dinner, but even the porch was vacant. It was as if an official decree had come down that everyone should stay inside this evening and mind his or her own business. He hadn't gotten the memo.

Rather than beeline toward the shed, Josh strolled around the left barrier of the compound. He lightly traced along the stone wall, letting his fingers guide him in the near blackness.

The wall pitched to the right and he turned, reaching out blindly to the stone so he could continue his walk. The shed came into view with a lone light bulb shining over the door. He kept his eyes focused, but eased his pace.

The barrier broke at the compound gate, and Josh paused at the massive wooden doors. He'd watched the gates open many times and one man could pull open each door. Could he fumble around in the darkness to find a latch? He wouldn't need to open it much to slip through. Then what?

He turned back to the shed. Using the light that spilled onto the ground from the house, he moved out of the shadows and crossed directly to the building. Five feet away from the shed, he paused and looked around. For so many people to live in a close quarters, he was completely alone.

Was this a trap? Would floodlights pop on the minute he

touched the door and the snap of guns rise above the whistling wind?

Josh shuffled forward two more steps before freezing again. Did he even want to see what was inside? Never before had he cared when men were brought to Vargas. Something was different this time. It was as if the whole *hacienda* held its breath; the people, the buildings, even the dirt courtyard sat in anticipated stillness. Like a storm was approaching. While everyone battened down to prepare for the worse, he rushed forward to watch it barrel for them.

The distinct spice of nicotine burned his nose. He jerked his head to the right and Vargas stepped through the haze of white smoke.

"Good evening," the drug lord said, exhaling another cloud into the dark night. "I thought you would be in bed like everyone else. There is something about a moonless sky that seems to send everyone to sleep early." Vargas walked toward him, his face lighting up in the orange glow as he took another drag.

Josh turned his back to the shed. "Can't sleep."

The boss studied him, grimacing as he withheld the cigarette smoke in his lungs allowing the nicotine to live up to its fullest potential. He laughed, the white smoke escaping both his nose and his mouth.

Vargas took another drag before dropping the butt to the ground. "You know what I find funny? For a second, I saw you as a child. Afraid of the dark, searching for his mommy." He closed the distance between them.

Dried sweat and tobacco flooded his senses as his boss clutched his face in his warm hands. His eyes glowed green in the darkness, as if powered from a light source within.

"You are standing here as a tow-headed little boy. Equally defiant and eager to please, both spoiled and oddly humble. You want it all and expect nothing." Vargas released him and threw an arm around his shoulder, guiding him as they walked away from the shed, and back to the house. "Some may think you came full circle," he continued. "That you've reached your point of maturation and started back down the hill toward your childhood. But, I know that's not true, Josh. I know all along you have been nothing but a smart, precocious child who minds his manners most of the time but every now and then gets caught with his hand in the cookie jar."

Josh finally exhaled.

The drug lord led him up the steps to the main house rather than around the back of the compound. They reached the door and Vargas pulled it open. The sudden brightness hurt his eyes.

"I can even imagine you on Christmas Eve. Shaking all of your presents, snooping under the tree. As you know, Santa is always watching you. Now, let's have a drink and cigars." Vargas turned to his study, releasing the front door to fall against Josh's shoulder.

Before he stepped inside the house, he glanced back at the solitary shed.

He'd never believed in Santa Claus.

## 18

Waking to the smell of frying bacon and coffee brewing went a long way in determining her mood. Amanda sat up and rubbed her eyes. After David had left last night, she'd sat at his kitchen table and waited.

And waited.

And waited.

When her blinks had become longer and she couldn't hold her head up, she'd gone in search of a bed. The second bedroom was completely empty, so she'd made her way to his room.

She never heard him come home. Maybe he'd stayed out all night.

Amanda didn't know him anymore. He looked like David, sounded like David. But he wasn't *her* David.

She smiled as he moved around the tiny kitchen, flipping bacon with one hand and stirring scrambled eggs with the other. She felt thrust back in time, back to when they'd spent lazy Sunday mornings cooking breakfast together. "That might be the best way for a girl to wake up."

He smiled over his shoulder. "It's nearly ready. Pour some coffee and have a seat."

The chair he'd knocked down was back in place. The shot glasses sat in the drying rack and the tequila was nowhere to be seen. It was almost as if last night didn't happen. Or, maybe it was *now* that wasn't happening.

Amanda felt out of time; standing there with David as he cooked breakfast, but instead of wearing his Phoenix PD uniform, he was dressed in Border Patrol green. The shooting felt real *and* imagined. Hank felt alive and dead. Josh felt within reach and a world away.

"About last night." She needed to rip off the emotional Band-Aid.

He set a plate of food in front of her. "I'm sorry." He took a seat across the table. "I said some stuff I shouldn't have said. Left when I should've stayed. You lost a friend yesterday, and I should've been here for you."

Amanda had expected another argument, even a minor one, not an apology. "Well, you had lot to process yesterday."

"I wasn't the only one," he said through a mouthful of bacon. "How're you holding up?"

Despite the emptiness of hunger and the teasing aroma of breakfast, she couldn't eat. Her mind was rolling through all she needed to do. Find Hank. Get back to Mexico. Find Josh. Bring Josh to David so he could arrest them both. It was only then, when she and her ex were tucked away in jail, could she allow herself to succumb to hunger.

"Can you take me back to El Paso today?" Where his words had been as soft as his scrambled eggs, hers came out like the hard shell. "I mean—"

"You're worried about Hank." David nodded. "I am, too. One of the other agents called in sick, so I'm picking up his shift. I'll check around though, see what I can find out."

There was a whole lot of *no* in those words. "That's fine, I've intruded enough. Can I borrow your phone and call someone to come get me?"

He laced his fingers together and propped his elbows on the sides of his plate. "Mandy, I'm afraid I can't do that."

She opened her mouth to argue, but he held up a palm.

"Hear me out. Whoever did this knows we got away. Let me get the lay of the land before we go charging into something."

Her mouth twitched as she absorbed his words. He was right. Even if the shooter didn't hang around, the place would be crawling with police. It wouldn't do Hank any good if Amanda went there and was arrested, if for nothing more than possessing a fake driver's license, which was left behind in her purse somewhere in Hank's office. "What am I supposed to do?" She broke off a piece of the bacon. Its allure was too much to resist.

"Trust me."

She looked across his sparse living room. She might not have been under arrest—yet— but she certainly felt imprisoned. What was she supposed to do all day? Pace the living room? Clean out the empty fridge? Mend the threadbare curtains?

If he hadn't been at Hank's office Amanda could very well be dead. Then again, if he hadn't stopped her in the parking lot she could already be in Mexico. That would've left Hank alone in the shooting. Even if he was dead, he wasn't alone when it'd started.

She'd put her life in his hands, but not the truth. Maybe it was time.

For a moment, he was there. Her David. With him she'd found herself. Her true self. Their brief relationship hadn't been perfect, but it was more real than the years she'd spent with Josh. "Okay, but first I need to tell you everything."

"Mandy—"

"I mean, you never got to the part about using it against me in court right? How much time do you have?"

David laughed and shook his head. "I don't have to leave for another thirty minutes." He scooted back from the table and grabbed the coffee, refilling both of their cups.

"Perfect." Amanda took a deep breath and looked down at her nearly-full plate. "After I left Phoenix, I realized the only way to fix all of this was to find Josh. The last day I saw him, he had a boarding pass to El Paso, so it made perfect sense for him to get this far and slip into Mexico. To meet up with a client of his." Her gaze wandered back to David. She didn't want to see his face at the mention of Phoenix, but he leaned forward on his elbows, listening intently.

"Who is the client?"

"Rafael Vargas."

His eyes widened and he exhaled. "Are you sure?"

"I didn't know who he was until I met up with Hank. His investigation was taking too long, so a few weeks ago, I started slipping into Mexico. I thought I was wrong, but just the other day I found him."

"You saw him?"

She put a small bite of eggs in her mouth, but they'd gone cold. "No, a girl at the supermarket in a town saw his photo and told me he worked for Vargas." Amanda could no longer sit still. Her legs ached for movement. To carry her out the door and across the river to finish her search for Josh. Instead, she grabbed their plates and went to the sink.

"And, it's not coincidental that you were shot at yesterday," he said the words she couldn't admit to herself.

The aluminum blinds over the small sink window were crinkled and snaggletoothed, and stared into the side of another trailer. "This is all my fault," she whispered. "I thought I was finally getting somewhere. I don't care who Vargas is or what he's done. I just want to get Josh."

There was no sound of the chair scraping across the linoleum, or vibration as David crossed the kitchen to stand behind her.

His presence enveloped, even if his arms didn't.

"Stay here today." His voice was low.

Goosebumps broke out all over her body as his breath tickled the back of her neck.

"My shift ends at four. We can figure out what to do next then. Don't open the door for anyone."

Amanda stood there for a long time after he left. After he locked the front door. After Hank's truck started up and gravel crunched as he drove away from her.

A year of missing him.

A year of dialing his number, but never being brave enough to hit send.

A year regretting the hurt she caused.

It felt like a sidewalk crack compared to the Grand Canyon between them when he left.

# 19

The Border Patrol agents in Vargas' employ were all the same. Young, poor and ambitious. For the most part, these men were smart enough to not visit the drug lord's *hacienda* unless the situation absolutely required them to risk getting caught.

Or, unless they were summoned.

It was rare for Josh to actually see one of these guys when they were on the compound. Security around him was tighter than usual when the Border Patrol called. Harboring a white-collar criminal must be a bit too much to turn a blind eye.

After lunch, he lingered around the spacious first floor of the main house rather than return to his room. He hoped the other residents on the compound would go back to their daily duties or indulge in an early *siesta* and forget he was there long enough to give him an opportunity to visit the man in the shed.

Vargas had kept him occupied until well past midnight. With each hour that'd ticked by, the boss brought out bottle after bottle of expensive sipping tequila. As much as Josh wanted to let the liquor take control and momentarily forget why he was drawn to the tool shed, he'd held back, letting the man out drink him two to one.

When the clock had inched closer one, Vargas had grown quiet, as if something that he'd tried to drown had managed to rise to the surface. Without a word, the kingpin had set down his drink and left his study, mumbling goodnight before slamming the door behind him.

Alone, Josh had refilled his glass with the most expensive tequila and stared out the window at the door of the shed until the eastern horizon showed the first hint of morning.

Whoops and whistles erupted from the front gate of the compound, pulling him back to his now-thwarted mission of sneaking to the shed. A rusty truck drove through and parked in front of the wide porch. A sandy-haired young man in a Border Patrol uniform hopped out of the truck and strode to the house.

Josh looked over his shoulder before quietly opening the door to Vargas' private parlor, the same room that housed the shrine to the patron saint of the drug cartels. The skeletal lady's dead eyes followed him as he moved against the wall. The waxy musk of her candles assaulted his nose, following him as he tried to move as far away from the corner shrine as possible.

Voices outside wafted in through an open window.

"Vargas wanted to see me." The man's confidence outweighed his years and his accent drew out the words longer than necessary.

One of the men lingering around the front courtyard walked toward the young agent. "Weapons?"

"I know better," he answered. "But y'all can check me anyway."

After several seconds passed, Josh heard a long, low whistle.

Footsteps echoed down the hall behind him, and Vargas appeared, as if he were an actor just waiting for his entrance cue. "Lloyd, thank you for coming at short notice." His voice was flat, as if the overabundance of tequila had robbed it of its normal inflection. "I see you were on your way to work."

"Yeah, sorry, I didn't have time to change." Lloyd's voice lost the harshness of derision, speaking instead with the softness of respect. "What can I help you with, sir?"

Vargas spoke to his men in Spanish. From his vantage point, Josh watched their dusty boots retreat to the side of the house.

"Come, let's sit in the shade of the porch." The boss' footsteps moved toward the chairs stationed in front of the window.

The back of Lloyd's blond head joined Vargas'.

Josh moved closer to the wall, hoping to blend into the beige stucco.

"Yesterday, my men attempted to thwart an attack on my business. In the aftermath, we discovered that someone very important to us was there." Vargas handed something to the dirty agent. "This woman was there, but got away."

The younger man's head bent and he held a small rectangle in his hand up close to his face. "Who is she?"

Josh leaned away from the cover of the wall to get a better view. Dropping to his hands and knees, he crawled between the upholstered chairs to the window.

Somewhere in his core he knew the answer, but he didn't want to look that deep in his soul.

"You can see her name there on the license, but she also goes by Amanda Martin."

The air in Vargas' parlor dipped several degrees, causing a shiver to radiate down his body.

*Oh. Shit.*

"Sir, please don't take this the wrong way, but how am I supposed to find this one girl in all of El Paso?"

The cartel leader passed something else over. "I can make it easy for you. There's a number she dialed recently. A lot. You won't recognize it, but it used to belong to someone you know. David Stephens."

The sheer curtain waved in the wind, tickling his arm as the soft fabric flirted with him.

"He's my partner." The agent's voice lifted in slight disagreement, the kind normally used by kids who don't want to take out the trash or clean their rooms.

He made it to the window and turned, bracing his back against the wall, slumping so the top of his head wouldn't be visible over the windowsill.

"I'm your employer, Lloyd." Vargas' words curled around a smile. "You will be fairly compensated when you bring her to me."

"Now wait a minute. I only provide you with information. I ain't one of your thugs. I don't kidnap innocent people."

The top of Josh's head prickled with Lloyd's protest. He was close to escape. Dealing with Amanda showing up wanting to kick his butt wasn't on his pre-departure checklist. Why did Vargas want her? Was it to control outside forces while he took over his father's empire?

Why in the world was Amanda wasting her time coming after him? How did she know where to look?

The last time he'd seen her, Amanda had known something was up, but she'd assumed it was another one of his dalliances. He could tell by the way she'd crossed her arms, waiting in his cleaned out office.

It was over, she'd had enough of his philandering. At least, that's what he'd thought. His photographic memory landed on his desk, where he'd carelessly left the boarding pass to El Paso.

*Shit. I may as well have written an address down for her.*

Even with the problem solved, a tingling sensation continued across the crown of his head. An involuntary shudder and he felt something tumble out of his hair and onto his lap.

Tail coiled, a four-inch-long scorpion faced him, ready to strike.

Josh tried to back away, but the wall wouldn't budge.

"You won't kidnap her, not technically. That's why my thugs, as you so eloquently call them, will be there with you," Vargas said.

Like a boxer circling an opponent in the ring, the scorpion spun around his abdomen. Even through his T-shirt and the waistband of his pants, he could feel the tiny pricks of the six legs as it crawled toward his groin.

*Oh not there, please, anywhere but there.*

Josh bit his bottom lip, willing the creature to keep crawling. Not long after his arrival, Pedro had killed a similar little beast just outside of his room and had taken the time to show it to him, explaining it was the one of the most venomous scorpions in this part of Mexico. While deadly to children, it would only cause pain and numbness in adults.

And, *that* was not an area where Josh wanted pain, or numbness.

The scorpion crept down his left leg, moving on the inside of his thigh. Obviously no longer sensing him as a threat, the scorpion lowered its tail, allowing it to trace lightly like a lover's fingertip.

He could feel the sensation building up in his thigh muscle. No matter how much he begged his ticklish skin to not jerk, his left leg flinched.

The scorpion struck, missing the delicate parts of his groin, but the stinger pierced his inner thigh, sending electric volts of pain throughout his body.

Metal flooded his mouth as he bit his tongue to keep from crying out. Before the thing could strike again, Josh backhanded it, knocking it to the floor between his legs. His right foot rose up and kicked it away, the cursed creature sliding across the tile toward a sofa.

"You fucker," he whispered through clinched teeth. His eyes flitted to the bony lady in the corner. Despite the fact that she was a statue without muscles or facial tissue, Josh swore she'd smiled. "What are you staring at?" he hissed.

"How am I supposed to take her with Stephens watching?"

Sweat dripped down Josh's forehead, making him jump at the fear that another scorpion was lining up to attack again. He tried to scoot away from the window, but only his right leg would respond to his brain's commands.

"Lloyd, must I do everything for you?" The cartel leader exhaled a dramatic sigh. "Amanda Martin is wanted for securities fraud in her country. Arrest her."

He made it to the adjoining wall, turning a hot cheek to the cool stucco and closing his eyes. His chest tightened, likely from a combination of exertion and the venom coursing through his body.

Pedro had said some adults had an extreme reaction, teetering on the brink of death.

His hair clung to his face, drenched in sweat.

"I'm Border Patrol, not police. How am I supposed to know this?"

"She was picked up by your agency just two nights ago. You recognized her. Or, if you prefer, you could just kill Stephens," Vargas continued.

Josh opened his eyes and saw his boss' profile as the man stared down the young agent.

"You have forty-eight hours to bring me Amanda Martin."

## 20

F our o'clock came and went with no sign of David. Amanda had already cleaned his trailer. Twice.

She rearranged his meager cupboards and kitchen counter, then moved everything back again. There was no washer and dryer, or she would've busied herself with laundry instead of worrying if David had been killed during the day. Or, had just up and left her.

*Karma is a pissed off ex.*

Finally, as the setting sun was about to kiss the long day goodbye, she grabbed a beer and sat outside on the wooden porch. Hank's black truck turned the corner and eased up the gravel road.

David got out, his green shirt untucked and his boots kicking up dust as they shuffled. He finally looked at her before he planted a foot on the first step. "Oh, hey." His words were slow, thick. "Sorry I'm late. Did you eat dinner?"

Amanda narrowed her eyes and chewed on the sharp words on her tongue. Despite the anger churning in her empty stomach, she held back on the scolding she'd practiced to the living room walls. "We're fresh out of saltines, I ate the last egg, but hey, we still have beer."

David nodded and half-collapsed, half-sat on the step next to her.

"Long day?" she asked.

He closed his eyes and rubbed his hands over his face.

She'd seen him tired before, but this was different. He was more than tired, more than exhausted. He looked as if he carried a hundred-pound weight across a hot desert. Even in the last remnants of twilight, he had dark circles under his bloodshot eyes. His skin was pale, nearly green and his breath came in shallow gulps.

"David, are you okay?" The other question sat on her tongue but wouldn't come out. If she asked and he answered, she could never go back to this moment. To not knowing. The weight he carried would be transferred to her, and she just didn't have the energy. Not now. Probably not ever. "Is it ...?"

He shook his head. "Couldn't find anything."

She examined each word as it sank in. He'd tried to find Hank, but he could not. So there was still a chance.

David had most likely started with the morgue, then hospitals. If he didn't find him there, maybe Hank went home, or somewhere else to lay low.

"Okay, he's not dead and he's not in the hospital, so we go look for ourselves," Amanda said, more to herself than the man sitting next to her. "This is good, right?" She glanced at David, but he stared down at his feet. "What's wrong?"

He took a deep breath, held it and opened his mouth, but instead of telling her what was on his mind, he just exhaled slowly and ran his hands through his hair. "I'm beat. I'll take the couch again." But, he didn't stand right away.

They sat side by side, watching the last light of the sun fade away.

He was pulling the aluminum door open before she could work up the courage to speak. "We can share the bed."

The creak of the hinges was her first answer. "Don't stay out here too long. I want to get an early start tomorrow."

The door clanged back into its frame. David's moods were a pendulum.

She was starting to get dizzy.

Water thundering through the pipes woke her the next morning. When she had finally calmed herself to go back inside, David had been on the couch, his back to the front door and a light, rhythmic snore told her he was either the best actor in the world, or was truly asleep.

While David showered, Amanda put coffee on. He may have rested like a fairy princess, but she'd gotten the sleep of a troll on night duty. Once the coffeepot was gurgling, she replayed their short conversation.

He was holding something back, there was no doubt about that. But what? Was the truth about Hank just too much for her to handle? Or, had he found out something about Josh that had the potential to break apart everything she'd worked for over the last year?

The slam of a car door broke the thoughts running through her head.

She listened for other sounds. Only David's shower and the brewing coffee buzzed in her ears.

*It's just a neighbor.*

Amanda reached for a mug, but a knock at the door froze her fingers. The blinds drawn, so all she could make out was a shadowy figure rapping on the glass.

Like the victim in a horror movie, she held her breath, afraid that the slightest exhale would give away her hiding place. The knocking stopped, and the shadow disappeared. Her whole body exhaled, eager for fresh oxygen to ward off the fuzzy stars.

David killed the running water as the knocking recommenced.

Afraid to take her eyes off the door, she backed down the hall to the bathroom. "David," she whispered. She reached out for the doorknob. It swung open just as her fingertips brushed it, causing her to jump.

"Who's here?" he asked as he tucked the end of a towel around his waist.

"I don't know. I was afraid to look."

A fist hammered on the door, the aluminum frame banging even louder. "Hey, Stephens, you in there?"

The clenched muscles beneath David's beard relaxed slightly. "It's Lloyd Carson, another agent. Go in my bedroom and don't come out. I'll get rid of him." He ushered her into his room and closed the door behind him, but the wide gap at the bottom of the door was enough for her to hear everything.

"Hey, Lloyd," David said. "What can I do for you?"

"You buy a new truck?" a youthful voice said. "You old dog. First you don't tell me about playing college ball, and then you go off and buy a truck without telling me. Really does make me wonder what other secrets you're keeping." Even though the man finished with a laugh, Amanda didn't like the undertow of his words.

"Eh, I'm in the middle of something." David's voice was tinged with annoyance.

"Oh yeah, I just wanted to stop by and say thanks for picking up my shift yesterday. What're you doing tonight? Want to head into El Paso, hit some bars? Maybe we can take your truck, check it out."

Amanda cocked her head at the door at the second mention of Hank's truck. *What is this kid's fascination with Hank's truck?*

"Lloyd, in case you can't tell, I was in the shower when you threatened to beat down my door."

"So what did that thing set you back?" the guy continued, as if having his own conversation. "I've been thinking about a truck like that. What's your monthly payment?"

Silence blew in from the cracked bedroom door. Amanda's eyes darted to the white bed sheet as she pulled her shirt over her head and unhooked her bra. She flicked her shoes off in two quick moves and dropped her shorts. The sheet wrapped around her twice and she knotted the top loosely. A tousle of her hair, and she was out the bedroom door.

"David? I thought you were coming back to bed, baby." She tried to make her voice heavy with sleep. Her cheeks were hot—

flushed, she hoped—so their visitor could take it as something *other* than her rising temper.

David turned and the man at the door peeked around him. He was at least a head shorter and fifteen years younger than her ex with a curly mop of dirty-blond hair. A slight smile slid across David's lips and his partner leaned against the doorframe.

"Well, hello there." Lloyd's eyes dropped from hers and took in the sheet. "Stephens, seems like there *is* more you're hiding from me."

"Lloyd stopped by to ask about your truck," he said as she joined him at the door.

She smiled up at him, relieved he caught on to her quickly-formed plan.

The younger man made no attempt to hide his wandering eyes. "*Your* truck," he said, shifting to squeeze past David into the trailer. "You look more like a sports car kind of girl."

Amanda arched her eyebrow and gave Lloyd a tight-lipped smile. "Why go for something fast when you can have something dependable?"

"I can be both." He leveled his gaze at her, his blue eyes scanned her face, as if memorizing every inch. "Want to go out for a test drive?"

"Has that line ever worked for you?" She rolled her eyes and crossed her arms in front of her chest with one hand still holding tight to the sheet. Despite the playful nature of his words, his face was hard and calculating. Her body began to tremble. She leaned into David to steady her shaking, the smell of clean radiated from him. A hot gust lifted her long hair from her shoulder and goose bumps broke out on her arm. "Come back to bed," she whispered, the huskiness in her voice surprising her.

"Bye Lloyd." He shut the door, forcing the younger man to back up suddenly or risk catching his fingers. He locked the front door and followed her into the living room, standing so close that the hairs on their arms could touch. David had an ear tilted to the door.

When his partner's truck door slammed and the engine started, he exhaled.

Amanda stared at the front of the trailer, wishing for X-ray vision to show her what the man was doing, who he was calling. The way he'd stared at her face was more than a kid hitting on someone, he catalogued it. "I don't like him."

"I've worked with him for six months, and like him less and less each day."

"I'm serious. There's just something ..." She took a breath. "Hank's truck ... Do you think he bought the act?"

"That was acting?" A smile tugged at his lips, but something pulled against it, making his face look like a theater mask.

*What was he hiding?*

Clutching the sheet tighter and tugging it to her chin, she pushed past him, her eyes locked on the floor. "You can have your room after I get dressed." Amanda headed down the hallway to his room. "I want to leave in ten minutes."

## 21

No matter how much she tried, Amanda couldn't get the young Border Patrol agent out of her mind. Lloyd's unexpected visit had unnerved David, too. At least that was what she assumed. His face whitened, and the muscles along his jawline formed a steel trap, locking away what he was thinking.

"You never told me." His voice sliced through the uncomfortable silence. "Where exactly in Mexico did you find Williams?"

"A couple of hours south from here." The scenery burned behind her sunglasses as she felt the heat of the sun, remembered the smell of sweat and exhaust. "A tiny town, not even a smudge on the map. It was... *La Paz de*..." There were so many towns she'd visited, so many *X*'s on her map. In the blur of the last two days, somehow the name left her. "I'm sorry, my map is in my car. I can tell you when we get to it."

David clicked his tongue. "Could you find it again? On a new map?"

She peered at him. He didn't look in her direction. It felt as if there was a glass barrier between them, like in a cab.

Or, a police car.

"Yeah, I think so. Why?"

He didn't answer until they pulled into a gas station on the outskirts of Presidio. "Why don't you go in, get a map. Grab something to eat and drink if you want." He handed her some cash, but didn't look her in the eye. "I'll wait here, and make sure we weren't followed."

Amanda peeked over her shoulder and out the back window. David still wouldn't look her in the eye. Her stomach knotted. What was she missing?

The metal bars on the windows of the convenience store stared at her in irony. Another barrier between them. When she entered, she felt protected instead of detained. After grabbing a couple of bottles of water, she lingered over the packages of chips and cookies. None of it looked appetizing. She glanced over the shelves and out the dirt-streaked front windows.

David leaned against the side of the truck with his phone to his ear.

She watched as he walked around to the back of the truck and squatted down. Was he looking for a tracking device? When he popped back up, his gaze met hers with an expression she's never seen before.

Detachment.

Amanda gasped, and lost her grip on the water. "Shoot," she mumbled as she chased a tumbling bottle across the dirty linoleum floor.

"You okay, miss?" the clerk called.

"Sorry. Slippery. Where are your maps?"

She followed the direction of his nod and found one of Northern Mexico. As the cashier rang up her purchase, she shifted her gaze outside.

David was in the truck, the cell still at his ear. A voice in the back of her mind shouted for her to run, that something was wrong. He could always look her in the eye.

*Except...*

She inhaled a jagged breath.

"Anything else, miss?"

"No, that's all, thank you." Her numb fingers reached out for the shopping bag. Feet on autopilot walked to the door, the metal handle felt hot under her cold hands.

David looked away as he continued his conversation.

"Miss?" His voice sounded garbled, as if Amanda was underwater. "You okay?"

The door swung away from her, and a tall cowboy stood aside, his fingers lightly touching the brim of his hat.

"Thank you," she said, forcing a smile.

There was no turning back. No hiding from whatever was waiting inside Hank's truck.

She took her time crossing the two parking spots. David's head still turned away, but he jumped at the sound of the door opening. "All right, well thanks for the time, Weatherby. I'll put in some extra shifts in the next couple of weeks."

He hit the end button cutting off a woman's voice.

"Who's that?" Amanda tried to keep her voice level.

He fidgeted with the A/C, blasting the cab with frigid air. "What? Oh, guy from work. I called to take a couple days off." He kept turning knobs, forcing currents of air to tickle her ankles. "Did you get a map?"

David avoided her as she worked up the nerve to call him a liar. Weatherby was very definitely a woman. What else was he lying about?

"Mandy." He turned to face her, but his eyes darted up and over her head. "The map?"

She fished it out of the bag and pulled it open. Her finger traced the mountain ranges and small roads before she found the town. "Here, *La Paz de Cristo*. That's the town where a girl saw Josh."

David took the map and studied it. "The Peace of Christ. They always said Vargas was a fan of theatrics. Seems he likes irony, too." He took a deep breath and tossed the folded paper on the dashboard.

"We're still going to El Paso, right?" The words didn't want to leave Amanda's mouth, but she was no longer in control of her destiny.

"What?" He spoke over his shoulder as backed out of the

parking spot. "Oh yeah, this is just for next steps. If we can't find Hank, we'll cross into Mexico and go after Williams."

"I can't. Not legally. No passport."

He waited for traffic to clear. "I know someone who works the border in El Paso, he can get us across."

She chewed on the inside of her cheek. As much as she wanted to do this, it felt wrong, as if they were on fast-forward. She needed a plan. She needed Hank.

She needed to be back in control.

Amanda exhaled a heavy sigh. "Let's think about this." She turned off the A/C so her words would be clear. "We've been reacting for the past few days, it's time to be proactive. If we don't find Hank, can we go back to your place? Strategize?"

He didn't answer. Instead, the truck sped up as they left the city limits.

"David, listen to me."

He flipped on the radio. A male voice speaking rapid Spanish wove with the hum of static.

"What's going on?" Her heart hammered against her seatbelt.

This time he cranked the A/C to high. Frigid air blew out, but that wasn't the cause of the goosebumps on her arms.

*Screw him. I can pretend he doesn't exist, too.*

Amanda rolled down her window to let some of the tension out of the truck. The dry air blasted past her, whipping her hair across her face and stinging her eyes. She let the tears wash over, mentally blaming the wind and her hair, but giving a little credit to David's icicles piercing her heart.

At first, she thought the dark figure moving on the desert floor was a large animal or her sore eyes playing a trick on her. Dodging cacti and ocotillo, it zigged and zagged with the agility of an elephant. But, the plume of dust in its wake indicated it was no mirage or animal.

Her head jerked to David, but he stared straight ahead, either not seeing or not concerned. When she turned back to the window, her hand cupped over her narrowed eyes, she made out the shape.

A van.

A large, black van bobbed through small ditches on a collision course with them.

"Stop!"

"What?" he asked, the sound of the wind whipping through the truck drowned out her scream.

She put up her window halfway, killing some of the roar of the wind. With each vehicle moving at high speed, they would collide in less than a minute. "Stop! Stop! There's a car coming."

He looked past her, out the window. By the widening of his eyes he saw it, too. "Hold on." He stomped the brake and downshifted the engine in one move.

Amanda's body strained against the seatbelt, forcing all the air from her lungs. The back end whipped around by the force of the stop, throwing her against the seat like a ride at an amusement park.

The van vaulted over the ditch and spun around the truck like a bull and a matador in a morbid dance.

In a matter of seconds, both vehicles stopped.

Hank's pickup hung off the road and the other vehicle centered on the highway facing the direction from which they came. No doors opened on either car.

"Are you okay?" he asked, glancing into his side mirror.

"I think I hit my head." Amanda winced. She touched her right temple.

"Don't move," David said before popping his door open.

"Wait."

He stared down at his lap. Still refusing to meet her eyes.

*Why won't he look at me?*

David always looked her in the eyes.

*Except...*

Except when he was breaking her heart.

## 22

D avid's boots hit the ground.

The van's doors opened. Four men got out, guns drawn. Spanish shouts ricocheted across the air.

Amanda couldn't interpret the words, but she understood the intention.

He kneeled on the isolated highway with his hands laced behind his head.

She bolted out of the truck. The sudden movement made her vision waver and her legs heavy, as if she were moving through water.

Two of the guns swung her direction. The same Spanish words were aimed at her.

"Get down on your knees and put your hands behind your head," David directed.

Her hands slowly rose as she went down next to him, the warm asphalt burning her knees.

"What did I tell you?" he whispered.

"You're talking to me now?"

David ignored her and returned his attention to the men. "Look, this must be some kind of mistake. It's just minor damage, no need to report anything." When the men didn't respond, he spoke again in Spanish.

One of the men reached into his back pocket and pulled out a cell phone. He thumbed the device for a moment, looking at Amanda before bringing it to his ear. His lips barely moved, but the sound of his voice carried across the isolated highway. A few words struck her.

*Tenemos la mujer.* We got the woman.

Her basic understanding of Spanish was all she needed.

"Is this my punishment for leaving Phoenix?" she whispered.

"What are you talking about?" David whipped his head in her direction.

Staring into his eyes, something she'd wanted for the better part of the morning, only jumbled her thoughts. Amanda could see the battle within him; anger, fear, remorse. Whatever love was left in him, he'd buried it. It was already decayed.

"You think *I* did this? Look around, Mandy." His face softened, but his voice was as sharp as a cactus needle. "The guns are on me, not you."

He was right. All four guns remained on him, *not* her. Fear climbed up her spine, one clammy hand after another.

"You..." Amanda tried to speak. Her lungs tightened around the words.

For the first time since the collision the idea they could die sank into her brain. All her mind could process was *death.*

Not hers death. David's.

David. Dead. The words flowed with the alliteration of a lilting poem.

*Breathe. He's still there. He hasn't left you. He won't leave you.*

Her heart sprinted, but her lungs declined to join the race. Humming filled her ears and her vision narrowed to the guns pointed at David.

*Nononononono. Think. Think.*

"Mandy?" His voice was thick with worry.

Amanda's legs twitched and tingled, begging to be activated, pleading to take her somewhere safe. Flight always won out over fight. Not anymore. Panic was always fluid. Something that flooded her, filled her, crept into crevices, growing her self-doubt.

She stared up at the cerulean sky and struggled against the panic, pushing back at it and trying to evaporate it. It was too strong. Another wave knocked into her, rocking her back on her heels.

Amanda was drowning in the desert. Her consciousness reached out for a lifeline and grabbed hold of a sound in the distance. "A car," she whispered, breaking the surface. "Can you hear it?"

"Yeah." His murmur danced with a breeze and fell lightly on her ear. "*Ella no puede respirar*," he shouted at the men. "She's hurt, let me help her."

"David, I really can't–I'm afraid I'm going to–"

"Shhh."

The sound of the oncoming car was a full roar.

Amanda wanted to turn to see their savior, but the four men seemed unconcerned.

Tires creaked to a stop and the transmission clicked into park. The driver killed the engine, stealing all sound, leaving only her shallow breathing to fill the air.

David's quick glance revealed he shared the same realization. The men weren't scattering like either had hoped. This wasn't someone to save them, it was someone to drive in another nail.

"What the *hell* are you doing?" A familiar voice traveled to her ears with the thumping of his boots. "Not here on the road. Get them in the van and let's go."

Boots came into her line of vision. Her eyes lifted, traveling up the thin legs and resting on the young face of Lloyd Carson.

"What have you gotten yourself into, Lloyd?" David's voice was low and tight with anger.

"I told you..." Amanda murmured between gasps.

David cut his eyes in her direction.

Lloyd stared down his nose at her ex, anger distorting his

youthful face. His flirtatious swagger was gone, and in its place was a harsh furrowed brow. He fingered his holstered gun, leaving her to question who he trusted least, them or the other men.

"How long have we been partners? Huh?" He paced in front of them, running his fingers through his hair. "A year or two?"

"About six months," David said.

"After all this time, I know nothing about you. I mean, someone else had to tell me you played at UT. Come on, man."

"*Señor* only wants the girl," the man with the cellphone spoke up. "Our orders are to kill whoever is with her."

"No." Amanda leapt to her feet so quickly her head swam. The guns swung in her direction.

"Mandy, sit down!"

"Don't shoot her!" Lloyd reached for his own weapon.

The air was void of sound after David and Lloyd's mingled commands.

"Whoa, whoa," Lloyd said to both Amanda and the men.

"No, please, not him." She tugged at the younger man's shirt. "You don't really want him to die. I know you don't."

"Doesn't matter what *I* want." His narrowed eyes covered up the trepidation she saw. "Orders are orders. They said to kill him, it's what we have to do. I can put you in the van so you don't have to see it." Lloyd grabbed her arm, his short nails digging into her bicep.

Her feet skidded across the asphalt. She pulled against him, her free hand trying to break his grip. Channeling a long-forgotten kick-boxing class, she launched a kick at the side of his knee.

He buckled, releasing his grip to grab at his knee, giving Amanda and opportunity to run back to David. "You bitch," he growled. Lloyd chased after her, reaching for her hair and doubling the long strands around his fist.

"I don't care how many guns are on me." David's voice cut across the road. Calm. Clear. Commanding. "You touch her and I *will* kill you with my bare hands."

Her head tugged back and Lloyd's syrupy sweet breath was in

her ear. "Try that again and you'll be wearing his brains." He untangled his hands from her hair and pushed her back to the ground. "Take them both," he said to Vargas' men. "I'm going with you to the *hacienda*. I'll explain to *Señor*. But, if she does anything, kill him."

Without another glance at the two captives, David's partner walked back to his truck and slammed the door behind him, his hand beating the steering wheel.

The four men exchanged glances. The one who'd made the call barked a command at the man closest to the van. He pulled open the passenger door and grabbed a duffle bag from the floor.

"Do what they say," David said. "I mean it."

Two of the men came to them, both holstering their guns.

"Stand," he commanded David in English. "Hands up and turn around. Both."

In unison, they turned to face Lloyd's truck, but he gazed out over the desert, not meeting their eyes.

Rough hands ran along the inside of Amanda's long-sleeved shirt, tracing the contours of her body over her tank top as they moved down to her shorts.

"It's okay, he's checking for weapons," David spoke at the sound of her gasp.

The man behind her said something in Spanish, but she didn't understand. "Hands," he said in English.

She let him guide her arms from behind her head to behind her back where they were tied with course rope. A glance at David told her his hands were also being tied and the man behind him held a black hood. "I didn't mean for any of this," Amanda choked on her apology. The hood went over her head, stealing the air, sound, David.

A pair of hands boosted her into the van, her knees burning as they skid across the metal. She tried to find a place to sit. A muffled crack and groan penetrated her ears as the van heaved. "David?"

Silence answered her.

She scooted until she ran into a prone body. With her hands still behind her, she felt along his T-shirt covered torso until she got to his chest. It rose and fell in shallow breaths.

He was alive.

"You behave, he lives," a thick voice spoke. "You don't, he dies and we feed him to the vultures."

**23**

---

The guard at the stucco shed was gone. That meant the man inside had to be dead. The heat climbed to three digits as the afternoon *siesta* bell echoed throughout the quiet desert. If the men of the *hacienda* didn't kill the man inside, the heat surely had.

Half an hour after *siesta* began, Josh snuck out of his room and across the courtyard even though he had to drag one leg. The sting from the scorpion had rendered his left leg numb from his groin to his toes. He'd stopped shaking and sweating sometime around lunch and some gentle pinching confirmed the scorpion's intended mark, his crotch, was still capable of feeling pain, and one day, hopefully, pleasure.

He pushed open the door, bracing himself, for what, he wasn't sure. The man sat on the dirt floor, his hands tied behind his back and his chin rested against his chest. The smell of acid mingled with the heavy scent of sulfur in the thick air. He covered his nose and mouth as he watched for any movement coming from the body.

*Dammit, I'm too late.*

A raspy breath startled him as Josh choked back nausea.

"Are you alive?" he whispered.

The man's one good eye opened and focused on his face. "Barely," he said.

Josh pulled the door closed behind him, leaving only a gap for sunlight. He knelt next to the man and swatted away flies before bringing the bottle of water he brought to his cracked lips. The man drank greedily. "Thanks," he breathed.

"Who are you?" Josh asked.

"Vargas send you in to interrogate me next? No offense buddy." Pain flashed across his face as he shifted on the floor. "But I don't think you can break me."

He tucked a stray strand of hair behind his ear and glanced toward the door. "He doesn't know I'm here. I've only got a couple of minutes, so let's cut right to it. Are you connected to Amanda Martin? I have to reach her because Vargas just sent someone after her. I need to tell her to stand down."

The man winced again as he took a deep breath. "That's creative. Pretend you care so I'll give up her location."

"It's not a coercion tactic. Her life is in danger and I need to warn her."

"Not if she's with Stephens." The man sat up straighter, gritting his teeth in the process. "He'd die before he let something happen to her."

"Seems he'll get his chance if you don't help me out." Josh swung his legs around to sit down next to the man. "Vargas gave the order to kill him and bring Amanda here. Last chance. Start talking old man or I'm heading back to the comfort of my air-conditioned room."

The man took a long labored breath. "I'm Hank Snare. Amanda came to me a year ago to find you. She was heartbroken over her role in your fraud and wanted to find peace by turning you in. She got close." He closed his eye and his chin drifted back to his chest. "Too close."

"Hey." Josh shook him. "Come on, stay with me. Where is she?" He patted the man's cheek, but drew back at the heat radiating under his palm. Hank was flush with fever.

Another breath rattled in the guy's lungs. "How can I be sure you're telling the truth?"

"You can't. You'll just have to trust me. Where is she? How can I get in touch with her?"

Bloody spittle dotted Hank's chin as a laugh erupted from his chest. "Trust. She beat herself up for trusting you. Poor girl couldn't sleep. Guilt ate her up inside."

Josh turned his head away to get a fresh breath of air and to make sure no one snuck up on them. He also didn't let the man see he had no visible reaction to Amanda's agony.

If she were truly pained, she would've questioned him on where her quarterly bonuses had come from. She should've lost sleep then, over how JWI stayed strong in a down economy when so many competitors laid people off, not now. Instead, Amanda had spent sleepless nights trolling online for shoes.

"We don't have time to debate right and wrong. If you tell me where she is, I can at least stop one, if not two, more people from getting hurt."

Hank's one-eyed blue-gray stare shot into Josh. It was so intense his hands went cold. Even in this beaten state, the man was a formidable presence. "She's across the border, in a town called Pardon Falls. But that doesn't mean she's there now."

"How can I reach her?"

"You can't."

"What do you mean I can't?" Josh glanced behind him again. He'd been in the shed too long. If Hank didn't share something fast, he'd have to walk out and hope Amanda could survive whatever was heading her way. "She's got to have a cellphone or something. The Amanda I knew couldn't live without her phone."

"Why do you care, Williams? Huh? Why now after all this time and all the crap you put her through do you care about what happens to her?" A wave of perspiration dotted the man's pallid forehead.

"She was just doing what I asked," he whispered. "She wasn't behind it. I don't think she even knew what was happening. So the least I can do is keep her alive."

Hank held his gaze until his lid wavered closed.

"Come on, Hank." Josh shook him again. "Just a little longer, and I'll let you rest."

The eye fluttered open.

He could tell the man struggled for even the shallowest breath.

"There is a bar in Pardon Falls, called *El Capitan*." Stagnant breath bathed Josh as he leaned closer. "The owner will know how to reach her. Just tell him..." His good eye drooped, only a slit of white beneath his bruised lid. "Tell him Sylvia sent you," he mumbled through cracked lips before his head dropped. The light lift of his chest indicated he just passed out.

"Are you kidding me?" His voice was louder than he planned, but he didn't bother tamping it down. "I risked my life to come down here and all you do is tell me to call a bar and say some chick sent me?" He popped up and paced the small shed, his anger rising to the temperature of the stuffy room. "Shit!" Josh threw the remains of the water bottle against the opposite wall and it rolled back to his feet before he kicked it again, hearing it roll into the darkness.

He backed out of the shed and gently replaced the latch, the sun-heated metal burning his hand. No wonder no one stood guard. The summer sun made it deadly for anyone to spend too much time guarding a dying man.

As he hobbled back to his main building, he mulled over how to make a phone call. No telephone lines looped into their isolated location. Instead, a small satellite dish in the back served as the hub for communication with the outside world.

In his mind's eye, Josh walked through the compound looking for a phone here, a wall jack there, anything that indicated a connection to the outside world. Nothing.

He'd have to convince someone to let him borrow a cell phone. Or even more daunting, steal one. But from who? He'd rarely seen people milling around making calls on cell phones.

"*Hola, Señor* Williams."

"Pedro." Josh jumped as the young man approached from the side of the house. "I didn't see you there. How's it going?"

"Good. Hot. I couldn't sleep. Is something wrong with your leg, *Señor*?"

"Me either." Only a partial lie. "Oh this, it's just sore muscles. Thought I'd come out and get some fresh air; stretch my legs." There'd be no shame in telling Pedro about the scorpion, but he didn't want to be a lame horse. He and the boy faced each other, both seeming to have more to say but neither wanting to begin. "Okay, I'm going to go back to my room and get some rest. See you later, Pedro." He took two steps toward the house but then stopped.

There were no retreating footsteps behind him, the boy likely sought him out in the quiet of the *siesta*.

Had Vargas sent Pedro to watch over him? Did he see Josh come out of the shed?

"*Señor* Williams?"

He closed his eyes, afraid to turn. This was where Vargas's men silently moved into place behind Pedro, guns pointed ready to fire at him for breaching the drug lord's trust and conversing with a hostage. He'd become more of a liability than an asset. Amanda had gotten too close. The drug lord wouldn't allow someone to be under his tutelage that could bring down his carefully constructed empire. "Yes, Pedro?"

"I, uh, wanted to thank you."

Josh whirled to find the teenager standing alone, looking down at his feet.

"Maribel is my sister. She told me you were kind. I hope the other men will be as kind as you." The boy turned.

"How many more men?" It was an inappropriate question to ask of a boy whose sister would have to pay an inflated price for their father's mistakes.

Pedro never looked at him, but the quiver in his voice told of the despair on his face. "It doesn't matter if it's three or thirty," he spoke into the desert wind. "I came here to keep her safe, but it wasn't enough. She will never be married, never have a family." The boy looked over his shoulder, his brown eyes squinting into the reflection of the cruel sun off the stucco building. "Her life changed when she was sent to you."

Blood thrumming through Josh's ears drowned out the sound of the teen's retreating boots.

## 24

The darkness was suffocating. The muffled voices of the men made her ears ring. Amanda was more motion-sick with each bounce of the van. Time lost all meaning. Only the numbers pulled her forward. "Seven hundred thirty-four, seven hundred thirty-five." Her throat burned with dryness, but she wouldn't stop counting.

Counting the breaths that David took reminded her he was still alive.

"Are you trying to drive me crazy? Because it's working." His words came out slow and groggy. "Where are we?"

She wanted to throw herself on him, to give him an awkward hands-tied-behind-her-back-hood-covered-head hug. That was if she could find a way to do so without becoming stuck on her back like an upside down turtle. "In the back of the van."

A light laugh tickled her ears from under the hood. "Did you get cracked in the skull, too?"

Amanda instantly relaxed at his teasing. It was nice to unwind the knot in her stomach, to feel the tension drain out of her shoulders. "How do you feel?" She asked when David stirred beside her. She was afraid he'd recoil when he was upright, but instead he settled in next to her, one of his bound hands finding hers and giving it a light squeeze.

"Like a defensive lineman hit me. I'll be fine. How long have we been on the road?"

How long had they been on the road? It felt like years. And, minutes. Time didn't follow conventional rules. "Maybe an hour," she said. "Let me put it this way, I'm wishing I'd gone to the bathroom at the gas station. I'm reaching critical need level." Amanda gasped, inhaling her own stale air. Wrapped inside that joke was an idea.

"Whatever you're thinking, no."

"This is going to work, I promise." She cleared her throat to wake it. "Hey, I need to use the bathroom."

"Really bad idea, Mandy."

"Shh," she hissed. It probably *wasn't* the best idea she'd ever had, but if it worked she could at least figure out where they were. "Can you pretend to still be knocked out?" She took another deep breath, preparing herself to speak louder. "Really, I need to go."

The driver responded with a swerve and Amanda fell into David.

"You think I'm kidding, but which one of you will have to clean it up?"

Muted voices volleyed and she felt the van slow. It pulled to the right, jostling her in the other direction.

"Be careful," David whispered. "And if you get a chance to run, go. Don't look back, Mandy." He pulled away from her.

The air shifted and she felt him stretch out beside her. A second later, the back door opened. The faintest hint of light teased Amanda from the bottom of the hood.

The same rough hands that'd hoisted her into the van grabbed her arms and dragged her out on her knees.

She fell to the ground, and the shock on her kneecaps hitting the hard gravel road made her cry out. Her shins seared and her feet tingled as blood rushed in.

The hood was ripped off. The two shadowy men standing above

her seemed to undulate as her eyes filled with tears at the assault of the bright sunlight.

"Up," a man commanded.

Amanda tried to stand, but the pain, tears and bound hands made it nearly impossible.

"Hurry."

"I've got it," she said, louder than necessary in hopes that David would hear her. She pushed the agony down, locking it in the place where her she kept the death of her friend Liz, homesickness of cutting herself off from her family, the guilt of ruining Shiloh's life, the anguish of leaving David and the torture of her part in Josh's crimes.

It was getting crowded in there.

The man untied her wrists and her shoulders groaned as she stretched. Lloyd crested a small hill and slammed on the brakes, forcing the men driving Hank's truck to do the same.

She turned her head and held her breath, hoping to avoid the cloud of dirt billowing her way.

"What are you doing?" The Border Patrol agent shouted. "Vargas is expecting us. We don't have time for sightseeing."

"Calm down," Amanda said. "Nature called."

Lloyd crossed his arms in front of his chest and widened his stance. He was trying to look more in control, but all it did was make him look unstable. "Well, what're you waiting for?"

"What? Here? Not gonna to happen." She stretched up on her toes, surveying the land around her. Craggy gray rocks contrasted sharply against the deep blue sky. Nothing taller than her knees grew around them, but an outcropping of rocks fifteen feet from the road suggested a bit of privacy. "There. I won't be far."

David's partner shuffled his feet and the men from the van looked at him for guidance.

"Fine," he said, drawing his gun.

The other two men flinched, once again proving there was no trust between her kidnappers.

Lloyd aimed inside the van at David's prone body.

The blood stopped flowing in Amanda's legs and her knees loosened.

"But you try anything, he gets shot. You run, he gets shot. You scream, he gets shot. You take longer than I think is necessary, he gets shot. You hear?"

She nodded and began her trek up the slight hill to the rocks. She silently begged the landscape to look familiar, for something to stand up and call to her, telling her she'd been here before during her Josh-searching journeys.

Nothing did.

It was one large, anonymous landscape.

Haze hung on the horizon to the south, but Amanda could make out another line of mountains hidden within the veil. If they went beyond that mountain range, they'd be boxed in. Remembering Lloyd's threat, she quickly finished and hurried back to the cars.

"All better," she said, forcing her voice to be steady, light. "Thank you."

"Whatever, show your appreciation by getting your ass back in the van." Lloyd avoided eye contact and instead he searched the road ahead and behind them.

She was better prepared when the hood fell over her head this time. The men were a little gentler when they tied her wrists together and hoisted her back inside, but the slamming of the back doors made her heart rattle.

Amanda scooted around the back until she felt David's leg and gave it a quick squeeze. His muscles tensed in response.

Once the rumble of the tires and the roar of the air conditioning filled the air, David sat up and leaned his covered head against hers.

"Well?" he whispered.

She took a deep breath and let the sigh answer. "Desert. Lots and lots of desert. It looks like we're heading southwest."

"Is it still just Lloyd and his buddies?"

"Yeah, but whatever you're thinking, no," Amanda repeated what he'd said.

"Mandy, I'm a dead man." His words were blunt and sharp. "We both know that. Let my death mean something."

His surrender stung. This man was her rock, the person who'd kept her moving forward when all she'd wanted to do was run back to him. Whether he'd wanted her or not. He had so many opportunities to quit on her, but now was not the time.

"As soon as I get a chance, I'm going to rush them," David continued. "I'll wait until I know you can break away, until I know you have a chance, but you have to promise me you'll run."

His statement hung in the darkness.

"Mandy?"

"No."

"What?"

"I said no." Amanda leaned forward, pressing her forehead into his. "You listen to me, David Stephens. You should've given up on me a year ago when I kept trying to brush you off, but you didn't. And, when you'd found out I lied about who I was, you broke up with me, but you didn't give up on me." Her words built quickly on a shaky foundation. "You didn't ask for any of this, so you're going to have to give me the chance to get you out of it." The mortar holding her together threatened to turn to dust. She swallowed hard, begging to keep it together, but her composure crumbled.

It no longer mattered that David couldn't look her in the eye. Whatever sin he was guilty of had been forgiven.

"But you can't give up now." The tears cooled her cheeks. She tried to take a deep breath, but there wasn't enough air beneath her hood and she choked, unleashing another more painful round of tears.

"I'm sorry, baby." David's whisper was warm and comforting. "You're right."

"I'm scared." Amanda's confession felt freeing, as if she was no longer burdened by the sin of fear.

"Good." He squeezed her fingers. "Fear and anger will keep you alive when I can't. Hold on to that and we'll be fine."

## 25

D espite the cloudless sky, Josh felt like a storm hung in the air, just waiting for the first crack of lightning to rip open and unleash a torrent of rain. It wasn't a thunderstorm he was awaiting. It was a hurricane. This one wasn't coming in from the Gulf, it was barreling at him from the north.

Hurricane Amanda.

No one spoke over breakfast. Children spent the day locked away somewhere rather than playing in the dusty courtyard. The uncomfortable hush that'd descended the desert hideaway was eerily reminiscent of the days in his childhood when his parents fought. This was a day for keeping a low profile and hoping Vargas forgot he was there.

Alone in his room, he turned to the one thing that could take his mind off the tension. Numbers. Josh liked that beneath his good looks and playboy lifestyle lurked a mathematical master.

In school, when all the jocks played dumb for the equally ditzy cheerleaders, he'd risen to the top by flaunting both his brains and his body. Women instinctively wanted a man who could be a good provider and showing his penchant for statistics and ability to do the most complicated equations in his head meant he was able to bang both the head cheerleader and the hot bookworm.

Instead of adding numbers, his mind calculated the time until Hurricane Amanda made landfall. Vargas had given that young Border Patrol agent forty-eight hours to bring her to him. Twenty-seven of those hours drifted by like the wayward clouds over the stark Mexican sky, each one passing by without so much as a glance to the people cast in its shadow. Josh hoped the next twenty-one hours would be just as unremarkable, but the pressure hanging over the compound was palpable.

Amanda was on her way.

After his third mistake in addition, he crossed his room and opened the French doors, releasing the cool air and frustration in exchange for the heavy heat and distraction. He gazed at the thick wooden gate.

Sometime today that gate would open and Amanda would cross into his world, or more realistically, into his hell.

His temper rose with the invading heat. Why couldn't she be satisfied with what he'd left her? Sure, the life she was accustomed to was gone, but so was his. She, on the other hand, had freedom. Freedom to live her life, freedom to fall in love, freedom from the fear that a simple mistake in addition or subtraction could be the end of her life.

Now, instead of worrying about paying the price for his own mistakes, Josh had to carry the burden that her slip-up could be his downfall.

"Damn you, Amanda." He looked down at the lonely shed knowing the man inside was the only link to her life after Chicago.

Hank had claimed Amanda was broken up over the fraud, but Josh knew the true reason. She'd found out about the others.

Her jealous streak ran deep. During the years they'd dated, she'd quizzed him repeatedly about his whereabouts, always suspicious he was seeing someone else or, as she'd guessed right a few times just carousing with beautiful young women. He should've ended their personal relationship not long after it started, but that was about the time his father had told him he had no intention of stepping down and, in a fury, his scam was born.

Josh couldn't give Amanda any reason to leave the company, so he backed off the wannabe models and doused her with attention. For a little while, at least.

"You come all this way to confront me about cheating," he said to the shed. "You self-righteous bitch. Dragging some guy Hank says will die for you. Whatever. His blood is on your hands."

Would both their blood be on his hands? Hank told him how to warn her. Amanda's arrival to this compound would change the trajectory of Josh's life. He'd be responsible for her, he could even lose privileges and no longer be allowed out. The groundwork for his escape from Vargas grew stronger, but her presence could put a permanent hold on it.

He gripped the balcony rail and hung his head. One quick phone call and he could continue on his life. He'd done it once before. A call to Roland Burrows to tip her off, hoping she'd skip town like he did had. It'd worked, in a sense. She'd left town. To come after him.

The chair usually occupied by his guard sat empty and the only movement down the hallway was the overhead fans spinning.

Adopting the posture of someone in charge, Josh skipped down the stairs, forcing his still numb left leg to keep up with his right, pausing at the bottom long enough to scan the foyer for movement.

Distant voices spoke quickly over the clanging of pots and pans from the kitchen to his right. To the left, a line of closed doors stood sentry. The first was the library, the place where he and Vargas had shared many drinks and cigars. Next was the boss' private office, a door that was always closed, locked and under guard.

Josh closed his eyes and let his mind go back to the study. He'd never seen a phone in the room, instead it had an old world quality to it, a place where modern technology had no place. The most logical location would be the office.

He filled his lungs with air to propel himself forward. The dark wood door stared back, heavy and uninviting. No guard stood outside, which could mean Vargas fired all his men or they were otherwise engaged in the search for his ex-girlfriend.

Josh swallowed as he reached for the knob, holding his breath before turning it.

The door swung open, and a beige linen suit filled his line of vision.

"Josh," Vargas said, taking a step back. "To what do I owe this surprise?"

"*Señor*," he paused, begging his mind to work faster. "I–"

A ringing phone cut him off. The drug lord held up a finger and turned his back to answer. The conversation in Spanish was quick.

"*Bien*," Vargas said after hanging up. "You have good timing, Josh. I was just about to send for you. Come, follow me to the library."

They walked side-by-side. His boss' green eyes watched him, because the limp was more pronounced after the momentary interruption in his blood flow.

A day after the blasted scorpion sting and Josh still had to drag his left leg around like he had a ball and chain clamped around his ankle.

"You're lame," Vargas said. "Do you need medical attention?"

*I need to have my head checked for being here.*

"No sir, I'm fine. My foot fell asleep."

The small library seemed out of place compared to the rest of the stucco compound. Floor to ceiling bookshelves were lined with linen-covered books in both English and Spanish. Deep leather armchairs begged for company and a tray with two glasses and a decanter of caramel-colored liquor beckoned.

"Share a drink with me. As they say, it is five o'clock somewhere." His boss pulled the stopper out of the decanter and poured each of them a generous drink. "*Salud*."

Josh watchfully met the drug lord's glass and waited until he saw Vargas' Adam's apple bob before opening his lips to the liquid. "What are we celebrating?"

Vargas drained the rest of his drink and poured a second, even more generous portion for himself. "I'm so glad you asked that question, my friend. I have a surprise for you." Vargas took a gulp from his fresh pour. "Although, I shouldn't let you have it. You're like a naughty child who snuck downstairs on Christmas Eve, aren't you? But that's okay. Being the forgiving parent I am, I will still allow you your present."

He stared into his glass. Josh suddenly felt like a mouse caught in a maze looking up at the cat's knowing grin who took more pleasure in drawing out the kill.

"Your silence indicates your chagrin," the drug lord continued. "I accept your apology."

"I'm not sure I'm deserving, *señor*." He employed his mother's abrupt accent to tamp down any emotion. "You've been more than generous as it is. I hope you haven't gone to too much trouble."

"You are wrong. You deserve this more than anyone else." He stopped to drain his second glass and put his finger to his lips.

Josh braced himself against the shiver that fought its way down his spine.

"I won't say anything else about that. I still want some element of surprise." Vargas picked up the decanter and tilted it to toward him.

He declined with a soft shake of his head.

The drug lord opted to drain the last of the liquor into his glass, filling it nearly to the brim. Vargas brought the glass to his mouth, but a knock at the door interrupted. "Ah, that must be your gift arriving. Wait here until someone comes for you." He tossed back the liquor and slammed the empty glass on the desk. "And, no peeking," he added before closing the door behind him.

Once the door clicked shut, Josh allowed the shudder to radiate down his body as he threw back the last of the liquor. He palmed the empty decanter, prisms of light played across the wall as he examined the cut glass. Like a pitcher on the mound, he flung the decanter into the fireplace. "Shit!" The sound of shattering glass covered his curse.

He couldn't save her this time.

## 26

The second half of the van ride seemed to fly by in minutes. Anger and fear battled inside of Amanda, making her head thrum with heated emotions. "David." She felt him straighten beside her. "If you have a chance to run, take it."

"Mandy —"

"No, I'm not giving up, I promise. Run, get help, come back for me. Okay?"

The covered head next to hers nodded.

A voice erupted at the front of the van. Quick Spanish swam around her head with only one word catching a snag in her brain. *Aqui.* Here.

"We must be getting close," David whispered. "Sounds like one of them asked someone to open the gate. Remember that, there's a gate that leads out of here."

She nodded, even though David wouldn't see it. Chilling apprehension replaced the stiffness in her bones.

The van stopped and the transmission snapped into park, rocking the vehicle back, jostling her into his lap.

Voices barked outside the vehicle. Time was running out.

"Fight, David," she spoke in one breath. Amanda might never

see him again, speak to him again. This could be their end. "No matter what, fight it."

The back door opened and she felt a void next to her as David was pulled out. Rough hands grabbed her arms and pulled her so hard that she landed on the dense dirt facedown. A sharp stone dug into her temple through the heavy hood and she bit her lip to stifle a shout. Her skin immediately warmed under the blaze of the hot sun.

She tried to feel him near her, but the air swam with so many bodies she couldn't tell which was his. Amanda sensed a shark circle in her midst.

Something about the way the voices silenced at once, like a school of fish that knew instinctively to swim away.

Without warning, she was pulled upright and the hood jerked from her head.

Her pupils constricted so tightly she could only see a hazy figure approach her. His white linen pants rippled in the wind and the high sun behind his head gave him an angelic demeanor but blocked his face. This had to be Vargas.

"Good afternoon, Ms. Martin." His words were lightly accented in Spanish. "My apologies for the less than luxurious traveling conditions, but my private jet was otherwise engaged."

Her skin broke out in goose pimples at his chuckle.

The radiance behind his head made it difficult to look up at him for more than a brief glimpse. Stinging tears leaked out of her eyes, both for the pain of the sudden sunlight and the ache of not yet catching a glimpse of David.

Amanda craned her head to the left to see if he was behind her, but the man's soft yet strong hands yanked her head up to face him. The blinding sun only made her want to crush her eyes shut.

"You should look at your host when he speaks to you." He squeezed her jaw.

The urge to spit on him swelled in her chest, but David's reminder to not provoke anyone echoed in her ears and she swallowed her saliva and her pride.

"Lloyd." Vargas turned his attention away from Amanda and

she snuck a glance to the right, blinking furiously to coax her pupils to open.

Finally, between the legs of Vargas' men, she saw David kneeling; the black hood still covered his head.

"Why did you bring me two guests?" the drug lord asked.

The younger man stepped beside her, his boots blocking part of her view of David. "I brought him to control her. Seems she lacked motivation to come quietly. Plus, she kicked me." The shaky voice of an adolescent replaced the authority in Lloyd's voice.

"She kicked you?

"Hard." His boots shuffled beside her, stirring a cloud of dirt.

Vargas *tsked* as he went to David and bent at the waist. He ripped the hood off and David stared stoically ahead, not making any sign that the bright light affected him.

Amanda wanted to call to him, but her throat closed up.

"She kicked you hard, huh?" Vargas asked. Without breaking eye contact, the drug lord snapped his fingers and pointed at Lloyd.

A giant of a man broke from the group and took two quick steps toward the dirty Border Patrol agent. The man kicked him so hard that the snap of Lloyd's femur echoed around the courtyard before being drowned out by his shouts.

"Harder than that? Lloyd, isn't this the same man I told you to kill?" Vargas paced in front of them.

Lloyd rolled on the ground, crying, clutching his broken leg between the kneeling Amanda and David.

As she continued to stare at David, Vargas' circle of disciples widened.

*David, look at me. You know I'm right here, please, just glance to your left.*

He ignored her mental pleadings.

"Answer me, Lloyd."

She broke from staring at David.

Lloyd curled into the fetal position, his agony-filled face looked even more youthful. He couldn't be much over twenty-one, still a teenager in some sense. He was a boy who'd made a mistake, got in over his head and trusted the wrong people.

He was someone's son, brother, friend. He was someone about to die because she wanted to keep David alive.

A weak, muffled voice answered Vargas.

"I can't hear you." He stood over Lloyd. "Speak with conviction."

The agent leaned up. "He's my partner. And, a damn good quarterback—"

A gunshot pierced the silence, followed by a sickening gurgle cutting off Lloyd's excuse.

"No!" Amanda whipped her head back around, but all she saw was a cloud of red dirt.

When the sand settled, David was kneeling beside her. Between them Lloyd kicked on the ground, his broken leg twitched at a sickening angle and his good leg pounding the hard earth.

"Mandy, don't look." He finally turned to her.

She'd already seen. Lloyd had been shot, but it wasn't fatal. Instead it'd struck him in the neck. He was choking on his own blood.

Her eyes fought against her desire to keep them on David.

Vargas kneeled at Lloyd's chest. "Lloyd, as far as I'm concerned, *I* am the only quarterback here."

The dirt irritated her eyes and they sealed off the world around her, forcing her to once again rely on her other senses.

Vargas made several more passes in front of David and Amanda. "Of all the times I encouraged Lloyd to think for himself," he said. "It breaks my heart that this was the moment he chose to heed my advice." The ground vibrated in-sync with his words, as if he took a step for each syllable. "Does it bother you to know you traded one man's life for another?"

Her bound hands went cold at the bluntness of his question. She felt him stop in front of her. The rustling of cloth and current of air on her face indicated he'd knelt in front of her. Amanda tried to wrench open an eye, but fresh stabs of pain pierced her scratched cornea and all she could see were the distorted features of a face.

"Josh will be so thrilled to see you," he whispered, his voice softening. He leaned closer, his breath drying a bead of sweat trying to escape as he nuzzled her neck. "But first, maybe we should spend some time getting to know each other."

Amanda's back stiffened as Vargas stood. Her chest heaved and acid flooded her mouth as she swayed, feeling that she could pass out or throw up. Or both.

"You've got me, do what you will," David growled beside her. "Just let her go."

Footsteps filled the air as the drug lord retreated. Once he'd stopped, the only sound in the compound was the whipping of his pants in the wind. Quick words in Spanish sliced through the air.

She eked her eyes open.

Vargas drew back a fist and laid a punch on the side of David's face, knocking him backwards. The man behind her ex lifted him to his feet. Another man stepped forward to land a punch to his gut, forcing a groan from his chest.

After the second hit, the man holding David released him, letting him hit the ground on his knees and double over.

"No please, stop," Amanda struggled to get to his side with her hands still bound behind her.

Vargas pushed her away, causing her to land on her backside.

"Please don't hurt him."

"That's sweet, Ms. Martin." He barely glanced over his shoulder. "But did you really think you can save him? *Otra vez.*"

Her jaw ached and stomach roiled as if she was the one hit.

*Think, Amanda. Save him. Something.*

Her mind spun like a dust devil, whirling on thoughts and ideas, hoping for something solid to hit her.

"They're coming," Amanda said. "But if you hurt him, you'll never find out more."

Vargas stiffened as the air froze around them.

David lifted his head slightly, cutting his gaze in her direction, but she shifted her eyes back to the drug lord, not wanting to see her ex's disapproval.

"Who? When? If you tell me now I can promise a quick end."

She opened her mouth, hoping her tongue had the answer.

"It's still a ways off, three, maybe four weeks," David said, spitting blood on the dirt in front of him as sweat traced a line down his face. "The U.S. government and *Federales* are working together on a joint raid. Sharing satellite data, intel."

Vargas lifted his gun and crossed to stand in front of David. For the second time that day, She stared at him with a gun pointed to his head.

The drug lord dug the barrel into his temple. "Who betrayed me?"

David's Adam's apple bobbed as he looked up at their captor. "Go to hell."

Vargas tightened his grip and dug the gun into David's temple until the skin around the metal went white.

Stars spotted her vision to blind her from whatever was about to transpire. "No, please." Amanda couldn't control the sob that burst from her chest. "Please, don't kill him. I'll do anything, just please don't hurt him," she prayed to the devil in front of her.

The leader paced a few more times, the gun clasped in his hands behind his back.

She could feel David's scornful stare on her, but she refused to raise her eyes to his.

Vargas stopped at the foot of the dying man, whose gurgles were now mere whimpers. "Seems I was a bit short-sighted, Lloyd. You brought me a perfect situation. For that, I end your suffering."

A final shot silenced the whimpering man.

Amanda finally lifted her eyes to David's.

"My apologies, *Señor* Stephens. I seem to not have an additional guest room prepared." He nodded his head and two men pulled him away.

"No, David." Amanda tried to jump to her feet, but stumbled back to her knees. "Please," she cried. "No."

Vargas squatted next to her, his face hovering just inches from hers. "I'm not going to kill him, *mija*. I'm going to put him somewhere safe," he cooed, only making her cry even harder. "Shhhh." The drug lord stroked her hair. "But if you lied to me to save your lover, I will cut off your eyelids to make you watch him die."

## 27

---

Josh waited hours in Vargas' study, pacing and straining to hear outside the four walls.

Pedro simply opened the door, made eye contact and turned with the understanding that he'd follow. At his room, the boy turned the doorknob and stepped back, allowing Josh to be the first to enter.

He pushed open the door and gasped. Lit candles littered his room and a table reminiscent of one from a romantic bistro in Paris occupied the clearing in the center. But...that wasn't the cause of his gasp.

It was the woman who sat in the chair facing the door, the crown of stringy brown hair greeting him.

"I tried to persuade her to make herself presentable for you," Vargas spoke over his shoulder. "But, I fear that the trip here took too much out of her."

Josh's feet carried him two steps into the room, but he stopped short of the table.

Her head remained down, eyes shielded by the hair cascading around her face. There was no doubt it was Amanda.

"You are probably wondering why she's here." The drug lord

followed him into the room. "Josh, women need to be cared for, made to feel like they are the only one on the planet. When you master that, you gain control over them."

The numbness from seeing Amanda washed away, and new emotions rode in with the tide.

Guilt. Anger. Fear.

He couldn't quite put his finger on the onslaught running through his head at seeing her for the first time in over a year.

"Get control over your woman, Josh." Vargas' hot breath seared his ear with the command. "Because if you can't, I will."

When the man stepped away from him, the temperature dropped.

The drug lord walked to the table and pulled a bottle of champagne from the bucket. "One of my finest bottles of champagne and some chocolate-covered strawberries to assist you."

"Thank you, sir," Josh's voice was a hoarse whisper. "I don't know what to say."

Vargas slapped a hand on his shoulder as he passed on the way out the door. "Either she's under control or you're both paying the price."

His skin burned from his boss' touch as the door clicked shut behind him. He studied her, waiting for some indication that she registered he was there.

Amanda's hair was longer than he remembered, and she'd ditched her high-maintenance blonde locks for what he always guessed to be her true color; light, coppery brown.

Her white, long-sleeved shirt was soiled with the rusty dirt of the courtyard covered a gray, sweat-stained tank top.

His eyes continued down, below the tabletop to her crossed ankles, allowing him to enjoy the view of her bare legs peeking out of khaki shorts with dirt covering one knee and dried blood on the other. Shapely calves disappeared into dirty, worn sneakers, a far cry from the tall stilettos she'd donned as part of her professional uniform.

Amanda's legs had always been his favorite body part. Josh appreciated she wore something to show them off, even if she didn't dress for him that morning, and her knees looked like they belonged to a clumsy tomboy.

He pulled out the chair across from her and joined her at the table. His nose wrinkled as dry sweat and something acidic, like bile, rose off her body. Guilt for failing to save her crept up his numb leg, giving him enough sensation to know it was there, but not taking hold. Could he have reached her in time anyway? Would she have believed him?

In all likelihood, it would've made her work harder to find him.

Josh held his breath to keep from retching at her smell.

A faint sniffle escaped her wall of tresses, igniting his anger.

"Well, I hope you're proud of yourself, Amanda." He leaned back and draped an arm over the back of his chair. "You fucked up and got yourself and God knows who else killed."

Her shoulders fell further, her forehead nearly touching the table in front of her as another whimper escaped.

He crossed the room to the waiting champagne bottle and grabbed a glass, filling it to the point where the foam crested the rim. "Cut the crap. I know you wanted this." His voice came out harsher than he'd intended. Josh reclaimed his seat and took a long drink, letting the bubbles tickle his tongue and fuel his anger.

This was his life here, his decision. Sure, it was also his prison, but he'd made this choice to be taken in by Vargas rather than face the SEC. He'd given Amanda a chance to get away and start her life over, and instead, she'd wasted time and money looking for him for some stupid vengeance.

*When did she become such an effing saint?*

Amanda's head lifted slightly, her bottom lip now coming into view beneath the hood of her drooped head. "He's going to kill him," she breathed. "I tried to save him, but he's going to kill him."

"From what I saw, he's already dead."

She winced.

"And, if by some miracle he's still alive, Vargas has you now. He's useless." Josh delivered the fatal prognosis with the clinical coldness of a doctor.

She gripped her stomach at the second, below-the-belt hit. Her body crumpled and she continued the slow fall to the floor, landing on her knees with her chest collapsing over them and her forehead to the floor. Her shoulders shook in a silent cry.

When the tears ran dry, Amanda righted herself and looked at him through red-rimmed eyes. Her face was caked in dirt, with pale lines cutting down where the tears washed part of her cheeks clean. The hair around her left temple was matted in blood. For the first time, Josh noticed red flecks of blood spattered on her right sleeve.

*God, what has she been through today?*

He drained his glass, hoping to numb any part of his mind that cared enough to comfort her. In the harshness of Vargas' compound, Amanda's presence only made him more vulnerable to the man's demands and manipulations. She was now his ward. Her well-being was *his* responsibility. Tamping down any concern would be the only way that he—and she—could survive.

She took a deep, wavering breath. "He lied to me," she inhaled. "He said he'd live." She pursed her lips and looked at the door. "That lying bastard."

"Well, that's exactly what Vargas is." Josh refilled his glass. "Even to himself." He poured a glass for her and offered it. "Want some?"

Amanda slapped his hand away, champagne splashing on his pants and running down her bare thighs. The glass landed on the floor in a resounding clink. "Go to hell," she snarled.

Josh laughed as he grabbed the bottle and took his seat at the table.

Her chest heaved, her breasts rising with each angry breath and her dirty cheeks flashed red.

Warning signs for a famous Amanda Martin temper tantrum, but it didn't mean he'd approach with caution.

Beads of sweat dotted the chocolate skin of the dipped strawberries, reminding him of one of his former lovers. He plucked one off the tray and popped it in his mouth, biting into the hard shell while his mouth filled with the sweet juices. It'd been so long since he'd indulged in something he considered standard fare for cocktail receptions and post-coital snacks.

With a second bite as sensuous as the first, he'd get an erection from food porn alone, proving that the scorpion's sting hadn't rendered him impotent. But, finishing off the first strawberry was as unfulfilling as a quickie in the coat closet with an ugly girl with a nice rack.

Josh dove in for seconds. "I would offer you one, but judging by your rising temperature, I think you'd just spit it at me and waste a perfectly good strawberry." He washed it down with a long drink of champagne. From the corner of his eye, he watched Amanda glare at him from the floor. "Hate me all you want, Amanda," Josh continued before biting into the third. "Months, weeks or, hell, even a couple of days from now you'll see I'm not the bad guy here." He offered the virgin strawberry to her lips.

She blanched and turned her head, and he devoured the entire thing in one bite, letting the juice dribble down his chin just inches from her stringy hair.

"You don't realize what a treat this is." He poured more champagne. The quickness with which he consumed the alcohol slowed his synapses, and it took a while for his hand to get the message to stop pouring as bubbles overflowed the glass. "After a few days of tortillas and beans, you'll wish I would've forced you to have one."

His ex-girlfriend knitted her brows together as his words sank in. He could almost read her thoughts.

This was her new life; stuck here in a ten-foot by ten-foot room in a desolate Mexican outpost at the mercy of whatever whim their madman, drug-lord keeper could come up with.

Another sip of bubbly gave birth to a new concept. What if Amanda's arrival didn't just signal her damnation? What if it meant *his* salvation?

*Surely between her and grandpa they know where we are and which way I should go to get out of here.*

Josh eyeballed the champagne remaining in the bottle and determined it was enough for a peace offering. He slunk to the floor sitting cross-legged in front of her and offered the bottle.

Amanda turned her head even further away.

"I'm sorry." He switched off his anger and summoned his little-used charm. "Let's start over." He stretched the offered champagne even further. "You'll thank me for this later. It took me over a year here before Vargas would share his tequila, and trust me when I say you'll need a drink." Like dealing with a scared kitten, he just held his hand out patiently, not moving while he waited for her to come to him before clenching her in his grasp.

Finally, she reached for the bottle, pausing before bringing it to her lips.

"Atta girl," Josh cooed. "I'm not the bad guy here."

She took one short sip from the bottle, grimacing. "I still hate you," she said, her voice raspy.

"I know."

She took a longer drink this time, so eager that the liquid spilled out of the sides of her mouth, the back of her hand caught the overflow.

Josh suppressed a sarcastic smile in favor of a sincere one. "Are you hungry? There're two strawberries left. They're yours." He reached for the plate and brought them chest-level to Amanda.

She took one and greedily ate it in one bite.

"Admittedly, they aren't as good as the ones we had when I whisked you to Paris for your birthday. Remember, they were dipped in dark chocolate from that famous little chocolatier?"

"Don't, Josh," she said with her mouth full. "I'm not walking with you down memory lane. The path I'll take will be vastly different from your little fantasy." Her voice was sharp and full of warning, silencing him, forcing him to retreat and regroup.

"You're right. I'm sorry, I just got carried away with seeing you." He bowed his head, but looked up at her from under his brow, giving what he guessed to be his best James Dean. "I missed you, Amanda."

She bent forward, plucking the final strawberry off the plate.

His nostrils filled with the odor of her sweat but he held his face steady; gagging would only break the spell he was casting.

"You know *I* know that is bullshit," she whispered. "Tell yourself that all you want. I'm going to figure out a way to get you back to the U.S. so you can go to jail." Amanda traced the tip of the strawberry around his lips before pulling it back to her mouth, biting into it.

For the first time in days, something stirred within Josh's groin.

She smirked and scooted away from him, not stopping until her back hit the closed French doors. "If I can't do that..." She took a long drink from the champagne, her knuckles white as they gripped the neck of the bottle. "I'll just kill you."

This was going to take a little work.

## 28

"Well, I sure as hell hoped I'd never see you again."

The voice startled David awake, like a bucket of freezing water, but he relaxed. It was Hank Snare, Mandy's injured PI.

The room was so dark that he blinked twice to prove that his eyes were able to open. His awareness traveled down his body.

He pushed himself into a seated position. Pain shot through his ribs and he gritted his teeth. A quick run of the tongue confirmed that they were all in place, but his mouth was flooded with the metallic tang of blood. David leaned against a wall only to be reminded of the blows to his back. He was hard-pressed to find a place on his body that didn't hurt.

Including his heart.

Being taken by Vargas' men had saved him from going through with his betrayal of Mandy. Just meeting her eyes pierced him with a blunt edge, he couldn't imagine what it would feel like when he'd pulled into the FBI office in El Paso.

"Forgive me for not bringing a gift," David's throat was raw.

A guttural laugh spewed from the man's chest and the putrid smell of decay assaulted his nose. Through narrowed eyes, he took in the man through the hazy darkness. Beaten and bruised, did he looked as bad as Hank? "We need to take care of that leg," he said while unclasping his belt buckle. A scarlet circle smeared one thigh and white glowed from the center of the wound.

The shootout that felt like years ago flashed through his mind. Hank was shot in the thigh and it was obvious the man had received no care for the gaping wound.

He waved him off. "Save that for yourself. It's too late for me. I can feel it in my blood. Doing the tango with the cancer." Another round of body-rattling coughs erupted from his chest. "I'd rather die by a bullet than delinquent cells. Where's Amanda?"

*Cancer.* It all made sense now; thin, gray skin tone, that painful cough. David couldn't blame the guy. A quick and meaningful death trumped being eaten alive by your own body any day.

"She doesn't know, does she?"

Hank took a deep breath and exhaustion floated across his face. "She was my last client. I got the diagnosis the day before she showed up." He rested his head against the wall of the shed and grimaced as he stretched his good leg. "Here she was, crying and upset, hating herself but willing to set things right. I just knew I had to do this one last case."

David sat back on his heels. That was what had drawn him to her. Sure, the physical attraction was strong, but her heart was bigger than the Texas sky. It was a heart that would love him with everything she had. It was a heart that no matter how hard she tried, she couldn't hide from him. It was a heart that even though he'd yet to shatter it, a crack had formed between them because of his call to Fallon.

"You didn't answer my question." Hank pulled him back into the hot shed.

"She's with Vargas."

"Vargas is using her. Josh Williams came to see me last night. He has got Williams under his thumb, but something else is in play." The old PI inhaled a deep breath. "Something Josh needs to be kept in line."

David exhaled and allowed his head to drop. Knowing the man

that manipulated Mandy for years was actually *here* deflated his lungs as quickly as a kick from one of Vargas' men. He tried to ignore that voice in the back of his mind that reminded him what he and Josh had in common. "So he does exist."

They sat in silence. Occasional movement from a corner sent chills down David's back, but Hank seemed immune to whatever scurried in the shadows.

"Stephens, don't take this the wrong way, but why are you still alive?"

"He thinks I have information about a raid. Mandy made it up, last ditch attempt to save me." He rubbed the raw skin on his wrists. "He killed someone in front of us, in front of her."

"I heard the shots."

"It was this kid, Lloyd. He joined the Border Patrol right out of junior college not long before I did. I don't think he was really bad, I think he just got in over his head." David replayed the gruesome scene in his head, wishing he could fast forward through the sound of the man drowning in his own blood. "The thing is, Hank, I saw it coming. I saw Vargas draw the gun and in that split second when it was coming, I prayed it was for Lloyd and–."

"Listen, Stephens, put that out of your mind. Out here, it's the survival of the fittest. You know that. Lloyd was a dead man the minute he made a deal with the devil. So, get over it and let's figure out a way to get you and Amanda out of here."

He pulled himself up to study their enclosure. His right knee wobbled at his first step, reminding him he needed to baby his old football injury in case they had to make a run for it. He crossed the small room in three steps.

The stucco walls were warm, suggesting that the outside sat in the direct sun. David felt along the walls for a light switch, but instead wiped cobwebs from his palms. The wooden door was the only way to escape and through the tiny gaps around the frame, the only source of light. He pressed his ear to the door, but only silence spoke to him.

"Don't bother," Hank said. "There's no doorknob."

His hands groped the wooden door for confirmation. The only way out was if someone was coming in. "How many stand guard?"

"One for the first day or so, but once they realized I wasn't going anywhere." The older man nodded to his festering thigh. "Someone comes twice a day to bring water and tortillas."

"Any way we can ambush him?"

"Can you deflect bullets?"

David let his back fall against the door, ignoring the pangs shooting through his shoulders from his bruised muscles. He aimed a punch at the wooden door, stopping the momentum just short of the hit. He needed to save his knuckles for flesh. "There's got to be a way."

The air was thick with doubt and fear. Waiting for an answer in that room was like waiting for the air conditioner to kick on. It wasn't going to happen.

He went over the layout of the compound in his mind. He'd only been able to take in part of the *hacienda* while kneeling in the courtyard. All the buildings were made of light pink stucco with the focal point a large Spanish-style manor.

David guessed the house to be where Vargas lived, and hoped Mandy was there instead of a similar room. He'd been dragged backwards, so they were kept somewhere to the right of the residence.

The silhouette of a structure to the left of the main building slid into his memory. The number of armed men that'd slipped in and out of his vision guarding this building indicated it must be the commerce center of Vargas's empire.

"Mandy saved my life today."

"Wouldn't surprise me. She's braver than any soldier I ever served with."

"She lied, about me having information. I'm worried. Vargas knows she lied, and he's going to make her watch as they torture me."

No sound came from the man in the corner.

"Hank?"

"Well, let's start working on your story."

## 29

J osh and Amanda stared at each other from across the room well into the night.

"You should get some sleep," he suggested. "You look like hell."

"Is that the line you're using these days?" Amanda answered. "I'm not tired. But don't let me keep you up." She watched as his eyelids fought sleep, like a toddler trying to stay up past bedtime only to succumb in a series of slow, heavy blinks.

He slowly shook his head. "Nah, I'm good."

"Are you afraid I'll kill you in your sleep?"

"You wouldn't do it," he slurred. "You're too good."

He was right. Amanda wanted to hit him and make him hurt as much as she did, but she couldn't kill him. The threat itself felt oddly satisfying.

Her enemy didn't sleep in the room with her. He slumbered somewhere else in the house.

"Sleep," she sighed. "I promise I won't hurt you."

Once Josh's breathing became steady, she allowed herself to lie on the floor of his room. With her ear against the tile, Amanda listened for any indication he'd been wrong; David's Texas drawl or any murmurings of his name.

Twice during the night she heard a man clearing his throat deep inside the grand house. The tenor reminded her of him. The few times she saw feet come to a rest outside their door she imagined them wearing David's boots. As the feet moved on, so did her hope.

She stretched out, unleashing a waterfall of blood to her fingers causing them to feel as though stung by a thousand ants. The cool tile under her cheek soothed her. An overhead fan remained still and the French doors opening to the courtyard were shut tight.

Sure that no movement would stir Josh; Amanda sat up to survey her prison. His second floor room looked out over the empty courtyard.

Directly in front of her sat the heavy gate that must be the one David told her to remember. A tall fence fortified the perimeter with a stucco shed sitting solitary on one side.

She pressed her face to the glass and could just make out another building to the other side of the main house.

Orange light from the rising sun cast a spotlight on the dark red bloodstain on the courtyard. Where was David's blood? Did Vargas drag him out to the desert where his body would dry and decay under the harsh southern sun? Was his death quick and painless, or did he suffer as Lloyd had?

Amanda took a deep breath and splayed her hands against the glass, hoping if David's spirit were still near that she'd feel some electricity.

She felt only a chill.

"They're going to ring the breakfast bell in about an hour." Amanda jumped at Josh's voice. "You'll feel better if you shower."

She sat on the floor and hugged her knees to her chest, catching a whiff of what must be penetrating Josh's nose. The room wasn't warm and stuffy; it was rank with her sweat.

A shower might make her less offending to Josh's senses, but it wasn't going to make her feel better and it wouldn't bring David back.

"I'm not hungry," she whispered.

"Missing breakfast isn't an option here. Vargas sees this operation as a big extended family and in *his* family, everyone eats every meal together. No exceptions."

She sighed and went back to watching the rising sun. It would be the first sunrise without David. No amount of dialing his number and hanging up would bring him back now.

*David.*

Two days was all it took for the feelings she'd buried to push through to the surface and bloom like a long dormant flower basking in the sun. He felt it too. She saw the way he'd looked at her in his trailer, desire darkened his brown eyes.

But something changed in him after that phone call. Was there another woman? Someone he'd started seeing after her? It would make sense. Guys like him didn't stay single for long. Whoever she was, she'd spend the rest of her life wondering what happened to David.

*He had the misfortune of running into a crazy old girlfriend.*

Fresh tears burned her eyes, but refused to fall down her face.

"I know it may not seem this way, but I'm just trying to help you." Josh shifted on the bed.

She could see from the faint reflection in the glass that he sat up in bed shirtless. His vanity had fueled early morning workouts when they'd dated, and by the muscle tone in his chest and arms, he continued some form of that routine here.

*He must hate knowing his good looks are going unappreciated.*

"There is a way to exist here. Maybe after some time, you can even thrive here," he said.

"I don't plan to be here long enough to thrive."

His bare feet smacked the floor as he crossed the room to sit next to her. "I know I don't have to tell you this, but Vargas is nuts." As he whispered, his eyes gazed over her head toward the door, as if he expected armed men to burst through at his blasphemy. "You have to play to his ego. If you make him happy, he'll make you happy."

"Sounds a lot like dating you." She looked to the west, but Josh didn't move until the breakfast bell rang.

He dressed in silence and when a knock at the door revealed a young man to escort them to breakfast, he offered a hand to help her off the floor, which she accepted only to keep from breaking open the thick scab on her knee.

"*Buenos dias, Señor* Williams," the young man said. "Hello *Señorita* Martin. *Bienvenidos*, I am Pedro." He bowed his head respectfully.

"Hi Pedro," was all she could summon.

As she followed them downstairs, Amanda craned her neck to any open door in hopes of catching a glimpse of David. The building was silent as they turned behind the stairwell and entered a large inner courtyard of the house.

Orange trees bloomed from large blue pots, a small bubbling fountain foamed in a corner and a wisteria snaked its way up a thick trellis. Four tables formed a square in the center of the courtyard and people quickly filled their seats.

She hesitated, looking through the corridors for any way to escape. As if sensing her thoughts, Josh grabbed her hand and began to lead her to a table.

"There are the lovebirds." Vargas stepped out of the shadow and into their path. "I must say, it's not a surprise at all to see you two looking exhausted. Please, join me at my table this morning."

"That would be an honor, sir," Josh answered, tightening his grip on her hand, he towed her to a table in the opposite corner. He only released her to pull out a chair for her, positioning himself next to Vargas at the head of the table.

"Josh, please be a gentleman and allow Amanda to sit next to me so we may get to better know each other."

"Of course, sir," Josh's voice tight and clipped, the same tone as when he addressed his father at the firm. The elder Williams had always been congenial to her, but she'd heard stories that when younger, he'd been brash and temperamental. The tree to Josh's apple.

Once seated, Amanda kept her gaze on the tablecloth in front of her, not wanting to meet the eyes of the man who'd killed David.

When his open palm came into her view, Josh leaned over. "We hold hands to say grace."

Swallowing back the acrid taste in her mouth, her put her hand in Vargas' cold one. His fingers enveloped hers and she feared she'd turn to stone by his touch.

"*Para nuestros amigos de América, voy a orar en Inglés de esta mañana,*" Vargas boomed. "Heavenly father, bless us for this day, nourish our bodies and our souls with your gracious bounty. And, thank you Lord, for blessing us with a new member to our family." He squeezed Amanda's hand and she involuntarily tightened her grip on Josh's hand. "In the name of the Father, the Son and the Holy Ghost."

The drug lord released her so she could cross herself, but she fought against her Catholic school upbringing and simply placed her hand in her lap. God wasn't in this courtyard with her.

"Tell me, Josh, Amanda, how was the reconciliation?" Vargas asked as he stabbed at a grapefruit with his spoon, the juice burned into Amanda's arm when it squirted. "I expected to feel the building shake last night." He leaned in closer, his voice barely above a whisper and his warm breath filled her ear. "I feel passion runs through your veins, Amanda. Maybe Josh will let me have a chance to test my theory."

Even though she told her body to not react, goose bumps broke out down her arms.

Josh leaned across her as Amanda stared at her plate.

"*Señor*, everything is under control. Thank you for giving me, us, the opportunity to... reconnect." A squeeze of her leg signaled to Vargas the sincerity of his response and told her to play along, but she was in no mood to listen to her ex suck up to a madman.

Vargas turned to the other guests at the table and spoke in rapid, hearty Spanish.

"I really don't care if you want to get yourself killed," Josh breathed into her ear. "But you are *not* taking me down with you. If I tell Vargas we're done, that means *you're* done. Got it?"

"What's stopping you?" she hissed.

They suffered the rest of the meal in silence. Josh devoured his breakfast; Amanda only shuffled the food around with her fork, wondering if she stabbed it into the artery in Vargas' neck if he'd bleed out before giving the order to have her shot.

The man must have felt her stare on his neck. His expressionless eyes studied her before he spoke in a flat voice void of the earlier bravado. "My apologies for our rocky introduction yesterday."

"Why am I here?"

"It's simple. You were looking for Josh. I had him." He shrugged as he sipped his coffee. "I wasn't going to stand in the way of a lovers' reunion."

"Don't misunderstand me. I'm taking Josh home with me."

Vargas chuckled as he draped an arm over the back of his chair.

"I didn't realize I told a joke." She fought the flush of adrenalin urging her body to flee. She couldn't let him call her bluff this early in the game.

"You women are all the same. You make your decision before weighing all the options. There are three men on this compound with ties to you. It's your choice. Are you sure *he's* the one you want to save?"

Three men.

Amanda's throat closed up.

*Three men?*

Josh took up one of those but who were the others? El?

She should've checked on him. Was David still alive? Or, Hank?

Her lungs burned, with anger as much as lack of oxygen. The rest of the courtyard went fuzzy and silent.

Except for the vein on Vargas' neck. It pulsed, a hint of blue beneath his caramel-colored skin. His blood swooshed. A beating sound with a whish beneath it, like a percussionist using a brush on a snare drum.

Her heart fell in beat with his, the sounds assaulting her ears in stereo. She had to make it stop. The vein, the sound. His heart.

Vargas plucked the fork out of her hand. Her knuckles still white from her tight fist.

# 30

Vargas was in no hurry to finish breakfast. For someone who ran an international drug empire, he luxuriated in a drawn out meal joking with his employees.

This was for her benefit, for her to see him as the benevolent leader. It didn't work. Amanda wished she'd stabbed him in the neck before he'd taken her fork away. Especially when he suggested that she had a choice.

*Choices come with a price here.*

Finally, he dismissed everyone.

Amanda and Josh sat at the table, each looking down at their plates. Anger at each other pulsed between them. If Vargas felt it, he ignored it.

"Josh, I would like you to join me in my study to go over financials," the drug lord said, studying his fingernails. "Amanda will be escorted back to your room, where I encourage her to relax. You look like you've not had a vacation in a very long time, *señorita*."

The men stood, but before turning away, Josh leaned down as if to brush his lips against he cheek, but instead planted a "Be good," in her ear.

Amanda craned her neck, her gaze following as they exited the courtyard through a door in the opposite corner from where Pedro had led her and Josh. She closed her eyes, mentally tuning her hearing to their retreating footsteps and hushed voices until only the sound of a bee buzzing in a nearby plant filled her ears. "What have you gotten us into, Josh," she whispered, allowing her shoulders to sag.

Her head whipped around as she studied the courtyard. Situated in what she guessed to be the center of the house, two more doors faced her, the sounds of pots clanging competed with tinny sounds of music from the open one. An armed guard stood unblinking at the other.

As soon as she stood, a man stationed at the door behind her grasped her elbow. "*Vámanos.*"

She stumbled as he pushed her forward, using the barrel of his gun to point to where he wanted her to go. Amanda walked slowly, using the shield of her hair to hide her wandering eyes. Back inside the main house, she noted the wide front porch facing the dirt courtyard. Men milled about. The sound of children laughing danced in her ears.

Her escort nudged her to walk faster, causing her to trip on the first step up the grand staircase. She cut him a dirty look over her shoulder, using the opportunity to get a better view of the courtyard and gate.

Halfway up the stairs he must've tired of her snail's pace. He gripped her by the elbow, and dragged her down the dark hallway, pushing her through Josh's door before slamming it behind her.

Without her ex's watchful eye, she perused his quarters. The bed remained unmade, the table from the evening before still sat in the middle of the room with the nearly-empty champagne bottle floating in a bucket of water.

The door of an armoire stood ajar. Amanda pulled it wider and studied his limited assortment of khaki pants and T-shirts. "The lack of Armani in your closet must be killing you."

In the far corner, his desk looked much like it had when they'd worked together. Papers were scattered in haphazard piles. She flipped through them, the numbers written in Josh's hand making no sense.

She flopped in his chair and leaned back. "What in the world are you doing here?"

Amanda sprung forward and kicked the trashcan under the desk. The tightly wadded piece of paper grabbed her attention first. Once she smoothed it, her breath caught.

Staring up at her was her.

She unrolled the others to find more pictures of her. Her in the dark green rubber boots and denim shorts standing with her back to the camera while she spoke with a group of men in front of a mechanic's shop. Then in the small store, speaking with the young cashier who knew Josh. A final one of her sitting in the back of the truck, her head against the back window, her cheap aviator sunglasses shielding her eyes from the sun.

Was Josh watching her? Had he ordered her kidnapping? Had he also ordered David and Hank's murders? Did he have more power here than he let on?

With a deep growl, she flung printouts from his desk, hoping a pair of scissors or letter opener would emerge. Sheets rained down around her, landing on the now cleared desk, but nothing sharp emerged. Amanda shook as she wadded up the pictures, taking a deep breath to keep from ripping them apart. "You son of a bitch."

She ran into his bathroom, ignoring the clattering as his toiletries fell from a small glass shelf, but no file or nail trimmer, not even a razor.

Her reflection caught her attention. Rage flushed her cheeks to an unhealthy shade of red, her chest heaved as she tried to control her breathing.

A year of her life had been spent looking for this man. A man she thought she knew. A man she'd maybe even loved.

But who was he?

Amanda took a deep breath. More importantly, who was *she*? For the past year, her goal had been to bring him back to Chicago to face those he wronged. But, the game was changing.

*She* was changing.

"You killed them, Josh. Prison is too good for you."

Amanda gripped the sides of mirror, the metal cutting into her fingers as she tried to pry it off the wall. Her cry of frustration bounced off the tile floor as she fled the bathroom, pulling open drawers, looking under his bed for anything she could use as a weapon as soon as Josh crossed the threshold into his room. "Come on Amanda, get it together." She paced. "Think, think. Ten, nine," she counted off her steps. "Maybe he didn't mean it. You know, just like he didn't mean to leave town the same day all hell breaks loose."

On her third pass by the table, she skidded to a halt, her eyes locking on the floating champagne bottle. She gripped its neck and clung to it while exhaustion washed over her. Amanda curled up on the end of his bed with the bottle cradled against her chest.

It'd been days since she slept. A short nap was all she needed. Just long enough to give her strength.

Her eyes fluttered open at the sound of the door clicking shut. The headboard stared back at her; she must've rolled over during her nap. Her fingers tightened on the warm glass. At least she'd held on to her bottle.

Footsteps approached. Slow, heavy. The click of the heel was different from when Josh had walked away in his loafers that morning.

Amanda kept her breathing slow and steady. She squeezed her eyes shut and tucked the bottle closer to her chest as rough fingertips brushed her hair off her face.

The fingers paused, then continued tracing a line down her arm hopscotching to her hip and down her leg.

Bile rose up from her stomach, but she begged her body to not react.

The bed behind her shifted as she heard the metal clang of a belt being unhooked. Tightening her grip, she rolled over, using her body's momentum to swing the bottle. A thud echoed as the bottle collided with a man's temple.

He fell backwards with a grunt and his head hit the tile floor.

Panting, Amanda scrambled to his side. It was one of the men from the van ride, the one who'd cracked his gun into the back of David's skull.

*David.* Tears flood her eyes as she pulled the handgun from the man's holster. He didn't deserve any of the mess she'd brought to him. The gun felt heavy in her hand, as if it was weighed down with the souls with the lives it stole.

Much like the lives Josh had stolen without even pulling a trigger. A tear splashed on the trigger, nudging her to what she had to do.

The door was ajar. She pulled it toward her and looked down the hall. Emptiness stared back at her.

## 31

The house was quiet. Desert heat fought with the cool breezes from the overhead fans. It felt as if the whole house was asleep.

Amanda paused at the foot of the stairs. To her right was the corridor she'd taken back from the courtyard. She glanced to her left, guessing that was the route where Vargas had led Josh after breakfast.

Light poured out from a cracked door midway down, illuminating the dark hall. As she crept closer, she heard Vargas' musical accent and Josh's strained, hurried whispers.

"Maybe they aren't making it up," her ex said in a high-pitched whisper. "Look, we can't be too careful. You have much to lose, *señor*."

"I have people working for me in every rank of the U.S. Border Patrol and the Mexican government. Why would some low-level agent know what they don't?"

Her hands went cold, the warm gun burned in her palm. She hadn't given her lie to save David another thought, especially since it failed.

"Well, I guess we'll never know, will we?" Josh said. Amanda imagined him leaning against the side of the desk, arms across his chest, shirt collar popped, looking like a smug frat boy.

She glanced down at the weapon in her hand. It fit into her palm neatly, almost perfectly. It was appropriate. The hunted had become the hunter. The victim, the aggressor.

The wronged became wrong.

The men's heads were close, bent over papers. They both looked up when she opened the door.

Josh's mouth dropped, Vargas' formed a tight, straight line. Their eyes darted from her face to the gun she held out in front of her bouncing from one to the next as she tried to decide who to shoot first.

"*Señorita*, I see one of my men was careless," the drug lord said, his voice calm. "If you would be so kind, please tell me who I need to punish."

"I took care of him for you."

The moment his green eyes locked with hers, she felt weak.

Vargas laughed and perched himself on the edge of his desk. "Well, for that I owe you my gratitude."

Amanda froze in the door. The gun swayed in her hands, as if it were the one in charge, not her.

In a way, it was.

"What happened, Amanda?" Josh stepped around the desk and inched in her direction. "Where did you get the gun?"

Her finger stroked the trigger. Not enough movement to fire, but enough for her ex to stop advancing. "Don't pretend you're inno-cent. *You* did this."

Josh held up his hands and nodded. His gaze darted to her left, into the hall and then quickly back to hers.

She moved all the way into the room and gently closed the door behind her.

Vargas plucked a balance sheet from the stack they were just perusing and studied it as if this were nothing more than an annoying interruption to their conversation.

A scream bubbled up her throat, full of rage and sadness. Amanda wanted to fire a shot into the bookshelf above his desk, if anything to prove to herself that it was real and not just a water pistol.

"Did someone hurt you? You've been crying." The concern etched between Josh's eyes looked real, but he was a master thespian. He worried about his own life, not hers and certainly not Vargas'. "*Señor* will take care of him for you. Just tell us who it was."

Her arms grew heavy as she refocused her aim. "Really? He'll do that? What if I told him it were you?" She reached around to her back pocket and flung papers that landed at his feet.

Josh barely glanced down before his face whitened.

He knew what she found.

"Deny it," she said, her voice breaking. "Deny it, Josh Williams, and so help me it will be the last words out of your mouth."

"Babe, listen—"

"Don't 'babe, listen' me." Her arms shook again as the words exploded out of her mouth. "How many people have you killed, Josh? Have you even bothered to think about that? When you ordered my kidnapping you killed at least three other people. And that's just *here*. Have you even thought about the people who died in Chicago?"

He winced from her verbal punch. When he met her eyes again, they darted back over her shoulder.

Was it a signal? Was he trying to tell her that someone was outside the door?

"Amanda, you are upset," Vargas cooed, releasing the paper from his hands. "Put the gun down. Let's sip some tequila and talk about this."

"I came here for Josh. You can let me leave with him and I'll happily forget where I found him."

"Amanda, look at me." Josh tried to refocus her attention. "Give us the gun. Don't do this."

Uncertainty clouded her mind. What if he was right about this being a prison? What if he wasn't a warden, but her cellmate? The gun dipped several inches, as if it too were uncertain of its intended target.

"Come, Mandy. That's what you go by now, right? It's what your lover calls you." The cartel leader pushed himself from the desk and crossed to the bookshelves, turning his back on her to pour a drink. "There's something sweet about that name. Innocent." Vargas pulled a sip of the liquor. "It's what your parents still call you. Despite everything you've done, you are still their little girl."

Her breath hitched as she absorbed his words. "What?"

"Amanda," Josh tried again, putting the weight of authority behind it.

"Your mom is a very beautiful woman. I can see where you get your strength and determination. My men spotted her in Juarez just a few days ago, searching for her wayward daughter." Vargas drained his drink. "Ah, now there's a thought. A mother-daughter reunion. Josh, you wouldn't mind would you? Although you seem hardly able to handle one Martin woman."

Amanda's eyes locked onto Vargas. The tears dried up as she squared her shoulders and straightened her arms. She wrestled for control, but she was punching above her weight class. "You bastard."

"Or, maybe your brother. He's following in your father's foot-steps to become a doctor." He poured another drink. "Speaking of your father, he's back to work now. It's been hard for him to accept that daddy's little girl was less than perfect."

"Stop it."

"Amanda, dammit. Look at me." Josh sounded distant.

"You really should call them sometime. The FBI isn't bothering them anymore. I'm sure they'd like to hear from you."

"Shut up." The words scorched her mouth.

"Amanda! Think about what you're doing." Her ex was losing the battle raging in front of him.

"They are just going about their business in suburban Chicago. The perfect American family. Fugitive daughter aside."

White-hot heat flooded her veins, pulsing from her heart, flowing down to her fingers and toes. A tiny bead of sweat cascaded down her temple, as if attempting to cool her anger but evaporating before it could reach her cheekbones. She was burning from within, but instead of turning her to ash, she felt herself turning to stone.

"It would make sense that you would want David to call you what they call you. As if it erases everything you did, all the money you stole, the lives lost because of you. *Mandy*."

Like a needle swinging to true North, the gun found Vargas.

It no longer shook.

Amanda's breathing evened out and her shoulders relaxed. The weapon liked what it saw.

"Point the gun at me," Josh said. "I'm the one you came here for. You said it yourself last night. You want to kill me, not him."

He was right. But she couldn't shoot Josh first. When it came down to it, she couldn't shoot Vargas either. No matter how much he deserved to die, *she* didn't deserve to add this to her conscience.

Her eyes collided with Josh's, silently begging him to save her.

His face softened and he cocked his head to the side. All those years of working side by side paid off, they still had a little bit of that connection, the ability to read what the other was thinking. He nodded and opened his mouth, her salvation just moments from being breathed into life.

"Man-dy." Vargas drew her name out. It felt tainted coming from his lips. "Mandy, Mandy. That name is so sweet, like suckling nectar from the juiciest fruit. Wouldn't you agree, Josh?"

Her eyes left her ex's face.

Vargas flashed a winning smirk at Amanda and brought the glass to his lips.

"It was the last word he spoke." The drug lord went in for the kill. "David, that is. The last word on his lips was your name. Too bad we can't ask him if it was as sweet."

The air left her lungs in an audible exhale. A heartbeat thudded in the room. Just one. It could've been hers. Or maybe Josh's. But not Vargas'.

She swung her shoulder in his direction and lifted her arms in one move. The gun took over, telling her it'd be all right. Amanda squeezed the trigger, and stumbled backward into the door.

Josh ducked on the other side of the desk.

A piercing screech rang in her ears, followed by a muffled howl. Her lungs inhaled the smell of gunpowder.

The pistol hung at Amanda's hip, satisfied with its job.

Vargas crouched beside the desk, gripping the left side of his head.

Behind her, the door burst open and men rushed by her.

They were shouting in Spanish.

The butt of one man's rifle rammed between her shoulder blades, numbness radiated down her arm. The gun fell and her knees hit the floor.

Josh looked over the wooden desk at her, his eyes wide in fear and surprise.

With help from one of his men, Vargas pushed himself up. Blood pooled on his beige linen suit and matted his hair. A bloody black mass filled the space where his ear should've been.

He took three steps toward Amanda, his face distorted with hate and pain.

She met his stare, her chin thrust out in determination.

Vargas kneeled in front of her, their faces just inches apart. "You surprise me, *señorita*," he panted, blowing a combination of cigar smoke and tequila in her face mixed with the metallic scent of his blood. "*Santa Muerta* accepts your sacrifice."

The man behind him tried to help him stand again, but Vargas shrugged him off.

He lifted an arm, the back of his hand colliding with Amanda's face, whipping her head to the side. "That is for my ear, bitch."

## 32

J osh hoped he'd be forgotten in the chaos that followed.

The men swarmed their fallen leader.

Vargas shouted commands in an angry cacophony of English and Spanish, but the ringing in Josh's ears was so pronounced the words floated by as if he was underwater.

Amanda knelt in the doorway, refusing to meet his eyes no matter how intently he stared at her.

"Do you understand what you just started?" he hissed at her. "There's nothing I can do for you. You know that, right?"

Her response was a slight shift of her eyes in his direction.

Before he could relay just how much she was screwed, a man pulled her to her feet and dragged her backwards from the office.

Only then did Amanda's eyes meet his. She didn't beg for help. She didn't plead for mercy. She seemed to be at peace with her actions and her punishment.

The hall's darkness swallowed her and another wave of Vargas' men rushed in. A protective shield formed around the boss, but he waved them off and walked out of the room.

Blood dripped from his matted hair and lines of red raced down the back of his beige shirt. Vargas looked lopsided from behind, his shoulder-grazing hair flared more on the right, but hung grotesquely straight on the left.

Before leaving the office, the boss glanced over his shoulder at Josh and his lips curled up in a snarling smile before he whispered to the man next to him.

The man smiled and nodded.

An electrical pulse flooded down Josh's body. "Wait, wait, let's talk," he begged as rough hands jerked him up.

The henchman reached around his back and pulled out a gun.

With his hands up and his eyes locked on the firearm, Josh allowed the man to lead him. He held his breath until he entered his empty room and felt the whoosh of air as the door slammed shut behind him.

A circle of blood stained the floor at the foot of his bed. The fallen comrade had been either retrieved or able to walk on his own after Amanda's escape.

Sheets of papers were scattered across the floor. Josh knelt down, scooping them into a haphazard pile. What good did it do to put them back in order?

He sat on the edge of his bed and looked, mentally telling his room goodbye. For over a year, this had been his salvation and his prison. It'd taken months of delivering consistent numbers and counseling Vargas on how to make smarter business decisions to gain the man's trust.

It'd taken less than twenty-four hours for Amanda to ruin it all.

Was that her revenge? Is that why she hadn't shot Josh?

It made perfect sense. He left her to clean up his mess in Chicago, so she created a similar situation for him.

Amanda was smart, but was she *that* smart?

Suffocating in the face of his imminent death, Josh pulled open the French doors and looked out over the vacant courtyard. He braced himself against the rail, feeling the weight of his head as it hung down.

What would it feel like to lose his head? Would he die instantly, or would there be a moment of realization that his head was no longer attached?

Or, what about being shot? He already knew what it smelled like and he could feel the jarring pop of a gun at close range. Would a bullet pierce his skull before those senses hit him?

He took a deep breath of desert air, closed his eyes and looked up at the afternoon sun. Despite the stifling heat, the sun embraced with warmth.

When his lungs felt like they would explode, he exhaled and lowered his face, fluttering his eyes open. His gaze landed on the stucco shed to his right.

Had Amanda joined up with Hank in that filthy shed? Or, had Vargas wasted no time in ending her life?

Josh rooted around in his heart, waiting to see if he'd feel anything if Amanda was dead. *Nothing.*

Was he really as awful as she said? Did *he* deserve the bullet that'd maimed Vargas?

The sun fell in the sky as he quietly considered if he deserved life or death. Even in the darkness of the night, the compound felt like a tight rubber band. Something was about to pop and it would either break or sting like hell.

He didn't want to be around for the snap.

Goose pimples covered his arms in the night air and he closed the doors. The soft, brown leather messenger bag sat untouched in the back of his closet, only holding his fake passport and a tattered copy of *Catcher in the Rye*. He tossed the book aside; Holden would understand, and filled it with the stolen money from his toilet tank.

Unable to sit still, he paced his room with the bag across his shoulder. At first, he made a conscious effort to step over the dried blood on the floor, but after thirty minutes of pacing, his body automatically took a larger step at that spot on the floor.

Somewhere in the house a grandfather clock chimed midnight. Josh hadn't eaten since breakfast, but it didn't matter. His stomach churned every time he thought about the smell of gunpowder and the sight of blood pooling on Vargas' shoulder.

At two o'clock, he felt brave enough to peer outside his door. No guard stared back. The compound was so silent, as if everyone had abandoned it but forgot to take him with them. He wasn't ready to leave. He needed that time before the sun rose when the night owls and early birds were collectively sleeping.

Josh sat on the edge of his bed, his bad leg aching from the incessant pacing, and stared out into the blackness of the Mexican desert.

Shortly before three o'clock, Pedro quietly opening his door interrupted his gaze into desert. "*Señor* Williams?" the boy peeked into the room before entering. Backpack straps clung to his chest, reaffirming the fact that the boy should be heading off to high school, not working for a drug cartel. "May I come in?"

"Pedro, what's going on? Why is it so quiet?" The hours of solitude erupted in a lava flow of questions. "Is Vargas ok?"

"Please, we must be quiet and be quick," Pedro spoke in a hush. "*Señorita* Martin is in serious trouble. We can save you all if we hurry." The boy's eyes fell to the bag at Josh's hip. "Are you leaving?"

"I don't know, I figured my time here was coming to an end," Josh folded his arms across his chest. "Assuming Amanda's still alive, she pointed a gun at me. Why should I care?"

Pedro glanced at the closed door. The boy was taking a huge risk being there even though he routinely saw to Josh's needs. "The men in the shed, *señorita*, you, they are going to kill you all at sunrise. In a ceremony, for *Santa Muerta*. You can't be here."

Mortality slammed into him like a freight train.

"What? Wait. No. But, I didn't do anything wrong." He sounded like a whiny child being punished for his classmates' misdeeds, but he didn't care.

Pedro just blinked his response. "*You* are the only one who can help, *Señor* Williams. Without you, everyone will die."

"I'm a son of a bitch, Pedro, not some hero. It won't work. We'll get caught, you'll get dragged down with us."

"You will die anyway, why wait for it?"

Josh took a deep breath. It'd be too easy to walk in there and walk out, but the troops were rallying around their wounded leader. What better time for him to find his way out of the compound? He ran his hand through his long hair, reaching for a rubber band from the desk and pulling it into a ponytail. It was stupid and would likely cost him his life, but he'd made that deposit a long time ago, it was only a matter of time before the balance would be due. "What's in the backpack?"

"Guns."

## 33

It wasn't the cold, hard floor of his cell that kept David awake and staring into the darkness. Nor was it the occasional scurry of something in the corner or the groans of a dying man.

It was the fact that he hadn't picked up one clue about Mandy since they arrived. The men who brought tortillas and water ignored his pleas to tell him something.

He pounded his fist on the wall behind him as thoughts rumbled through his brain. David went through what he knew about Vargas. The man was a relative newcomer on the drug scene and had risen to one of the most ruthless in northern Mexico in less than five years. He was an American citizen with a Mexican father, making him a thorn in two governments' sides, and he rarely, if ever, left the compound.

There was one bit of Vargas' background that forced him to grind his teeth; he was known for putting young girls to work as prostitutes to pay off their fathers' debts to him.

David would rather put a gun to his own head to release her from Vargas' hold than imagine Mandy giving herself to someone just to keep him alive.

A groan broke his suicidal contemplations. The infection in Hank's leg was getting worse. Heat from his forehead burned the back of David's hand every time he checked him, confirming that the infection likely spread to his blood and the man was in sepsis.

"Hey, Hank. How are you holding up?" He brought a cup of water to the man's lips, but instead of drinking, the precious liquid simply rolled down the side of his face.

"How's Amanda?"

He shouldn't lie to a dying man, but the truth would only make it worse. "She's fine."

"Of course she is. She's smart. Won't get herself in trouble," Hank struggled to say.

"I've got to get out of here."

"Yes, you do." The man's head fell to the side.

Resolve replaced resignation and he crept to the back of the shed, feeling along the ground for anything he could use as a weapon.

Finally, his hand grasped a wooden handle and his fingers confirmed it to be a garden spade. He tucked it into the back pocket of his jeans and resumed his spot on the floor, his back against the wall and his eyes peeled to the door.

It didn't matter that it was still several hours from dawn, the next person that walked through that door was going to get a spade to the gut.

The click of the door handle jolted David awake. He didn't remember dozing off and had no way to determine for how long. He scrambled to his feet and stood flush against the wall next to the door. A single beam of light shone into the dark shed as it opened.

"You told me he's here. What happened to him?" Someone spoke with no hint of a Spanish accent.

"He was. I brought him dinner just a few hours ago." It was the boy David had seen earlier in the evening. "Hurry, close the door."

Once the door shut and light flooded the small shed, David grabbed the person closest to him. The teenage boy was a head shorter, and his bulky backpack prevented him from getting much leverage with his hostage. "Who are you?" David demanded, pressing the edge of the spade against the boy's neck.

The man shined the light in his face, forcing his pupils to dilate. "Drop it," he commanded.

"Answer my question."

"We're here to help," the boy said. "Please, *Señor* Stephens. We are friends."

"Don't shine that in my face," David growled.

The man moved the flashlight to shine up, washing the small shed in the soft yellow glow.

David released his hold and blinked until his eyes grew accustomed to the light.

The boy moved beside the blond man. Unlike the men David had seen in the compound, this man was clean-shaven and clad in chinos and a T-shirt with his hair pulled back into a ponytail.

"Amanda has only a few hours to live. All of us have only a few hours to live," he said. "We have to hurry."

David crossed his arms with the spade still firm in his right hand. "You're Williams, aren't you?"

Josh stood just a couple of inches shorter and his shirt and pants seemed a bit too big. As if sensing being sized up, he too crossed his arms and straightened his back.

David nodded at the worn leather messenger bag slung across his body. "You leaving?"

"We're all leaving."

"Why should we believe anything you say?" he countered.

"You can't afford not to."

"*Señors*, please, we must help her," Pedro broke in.

"What's wrong with Mandy?" David asked.

"Her name is Amanda," Josh scoffed.

"She shot *Señor* Vargas's ear. She will be killed at sunrise. In a sacrifice," the kid's eyes were wide with fear.

David remembered the boy. He'd brought extra water with their tortillas, his brown eyes were warmer than many of the others he'd seen since his arrival. "All of you will be killed."

"Is she hurt?" he asked.

"I don't know. They are holding her in a cooler in the kitchen. Turn off the light, I think I hear someone."

Josh obeyed.

David held his breath, listening for any sounds outside the shed.

"Pedro," Josh whispered. "I think it's just a mouse or something. We're the only ones awake." He flipped on the flashlight and the nervous boy sighed.

"So what do we do once we get her?" David asked.

"Leave. All of you." Pedro gestured to the feverish Hank. "Tonight."

"How?" Josh asked. "We can't just walk out of here."

"You drive." He pulled a set of keys out of his pocket. Keys that David recognized from being in possession of Hank's truck. "His truck is behind the kitchen. I will open the back gate for you."

"It won't work," Josh finally said. "The place has night watchmen, and after Amanda's stunt they will be on high alert."

David pursed his lips and stared. "As much as I hate to admit it, he's right. We're outnumbered." He stared down at his boots and inhaled a lungful of stagnant shed air. Finally a way out and an opportunity to save Mandy, but he couldn't do it without jeopardizing the life of this boy.

"You need a distraction," Hank spoke from the floor.

"Like what?" Despite his best effort, the words came out cynically. "Fireworks?"

"How about an explosion?" Josh asked. "Because firing into a meth lab should set one off, right?"

He snapped his head up and narrowed his eyes. The man seemed to be a little too eager to offer that solution. "That's a really bad idea."

"Do you have a better bad idea?" Williams crossed his arms over his chest and leaned against the wall.

"Quit bickering like two hens." Hank pushed himself into a seated position, wincing only once. "Let's figure out a way to get home."

David squatted next to the older man. "All right, but we have to work together if we want to get out of here."

"Well aren't you the Boy Scout." Josh knelt on the other side of Hank, obviously ignoring the look David shot him. "Pedro brought two guns with him."

"Good, we'll need those," Hank said. "Now, Pedro, sketch out for me the layout of where they're keeping Amanda and where the guards are."

David marveled at the injured PI's strength. He'd pushed aside the pain and fever of his infection to take the helm of their escape.

As Pedro sketched on the dirt floor, David noticed Hank's eye seemed less clouded and his color looked better than he'd seen since his arrival. Even his swollen left eye fluttered open. Maybe the thought of going home had helped break his fever.

"The kitchen is in the back of the main house with a door that opens to the back courtyard. *Señor* Vargas instructed *señorita* to be placed here." The boy pointed at an area in the corner closest to the door. "It's a large refrigerator."

"Is anyone guarding her?" Hank interrupted.

"No need, it locks from the outside." Pedro tapped a large square in the right hand corner of his diagram. "Your truck is in this garage."

Josh leaned across the dirt map and made a circle with his finger, directly across from the garage. "And, this is the lab. There's someone guarding it, but the others are walking around like hazmat."

Hank studied the diagram for a moment. "Well, it looks fairly simple. One of us needs to get Amanda to the truck, someone needs to take one good shot at the building and we need someone to open the gate."

"I'll go after Mandy," David said on the tail of the ex merce-nary's words.

"Aren't you a cop?" Josh asked. "You should be the one taking the shot. I'll get Amanda and get her to the truck."

"Like hell you will. Why should I believe *you'd* save her now after you left her in Chicago?"

"So you're going to let your machismo kill us all?"

"What is that supposed to mean?" His voice was getting too loud, but he didn't care. If it was up to him, he'd get Mandy and Hank and get out of there while Josh stayed where he belonged.

Bringing him to justice be damned, this place was a tougher sentence than any prison.

"If you two don't settle down, we'll never even get out of here."

David looked down at Hank's chastising.

"We'll just revise the plan. Pedro, think you can help a crippled old man get close enough to get a couple of shots off?"

Pedro held Hank's stare for several seconds as an unspoken conversation passed between the two. Finally, the boy nodded.

"Great. Give me one of those guns, Stephens you take the other, and try your best to not use it on Williams. We have to get the timing perfect."

David and Josh nodded.

"You get her and make your way to the truck, but don't start it up until the explosion. Pedro, after you get me in position, I want you to make your way to the gate."

"I'll stop to pick you two up on my way out," David said.

They all exchanged glances and Hank nodded.

"Okay, any questions? Someone give me a hand."

Pedro and Josh jumped up and made their way to the door while David heaved Hank to his feet.

"Hank, you okay to do this?" he whispered.

"I'm fine. Stephens, there should be a 9 millimeter under the driver's side seat, fully loaded unless these goons messed with it. You're going to need a weapon."

"What d'you mean? We have two." Before the words left his lips David understood what'd passed between Hank and Pedro.

They didn't expect to join the escape, and in all likelihood, both would be killed for their role.

He swallowed his argument and nodded.

"Take care of yourself. And, try not to kill Williams before you turn him in. Pedro, lend me a shoulder?"

Hank tottered off with the boy leading the way, leaving Josh and David alone in the shed.

He cleared his throat. "Well, you ready?"

Josh walked out of the shed without a glance behind him.

## 34

*Keep moving. You have to keep moving.*

Amanda commanded herself to run in place, but the arctic temperature in the cooler made her bare legs feel heavy. With her hands tucked under her armpits, she paced, passing boxes of fruits and vegetables in the closet-sized room. The dry air burned her throat, which was already sore from screaming for help and cursing at Josh.

After another set of jumping jacks, she perspiration pricked her forehead. Her cheeks flushed with some heat.

"Finally," she said, pulling the long-sleeved shirt off her shoulders and wrapping her hands in it. The cool air bathed her warm arms and tickled the little bit of skin exposed. She resumed pacing and after several more minutes, sweat made its way down her stomach. "I'm overheating."

Amanda crouched in a corner farthest from the vent blowing a steady stream of cold air. Her eyelids were slow to lift with each blink. Despite her temporary warm-up, she didn't want to backtrack to freezing during her rest. Her tongue tenderly touched the cracked corner of her mouth finding the slight tang of copper from the bloody lip Vargas had given her.

Part of her wished she hadn't shot him, but the other part cursed her for missing his head. She hadn't decided who to shoot until the moment he'd spoken of David's last words. Josh had been saved by the fact that she had nothing else to live for.

An avalanche of exhaustion descended upon her. Her body swayed back and forth on the balls of her feet. She swung forward to her knees before falling to the side and curling into the fetal position. Her eyes closed to the hazy gray freezer.

Behind her eyelids, she found warmth. The sun-soaked sand squished between her toes as she strode barefoot on the beach. From under the brim of her hat, she could make out a figure walking toward her with his back against the sun.

She ran to him with a smile, her feet kicking up dry sand. The more she ran, the farther away he seemed. With each step, the sand burned hotter. The sun no longer gently warmed her skin, but steam rose from the heat of the unforgiving star. Sweat poured down her face and there was nowhere she could go to escape.

Amanda jerked into a seated position.

"Mandy, it's okay, it's me." David knelt beside her and his warm hands cupped her face. "We have to go, I need you to walk. Can you do that?"

She nodded, but what was real and what was a dream? "I walk into the light?" Her voice was barely a whisper.

Death was comforting with David at her side.

He smiled and stroked her hair. "No, baby, not yet. Not if I can help it." He reached for her hands and smiled again as he unwrapped her shirt from them. "Good girl, you wrapped your hands. Does it hurt if I take this off?"

Amanda shook her head and David continued to uncoil her shirt. "But I don't understand. Why is it so cold in Heaven?"

"Hurry, we need to get out of here." Another voice filled the room from the door.

"Who's that?" she asked.

He didn't answer.

She took two heavy steps past David and stumbled, but another set of hands caught her before she fell into a metal shelf stacked with canned goods.

"You need to hold on to her," the other voice hissed.

Amanda righted herself and looked into Josh's cold eyes. "If I'm dead this must be hell."

"It's good to see you, too," he said.

"You get Mandy, I'll follow behind. I can't shoot if I'm holding on to her."

"Shoot? David what's going on?" Amanda reached out for him, but Josh grabbed her hand. "Ouch, my fingers." If he heard her, he made no indication.

The warm air of the kitchen made her confused skin break out into goose pimples. The room was dark, only the light of the slivered moon guided them to the back door.

Josh looked through the small window, and then pushed it open. Behind Amanda, David had a gun drawn.

"Clear?" he asked.

"Yeah," Josh answered.

"Hank's truck is the black F-150. Looks like that's it in that second bay in the garage," David said.

"You think Hank and Pedro are in position yet?"

"Hank's alive?" Amanda's earlier hoarse voice found renewed strength, but both Josh and David shushed her.

"Yeah," David answered.

"Barely," Josh said on top of him.

"Let's make our way to the truck, but stay in the shadows and keep low," David commanded.

Josh grabbed her hand again.

The desert air was a warm shower to Amanda and her eyes took a moment to adjust to the shadows of the courtyard.

They came to the end of the house and the end of their cover.

"We're going to be exposed between here and the garage," Josh whispered over her head. "That's a good twenty feet. We won't make it. Someone will see us."

He was right. Even with the dim light from the moon, it would be a risk running out in the open. Anyone standing guard would have a clear line of vision for three people trying to steal one of their cars.

When she looked up at David, his jaw muscles flexed.

"I'll go first to make sure it's clear," he said

"No." Amanda couldn't contain her objection. "You can't. You'll get shot."

For the first time, he looked her in the eye and smiled. "I'm trained for this so I'm going to take every precaution, but you have to do something to keep me safe. Sprint, like the end of one of our runs. The faster you run the less time I'm exposed."

She nodded. His honesty calmed her thundering heart. A little.

"But, you also need to keep running, don't look over your shoulder, it slows you down." He looked up from Amanda to Josh. "I'm going to run out to the middle, when I signal, you high tail it over to the garage. I'll be right behind you."

She took one more look at David, and his eyes met hers. A day earlier she hadn't trusted him. It felt like a lifetime ago that she was afraid of him, afraid of that little voice whispering in her ear. Up until now, she'd been afraid he was dead. Her mind ran through a range of emotions like a pianist practicing the scales.

"Is it true you shot Vargas' ear off?" he asked.

"Yeah."

"That's hot."

She couldn't help but smile as she turned back to face a scowling Josh.

"Cute. Can we get the hell out of here?"

"Ready when you are," Amanda answered, begging her frozen legs to not hold her back.

"Let's do this." David pushed past them before she could change her mind.

As planned, he ran into the clearing and waved them forward.

Amanda let go of Josh's hand and propelled her body forward, but it was too much and she found herself falling forward. Her hands caught the ground and tried to move in sync with her legs, but her ex scooped her up before her face joined in the tumble.

"Really Amanda?" Josh growled.

"Get into the shadow," David whispered behind them.

Amanda held her breath until she reached the shadowy fringes of the garage. As David turned to run, voices betrayed the silence of the night.

Whipping her head to the north, she saw a beam of light cut across the dirt. "David, hurry."

He froze, crouched low, and lifted the gun.

Another voice called out to the first and the beam of light shot out again. Then the air was once again empty.

A heartbeat later, David ran to them.

With their backs again the wall of the garage, the three of them heaved in unison.

"That was close," David said between pants.

"What now?" Amanda asked. No one had stopped long enough to tell her the plan, other than Hank was alive and somehow part of the escape.

"We need to get to Hank's truck and wait for him to fire on that building over there." David nodded in the direction of a building across the courtyard.

"Why *that* building?"

"Because it's highly unstable. We need to create a distraction so we can get out of here."

"What happens to Hank? I need to see Hank," she said.

When David didn't immediately answer, Amanda saw him lock eyes with Josh.

"I promise I'll do everything in my power to get him out of here, but he wants you safe above everything else." He leaned down to be eye level with her.

She shook her head as ice-cold tears rolled down her cheeks. She couldn't let him walk into certain death, not for her again and not without saying goodbye.

Hank had been her father when she couldn't bring the mess of her world to her parents. He was the one person she'd trusted with her life when she'd walked away from the other person she trusted. The PI had worked harder for her than she deserved, and now he was going to fight on her behalf even if it meant he lost his life.

"Amanda, he wouldn't make it home anyway." Josh added. "He was shot when they took him. If he made it out of the compound alive, he'd be dead before we could get him across the border. He knows that."

Amanda reclined against the wall, banging her head as she absorbed their words.

"Let's get in place and wait for the sound of Hank's gun before we get in and start the engine," David said.

They moved in the shadows to the truck. Amanda stood next to Josh on the passenger side and she watched David through the cab of the truck.

"So, how did tall, dark and handsome woo you? Did he save a kitten from a tree?"

"You can be a real ass, you know that?" She refused to look at him, instead focusing on David's pacing. "He isn't a narcissist like you."

Several more minutes passed and she could feel Josh getting anxious.

"Something's wrong," he muttered and walked around the front of the truck toward David.

She followed.

"Something's wrong," he repeated to David.

"I know, I feel it, too. He should have made it by now."

"Cover me," Josh said.

Amanda's eyes ached as she rolled them. "To do what? Go find Vargas?"

"I'm going to find Hank, then we'll blow up that building."

"But you don't know how to shoot a gun."

"It doesn't matter. I just need to hit something that makes it go boom. Back me on this, Stephens."

David scanned the dark courtyard. "Hang on," he said. In one move, he opened the driver's side door and flicked off the dome light. Seconds later, he pulled a gun from the floor and checked it before handing it to Josh. "There's a round in the chamber, so be careful. I'll cover you until you get to the house, but beyond that it won't do you much good. I'll follow the original plan, once we hear the explosion we'll start up the truck. Run to the center of the court-yard, we'll pick you up."

Josh nodded as he took the gun.

Amanda grabbed his arm, the sharpness of her earlier tone feeling duller at the realization that he was serious. "Are you sure about this?"

He jerked his arm away. "You call me a narcissist, but yet you question when I do something for you. You're quite a hypocrite, Amanda. I'm ready," he said to David.

The two men ran into the open.

David held his gun high.

Once Josh made it to the house, David ducked back into the shadows of the garage.

"Josh." Her voice finally found its strength. "Be careful."

He nodded once and ran into the darkness.

## 35

"He's not a narcissist like you," Josh mimicked under his breath as he crept along the back of Vargas's main house. The messenger bag felt even heavier away from Stephens and Amanda.

If caught, he couldn't blame all the stolen money on them. "What if instead of saving your butt, I wake Vargas? You certainly *expect* me to do that."

Even if he did so, it didn't necessarily mean he'd be saved. He already had a sunrise date with the bony saint. Alerting Vargas would only endanger Pedro, who'd been nothing but kind to him.

Josh made it to the small back porch. In the shadows of the garage he could make out two figures standing close to Hank's truck. He would've felt better about the whole stuck-with-Amanda-and-her-boyfriend thing if the guy showed any bit of weakness.

David's taller shadow reached for Amanda's and pulled her to him. The two figures merged into one.

A voice tugged at his ear. *This man loves her more than you ever could.*

"Go to hell," he whispered to the voice. "She tried to kill me."

He focused the building. Was it just TV dramatization that meth labs could blow? What if they missed and only pissed off the drug lord even more? He was a numbers guy; did he even know what he was looking at in the first place?

Josh moved along the back of the house and came to the edge where the shadow broke off and the glow of a floodlight lit the ground in front of him. A man sat on the building steps, but appeared to have dozed off. Through narrowed eyes he could make out shadows moving inside. It came as no surprise that the lab was an around-the-clock operation.

He waited a few seconds before he stepped out of the shadow and into the clearing. To the left he spotted the closed, smaller back gate of the compound. He hoped Pedro was lurking in the darkness near the gate ready to open the door to freedom.

"Dammit, Hank, where are you?" Josh sighed under his breath. He didn't need Hank, he had a gun and a good idea of how to use it. Bringing Hank home, even if it meant the old man died on the way back, would give him a leg up on Stephens. At this point, every inch of leg he could get higher meant that Amanda would forget her vengeance quest against him.

Plus, he liked the symmetry of his head.

Josh trotted in the moonlight along the western side, moving toward the vast front courtyard. There was no shadow to crawl in here.

As he neared the front porch, Hank's slack body reclined against the side of the house and the gun hung loosely in his right hand.

He knelt by Hank and dropped his head. The only dead body he'd ever seen was his grandfather when he'd traveled back to Germany at age five or six. He remembered aunts, uncles and cousins all speaking to him in a language he barely understood.

Josh closed his eyes as he contemplated his next move. He'd never wanted to take Hank's role as the shooter. That was just for show. Now he had to summon the courage to actually do it.

*I should have recommended Stephens for this job.*

He was nearing the end of his silent pep talk when a clammy hand grabbed his arm, forcing him to lose his balance and fall back in the dirt. "What the—Hank, I thought you were dead."

"Close. I needed to take a break. Did you get Amanda?"

"Yeah. Any later and we'd be dealing with her hypothermia. Where's Pedro?"

The older man took a deep breath and closed his eyes. A deep rattle accompanied his exhale before he spoke. "He got me this far and I told him to go along the fence line to get into position. It's safer for him and would give him some chance of being able to leave with you. Where are Amanda and David now?"

Josh pushed the image of the conjoined shadow from his mind. "Waiting at your truck. Too much time passed, I had to check on you. So, what do you want to do? Sun's gonna to be up in an hour."

Hank nodded and pushed himself into a more upright seated position. "Want to help a dying old man finish his last mission?"

He stood and pulled the man up, standing on the side of his bad leg to serve as a human crutch. They slowly made their way toward the lab.

"See anyone standing guard?" the PI asked.

"Yeah, one man on the steps. Looked like he was asleep. From the shadows inside, there's at least one other person."

They made three more labored steps before Hank's good leg gave way and they both fell to the ground.

"Come on, Hank," Josh said heaving them both to their feet. "You have to be careful. Someone will hear us."

"I'm sorry, I need to rest again."

"In a bit. We're almost there." He braced himself under the man to keep him upright. "This isn't just about the gunshot, is it?"

Hank sighed and shook his head. "Cancer. Eating me alive."

Clarity slammed into him. Hank didn't expect to survive the escape. "So, that old saying about going out with a bang instead of a whimper?"

The man laughed, a painful sound that made Josh's lungs hurt. "You got to make sure you get the boy. Before you leave. Vargas will skin him alive if he thinks he betrayed him."

Josh's words and promises had little market value. He simply nodded. He'd never reneged a nod.

They took two more steps when the sudden sound of a door opening cut through the quiet. Josh drug them back into the shadow just as two men came outside, the top half of their protective suits peeled down to the waist.

One of them kicked the man asleep on the steps, knocking him awake. The threesome walked down the steps and moved about ten feet into the center of the yard where tiny flares illuminated their faces as they lit cigarettes.

"What do we do now?" Josh mostly spoke the question aloud to himself, but Hank's clear answer startled him.

"We give them a minute to finish their smokes and then we shoot them."

"Just like that?"

A cold hand gripped his shoulder. Perspiration glistened in the dark and his gray face reminded Josh of the man in the moon from the old silent films he watched with his dad.

"Make it easy on her."

"Make what easy?"

Laughter erupted from the trio. They tossed their cigarette butts on the ground and headed back to the building.

The man that had been stationed as the guard said something to the other two and ran to the back of the building.

"Well, well, our lucky day. Our guard is taking a leak so no one is minding the store," Hank said. "I want you to help me get about ten feet away from the front of the building, and then head back to the garage. Don't even bother checking on me after you hear the explosion. If that doesn't kill me this damn bullet wound will before sunrise. And, I've always got the cancer as a backup plan."

Josh nodded and they hobbled into the open dirt courtyard.

"I want you to make the trip home easy on her," Hank said, giving him a hard look. "Okay, this is good. Leave me here and get your butt back to the garage. Remember what I said. Just get the hell out of here."

As soon as he stepped back into the shadow the growing sound of whistling flooded his ears.

The guard came around the corner and stop in his tracks at the sight of Hank's unsteady arm pointing at gun at the building. The man said something to Hank in Spanish and drew a gun.

The PI adjusted his aim from the building to the guard and fired. The kick from the gun made him stumble backwards and the errant bullet blew into nowhere.

At the sound of the man's shouts and the gunshot, the other two men came outside, both with larger guns.

Hank righted himself again, but in his hesitation the two men on the porch lifted their weapons. His body danced as bullets hit.

Somehow, whether by a final dying conscientious action or by a muscle jerking in his finger, there was a flash from Hank's gun and one of the Vargas' men grabbed his knee and toppled over.

An eerie silence washed over the night. The two unwounded men quickly ran to check on their fallen brother. It was a matter of seconds before the entire compound would be a flurry of action and their chances of escape would fade into the desert night.

Josh tightened his grip on his own gun and ran into the middle of the courtyard, but his scorpion-stung right leg still operated on a delay. He refused to look down as he passed Hank's body, not wanting to see what the future held for *him* if he failed.

The wounded man was howling so loud that the crunch of dirt under Josh's shoes went unnoticed. With his left arm bracing his right, he lifted the gun and squinted to give himself a better view. One quick pull of the trigger and the man on the left fell in a heap over the other injured man as a bullet ripped into his back.

Josh aimed at a window on the right side of the porch, begging the bullet to find something highly unstable.

Out of the corner of his eye, he saw the remaining uninjured man look up.

If the man actually shouted "no" it was lost in the crack of a second shot from the gun.

Josh fired again and the man dove off the porch.

His arms burned as he lowered the weapon and took a step back.

"Come on, come on. Blow already," he whispered.

The shots must've missed anything flammable. Instead of squashing the hornet's nest, all he'd done was succeed in getting them sufficiently pissed off.

Josh gritted his teeth, raised the weapon and took two steps forward to shoot again. When the first flare flashed in the window, he thought he'd pulled the trigger, but a second later a blast of hot, noxious flames flowed out of the windows. He twisted his body to run from the lava-like blast, but his contorted body left the ground and flew backwards, landing hard on his left shoulder as flaming rain fell over him.

*Crawl,* he commanded his body. *You have to get to the center of the courtyard.*

His right hand reached forward and pulled at the dirt beneath him, moving him only an inch or two. He tried to move his other arm, but it had a numbing, tingling sensation. Afraid to look down and find his left arm missing, Josh reached again with his right, but he only moved another inch.

Shouts and whistles penetrated the ringing in his ears. He lifted his head to get a better view, but he couldn't tell if the fire was the glow behind him or the one coming at him. Through narrowed eyes he saw the light in front of him was actually two lights moving closer.

The ground shook as the truck made a hard turn and stopped just feet from where he lay. A pair of boots ran toward him, scooping him up and dragging him to the truck.

"Come on, let's go," the muffled voice said. "You did it, let's get out of here." Stephens boosted Josh into the back of the truck. "Once we get clear I'll re-set your shoulder, just hang tight."

Behind him, men poured out of Vargas' compound like angry ants protecting their colony. "Pedro," his voice burned as it escaped his throat. "Stop for Pedro."

David nodded and ran back to the front of the truck. Seconds later, the vehicle lurched and a cloud of dust kicked up behind them.

Josh held himself upright as the truck sped to the opened gate.

More men ran to the burning building, but another explosion sent them retreating back. A few splintered and ran after the truck. The vehicle paused as it neared the gate and a figure darted from the shadows to the truck.

Pedro smiled as he hoisted himself on the back bumper, dropping his backpack in the bed, but the boy jerked and then fell, revealing the snarling cartel leader.

As the truck sped away into the dark desert, Josh passed out with Vargas' silent promise charging through his ringing ears.

*We will all die for this.*

## 36

T he needle on the gas gauge danced provocatively with the E. David eased up on the pedal. After their escape, he'd driven south too long before cutting back to the east and heading north.

Light broke the horizon. His knuckles tightened on the steering wheel. The drive south wasn't completely in vain, this route took them away from the more crowded freeway and spit them out on a one-lane desert path. While there was some truth to safety in numbers on the freeway, taking a more crowded route also meant every car was a potential threat. On the back roads, he'd have a fair warning if anyone popped up.

His eyes left the road long enough to glance down at Mandy sleeping in the seat next to him. He fought the urge to reach down and stroke her head; afraid his slightest touch would wake her. She needed sleep. He needed sleep too, but it would be at least three hours before they crossed the border into Texas.

Who was he kidding? They weren't going to make it back in three hours, at least not in this truck. He should've known better. Their kidnappers hadn't stopped for gas on the way into Mexico, instead they'd drained Hank's gas-guzzler below the quarter tank mark.

The needle ticked closer to *empty* and he eased up again. The sky grew another shade lighter in the east as David gazed to the dark road behind them. He didn't see a deserted road, he saw the widening eyes of a teenage boy as a bullet cut through his back. It was *his* fault Pedro was dead. He should've sent the boy back to bed rather than enlist him in their escape.

The sun cast its radiance upon the Mexican desert and his eyes made out a building on the horizon. Another mile closer and shade lighter and he two metal boxes stood sentry in front of the building.

Likely, the gas station was still closed this early, but if he couldn't figure out a way to steal gas they'd sit it out until a worker showed up. And then what? He didn't have any *pesos* on him.

Vargas' men took his wallet and phone. David shook the doubt from his head. He'd deal with the 'what-ifs' when the time arrived.

He misjudged the distance on the flat Mexican highway, and by the time they arrived at the gas station, the engine choked to a stop.

"Are we home?" Mandy mumbled as she pushed herself up.

"No, we need gas. Stay here."

He popped open the door and trotted across the dirt parking lot. The dirty windows of the station were mostly shattered, and thick bars covered the glass door. It'd been many years since this place was functioning. "Dammit," he cursed under his breath.

David avoided Mandy's eyes and retreated back to the gas pumps. One still had its nozzle properly in place. He pulled it out and flicked the switch up and pulled the trigger, but only the faint fume of gasoline flowed from the opening. He threw the hose on the ground and gripped the sides of the pump.

*Stupid. I know better.*

A hand touched his arm and he took a deep breath before facing her.

"What's wrong?" Her pale skin bathed in a warm light under the rising sun, skin that would surely burn to a crisp under the hot desert sun.

"We're out of gas and this station is out of commission."

A sympathetic smile slipped across her lips as he watched her consider their situation. She opened her mouth to speak, but a groan from the back of the truck interrupted her.

"Guess Williams is awake. He dislocated his shoulder. I have to reset it. I need your help and it's not going to be pretty."

Mandy nodded and he pushed past her to pull down the tailgate.

David grimaced as Pedro's blood-splattered backpack tumbled on the ground. He ran his fingers over the dark green nylon. An innocent life taken senselessly.

Josh groaned again, his left shoulder hung down and the man was pale with pain. "Where are we?" he rasped.

"Still in Mexico. Listen, you're a little banged up but you're gonna to be okay. First, we need to set your shoulder. Can you sit up?"

In the quiet of the desert, David kept his ears tuned for any humming sound while his eyes focused on the damaged shoulder.

Mandy climbed into the back of the truck with them. "Have you done this before?" she asked.

"I've had it done to me after a bad hit during two-a-days in high school. While I get it back in the socket I need you to hold him down. Sit on him if you have to. Josh, I'm going to move your arm around to get it back where it belongs. If you sit still, it will be over really fast."

David lifted his forearm and bent it at ninety degrees. Then he crossed the arm in front of Josh's chest with one hand while feeling the out of place joint with the other. It hung loose from its socket, but the ball of his shoulder made no movement back into place. As he moved the arm to the left, Josh groaned.

"You're hurting him," Mandy hissed, but David ignored her.

He moved the forearm back to Josh's chest and finally he felt movement in his shoulder.

"Almost there."

The joint refused to go back into place after several more passes. He should've reset it immediately, but there was no way he could've done so without risking all of their lives.

David leaned back on his heels and made eye contact with Mandy. "I'm going to have to try something else." A bulky messenger bag sat between them, preventing him from getting close enough to put force behind it. "Let's get this out of the way," he added, reaching for the strap.

Josh reached forward with his good hand and pulled the bag into his lap. "It's not in the way," he snarled.

*Whatever.* "Hold him down really tight for me. On the count of three. One. Two." He twisted the man's arm and jammed his stubborn shoulder back into its socket.

The pop reverberated through the desert as Josh fell into Mandy's lap with agonizing cries. "What the hell? You said on the count of three." He cradled his left arm and Mandy looked down at him, stunned.

"If I would've waited until three you would've tensed up and it would've hurt a lot more," David coolly responded. "How does it feel?"

"It hurts, you son of a bitch," Josh spat. "My hand tingles. What did you do?"

"That's good. It means its back in place, blood is flowing like it should." He felt Mandy's eyes boring into him and he looked up. "What?"

"Was that really necessary?"

"Fixing his shoulder? Yeah, I should've done it a couple of hours ago, but we were too busy trying to escape. The dislocation was worse than I thought. Why are you so concerned about his comfort all of a sudden?"

Her hazel eyes said it all. He'd been intentionally too rough with the injury. Running out of gas was David's fault. They wouldn't be in this predicament if he'd paid attention to the desert floor when Vargas' men came barreling after them. Disappointment in her eyes made him shiver.

"Your shoulder will be fine. Try not to move it. As soon as we get across the border, we'll get you to as hospital, but I promise you, it's better that I set it now than to have you nursing a dislocated shoulder until we get home."

Josh didn't look at him; instead he kept his head buried in Mandy's lap.

"Could he use a sling?" she asked. She didn't wait for his answer before pulling off her long-sleeved shirt and securing the sleeves around the man's neck.

"What're you doing? Your shoulders are going to blister under this sun."

"Josh needs it more. Anyway, I owe it to him. I did point a gun at him yesterday." Her chin tilted up and her lips pressed together in a thin line.

David knew this look. This was Mandy's end-of-conversation-I-win look. Rather than get into an argument, he jumped out of the back of the truck.

"How long until we're back in the U.S.?" Josh's quiet voice broke through the silence.

She looked down as she adjusted the make-shift sling, leaving David to answer.

"I don't know. We ran out of gas."

He sat up suddenly, knocking Mandy against the side of the truck bed. "Are you kidding me? We're dead. I don't know why you even bothered putting me through that hell. Vargas is going to find us and not just kill us, but torture us first and then kill us. I can't believe you'd strand us out in the middle of nowhere."

"Screw you, Williams. I should've left you on the dirt where you landed." David strode past the dry gas pumps and his boots crunched on the broken glass of the busted out windows as he walked around to the back.

Mandy's shouts floated through the desert but failed to infiltrate his ears. "David, wait." She grabbed his arm. "He's an ass, ignore him."

He whirled and she took a step back. "I can't ignore him, because he's absolutely right. I'm sorry. I thought I could get us home safe and sound."

"Since when did getting us home rest solely on your shoulders?" She looked to her right and her eyes rested on the carcass of a rusty old sedan lying behind the gas station. "You think that thing has any gas left in it?"

He followed her gaze. "Don't know. And the chances that the keys are sitting in the ignition are probably even less likely."

"Who said we need the keys? Maybe we can siphon the gas out. Bring the truck around back and I'll look for a hose."

David didn't bother glancing at Josh as he climbed into the driver's seat. The truck coughed to life and he was parked it next to the rusted out sedan. It was not only a good idea to try to siphon the gas, it was smart to move the truck off the road in case some of Vargas' watchful eyes drove by.

After an hour of searching, they couldn't find a hose to siphon the gas out of the car.

"It would be too good to be true if there was actually any gas in there anyway," she said as they joined Josh in the western shade of the truck. Sweat glistened on her chest and her gray tank top had a deep V of wetness.

They sat on the ground, staring out onto the Mexican desert. No hum of a car filled the air, no sign of a helicopter or airplane cut through the sky above and barely a jackrabbit scurried across the desert floor. Only the watery waves of the rising sun bouncing off the hot dirt kept them company.

"How's your shoulder?" Mandy was the first to speak.

"Better."

"I'm sorry I threatened to kill you," she added.

Josh hesitated. "I'm sure there's an etiquette book with the appropriate response," he said. "Given the circumstances, you're forgiven."

"Good. Now apologize to David for what you said, and thank him for saving you and fixing your shoulder."

"What—" He snapped his head at her.

"Do it or we'll leave you here to cook in the sun for the vultures." She kept her gaze straight ahead and didn't meet his bewildered eyes or David's smirk.

"Sorry," Josh mumbled. "And, thank you."

"Very nice. Josh, thank you for saving us from Vargas. David, would you like to add your appreciation now?"

He swallowed his gloating grin and bit back the sour taste. "Williams, thank you. I can honestly say we wouldn't be here without you." He cleared his throat in hopes of disguising the facetious undertones.

"Very good." Mandy's voice had the cheerful praise of a schoolteacher. "Josh, would you like to talk about why you had pictures of me?"

*Pictures?*

"Amanda, I swear to you, I had nothing to do with it."

"I won't give a second thought to leaving you here."

Josh leaned forward, obviously trying to catch Mandy's eye, but she stared straight ahead. "What? You can't mean that."

"The truth."

"Vargas came to *me* with those pictures. He was using you to control me. I tried to find a way to warn you. I swear on my life."

She pursed her lips and looked out over the desert floor, as if considering the likelihood of the story. After several long seconds, she sighed. "I'm not saying I believe you, but we don't have time to debate it. We need to figure out how we get home. This isn't one person's responsibility." She glanced at David. "It's going to take all three of us working together. I take it you both are in agreement?"

David shot her a look at the same time Josh did. "Yeah."

"Sure."

"Okay, so it appears the only way we have to get out of here is to walk."

"In this heat?" Josh asked.

"You can't be serious," David said.

"All right, what do *you* propose?"

A light breeze shuffled a cactus bush as he contemplated their options. She was right. The only way was to set off on foot and head north. Maybe, if they were lucky, someone would find them before they got lost in the desert.

"But, we need to move at night and rest during the day," David said finally.

Several more minutes ticked by before Mandy jumped to her feet and dusted off her shorts. "Come on, I need your help with something." She tugged at David's sleeve. "Don't move," she commanded Josh.

David frowned, but followed as she walked back to the front of the closed up shop.

She stopped in front of one of the windows and gnawed on her bottom lip.

A question faded from his throat as she balled up her fist and punched out the remaining glass from one window, creating a wider gap. "Give me your shirt," she ordered.

"What are you doing?"

"If we're going to be wandering around the desert we need water and food. I'm gonna see if there's anything left inside, but I don't feel like ripping open an artery before we even start."

He smirked and pulled his T-shirt over his head, laying it across the windowsill. "Take charge Mandy is pretty hot."

She smiled back at him. "Keep it in check and give me a boost, cowboy."

David hoisted her up and through the broken out window, cringing when her back came close to scraping on a sharp point.

Moments later, Mandy appeared at the door, unlocking it.

He shook out the glass from his shirt, but didn't immediately put it back on. The air in the building was hot and stagnant. "You take the food shelves, I'll check the coolers," David said. The store was dark and dirty, and the coolers were mostly empty with shelves missing or caved in on one side. He pulled open one dirty glass door only to be assaulted by the pungent smell of soured milk. "Oof," he said, wincing as his stomach roiled. "Don't open that one. Find anything?"

"Nope. Pork rinds may be the safest thing to eat, if you consider them safe."

David opened another cooler and his hand wrapped around a bottle of warm soda. He twisted open the top and smelled the sickly sweet liquid. "I found a few sodas."

"Yeah?" Mandy came around the corner, a fresh layer of sweat glistening on her chest. "Will that do us any good?"

"The bottles perhaps. Let's see if there's any running water in this old place."

She disappeared around a corner and he began perusing shelves. Like the coolers, the shelves were mostly empty. From the faded ink on the price tags, the store had closed down some years ago.

He passed a shelf with a loaf of bread, but it crumbled beneath his grasp when he reached for it. David turned a corner and studied another empty section of shelving, nearly passing it by before he stopped.

Tucked away at the back of the shelf sat a solitary bottle of tequila. The amber liquid clung to the long, lean lines of the bottle and the seal on the cap was fully intact.

"I found a sink."

He jumped at the sound of Mandy's voice, breaking eye contact with the bottle.

"Turned the faucet and nothing. What do you think?"

"Well, old warm sodas are better than nothing. We may even be able to find a spring clean enough to drink out there." He pulled the T-shirt over his head. "I'll come back with the backpack and fill it up with sodas and pork rinds. You should rest before we set out. We've got a long walk ahead of us."

Before following her out of the store, David turned back at the bottle, begging it to wait for him.

## 37

D avid and Josh both slept soundly through the day. The sun climbed over the truck and their shade gave way to the blinding sun, Amanda woke them and, like groggy children, they tottered to the other side of the truck.

She dug through Hank's truck looking for anything they may need on their journey. Duct tape tumbled out of the glove box. A flashlight revealed itself from under the seat and a road map of Texas was shoved in the door.

Amanda collected her bounty on the seat of the truck and perched on the back steps of the boarded up gas station.

A warm breeze blew through the desert, whistling through the busted out windows and lifting the tangled strands off her face. Her best guess put them about two hundred miles from Texas, give or take. Luckily none of them had hurt their feet or legs in the escape, but she had to take into consideration David's bad knee.

If they walked at a conservative yet brisk pace, they could possibly cover three miles an hour, but with the short summer nights they'd only be able to trek about twenty miles before sunrise. Amanda was no mathematician, but there would be no way they could survive the desert in the time she estimated it would take them to walk home.

She rubbed her face, wincing at the cut on her lip. She wanted to sleep, to drift away in an oblivious slumber, but that wouldn't happen. Behind her eyelids was not the pastoral scene of sweet dreams. Behind her eyelids was her friend's body barraged by bullets and left behind. She saw a young boy, eager for a life of freedom instead have that very life cut short for helping them.

Amanda wasn't going to sleep.

Not then. Maybe not ever again.

The only thing keeping her from losing it was readying for their trip home. As long as she kept her mind occupied, she wouldn't break down.

She mentally walked through the meager supplies they'd managed to round up. How long could it last them? Would it hurt to die of thirst or starvation? Would she know if she started losing touch with reality before heat stroke hit? They couldn't die out here. Hank hadn't died just to let the desert kill her. There had to be a way.

Josh was the first to stir from his afternoon slumber. His eyes fluttered open and focused on her face for several minutes before he pulled himself up with his good arm and joined her on the back steps. "What time is it?" His voice was heavy and he rubbed his left shoulder.

"Last time I checked it was almost four."

"Is there anything to drink?"

Amanda handed him a soda. "We have five total, so you need to make it last as long as possible."

He took the bottle and sipped cautiously.

"I don't think I could've done it," she said while he had the bottle at his lips. "No matter how much I wanted to, I wouldn't have been able to shoot you."

"That's comforting, I guess," he said after sitting in silence for several minutes. "I was planning on getting Hank to the truck for you. They shot him. I'm sorry. I tried."

A knot closed up her throat at the mention of Hank.

"Seeing you in charge earlier made me realize how much I missed you," her ex continued. "The smart, tough Amanda Martin, always in control. Always on top of her game."

"Is that the only way you see me?" she asked quietly.

"What other way is there?"

Amanda considered his response while watching David sleep just a few feet from where they sat. *He* didn't know her as Amanda Martin, he knew her as Mandy Jackson, the semi-neurotic, small-town reporter who'd held back on a relationship to keep from exposing her demons.

Now, she felt like an amalgamation of the two women.

David shifted in his spot, as if he were about to wake, but instead turned his head and settled back into his slumber.

There was one part of Mandy Jackson that followed her into Mexico; her love for David coupled with her hesitation to allow herself to succumb to her feelings for his sake.

"You know what's funny?" Josh's voice shook her from her thoughts.

"There's something funny?"

"I was just thinking this isn't very different from our last vacation together. Remember that trip to Sedona? It was hot and dry and dusty. You sat in the shade with a long-sleeved cover-up and this big floppy hat that made you look like someone's grandmother. I made fun of you for putting on SPF 100 every hour."

Against her better judgment a smile spread across her dry lips. She'd been pestering Josh to get away for Labor Day weekend and he'd surprised her by flying her to Arizona on the tail end of a meeting with one of his clients.

"Who was it you were meeting with, anyway? Oh that's right, the same man who wants us dead. So you're right, this hell is just like our last vacation together." She turned in time to see the dark cloud cross his face.

"I need to take a leak." He pushed himself off the porch and headed around to the front of the building.

"Sounds like someone crashed and burned on his trip down memory lane." David's mouth opened but his eyes remained closed.

"How long have you been awake?"

He stretched and yawned. "I don't know, maybe about the time Williams woke up."

"So you decided to sit there and eavesdrop? Nice."

"I was trying to go back to sleep. You two kept me awake."

Her other ex pushed himself off the ground and joined her on the steps, taking the place Josh had vacated. "How're you doing? Do you need to take a nap before we head out?"

"I'm fine. I found some stuff in Hank's truck. Let me show you."

David followed her to the truck. "Flashlight will come in very handy, so will the duct tape."

*Men and their duct tape.* "Really, MacGyver?"

"When you rub a blister from walking, you'll be begging me for some duct tape." He opened the map and frowned. "Nothing on here for Mexico. Where's Williams?"

"He went around the corner to use the bathroom."

"How long ago was that?"

"I don't know, you tell me. You were listening, so your guess is as good as mine."

He dropped his arms to his sides and Amanda met his brown eyes.

At once they both took off running around the corner of the building, nearly colliding with Josh as he walked back in their direction.

"What's going on?" he asked.

"I was going to ask you the same. What took so long?" David crossed his arms and straightened his back.

Josh's eyes narrowed as he lifted his head to be in line with David's. "What are you insinuating? Oh wait, is that too big of a word for a dumb jock? Should I speak in simpler terms?"

David growled.

Amanda pushed herself between them. "Guys. Stop. We were getting worried, is all."

Josh folded his right arm over his injured left and spoke over her head. "If you must know, it takes a little longer when you're down an arm. What did you think I was doing?"

David's sudden intake of breath indicated he was about to answer. A jab to his ribs seemed to change his mind.

"We need to get moving," she interjected.

They walked to the back of the store and David opened the door to Hank's truck. "Mandy found some stuff in here while we were napping."

"Her name is Amanda."

"How is that relevant to what I'm showing you?" He rolled his eyes. "And she's Mandy."

"It's relevant because I'm going to correct you every time you say it until you can get her name right," Josh bit out.

"Seriously? You're arguing over *my* name?" Amanda contemplated storming off, but in the flat open desert it wouldn't have the desired effect. "You're both right. Everyone called me Mandy growing up. I went by Amanda professionally. You're going to drive me crazy if I have to listen to this for ten days." She turned her attention back to readying their gear, but the air around her froze. She looked up and saw both her ex's eyes locked. On each other.

"Ten days," David said. "Is she right?"

"We've got to be a couple hundred miles from the border."

"At best we could cover fifteen, maybe twenty miles a night."

"Her math is right," Josh concluded. "We'd be lucky if we made it in ten days."

"We won't make that without water," David breathed.

"And you're sure there's none inside?"

"All that was left were these sodas. The sink was dry."

Silence descended on them again as the sun dropped toward the horizon.

"So, what do we do?" Josh's voice was uncharacteristically humble.

Amanda shook her head. The self-doubt that volleyed between them questioned her confidence. Circumstances over the past year gradually chipped away at her control freak nature, loosening stones here and there while a potential avalanche of no longer caring teetered precariously. However, she wasn't prepared for the rockslide, not yet, not while she could still control their fate.

"We walk," she handed Josh a package of pork rinds. "And we try not to kill each other." She handed David the flashlight and duct tape for the backpack. "Josh, what do you have in your bag?" Amanda nodded to the messenger bag slung across his good shoulder. Even when he'd napped, he held tight to the bag, like a security blanket soothing a scared child. "Anything we can use?"

His face whitened and he moved the bag in front of his body. "I didn't take much with me when I left Chicago, and what few possessions of monetary value quickly went missing. Forgive me for wanting to bring back a few sentimental things."

She glanced at David. He only shrugged. "It looks like this road heads due north, so let's follow that and see where it gets us."

The sun dipped below the horizon and the slight moon was slow to show itself. Blackness descended over the desert and David flicked on the flashlight every twenty paces to scan the ground ahead. "We're going to need some help," he said a few hours into their walk.

"How do we know who to trust?" Josh asked.

"We don't."

## 38

The sun peeked over the eastern horizon. Josh could barely step one foot in front of the other. He was surprised it was to his right, sure they'd veered off course sometime during the night and were heading in the wrong direction. They never saw another living being, although they did hear some rustling in the thick bushes.

"We need to start looking for shelter," David said.

"I'd give anything for another old gas station right now," Josh answered while rubbing his sore shoulder. The pain had dulled to a low throb, but the memory of the blinding pop haunted his muscles.

Amanda grabbed the flashlight from David and lit up the desert around them. A mesquite tree towered over the loamy floor to their left. Considering the terrain, towering was only about six feet over its squat peers.

"That'll do," David said. "Come on, let's rest up."

They walked over in the graying dawn and cleared a spot on the ground. Amanda hadn't spoken in hours and exhaustion was painted on her face.

"Why don't you guys rest first," Josh suggested. "I'll keep watch for a few hours."

David gave him a wary stare, but handed over the gun. It was obvious that he didn't trust him.

Truthfully, Josh didn't blame him. While it was somewhat awkward navigating his zipper with only one hand, it didn't take him as long as he'd acknowledged. The bulk of his time had been spent trying to get the busted old payphone outside the gas station to work. It'd been an impulsive act. If he had gotten a dial tone, who would he call?

The safest bet would've been to call Vargas and let him know he was kidnapped by Amanda and David and needed his help, but if any of the men had survived the blast outside the meth lab, they surely had shared that Josh was the shooter.

He took a place on a small rock formation about fifteen feet away and nibbled on stale pork rinds while watching Amanda sleep with her head on David's shoulder through the loose leaves of the Mesquite tree.

If it wasn't his ex-girlfriend with her new boyfriend he would've thought the image endearing. Considering the situation, it only made the salty sustenance in his stomach turn.

His hip sweated underneath the messenger bag. Only time would tell if which side of the idea spectrum a bag stuffed with stolen *pesos* would fall. If the money could be used to bribe someone to get him home, it would be a brilliant idea.

Or, if Vargas figured out his numbers were as fake as a stripper's tits, then, well, Josh would figure that out when the time came.

He unscrewed the top to his flat soda and took a long drink. Sure, resources were limited, but chances were the drug lord and his henchmen would catch up to them before dehydration set in. Why bother making himself uncomfortable? Plus, the caffeine in the drink would help keep him awake during his guard shift.

Sometime around noon David stirred and joined him on the rock.

"You should save your soda for when you really need it," the man said, nodding at the nearly empty bottle sitting next to Josh.

"Needed something to wash the pork rinds down."

"We can survive hungry a lot longer than we can thirsty."

"I'll remember that, Boy Scout."

The man sighed. "Why am I even bothering?"

They sat on the rock for a while longer as the desert heat reached blistering levels.

Josh scratched at the stubble cutting through his face. An iguana scurried from cactus to cactus, pausing in the shade. "So, you and Sleeping Beauty a serious thing?"

"Don't see how that's any of your business, Williams."

He polished off the last of the soda. "Word of advice, ex-boyfriend to current whatever-you-are, watch the temper. It makes her crazy."

"You want to try saying that to me when we're *not* running for our lives?"

Josh tried on his best innocent face. It still fit. "No really, Stephens, I promise I'm not being an ass. I just, well, you know, she pulled a gun on me, and shot Vargas' ear *yesterday*."

"You ever consider you and Vargas have something in common?"

As much as he hated to admit, leaving with Amanda and David had been his only option. Eventually Vargas would figure out Josh was stealing from him. If he hadn't already.

But, it was much more hazardous to be no longer working with him and possess knowledge of his empire.

He had a double bull's-eye on his back.

"Do you hear that?" David whispered.

Josh shook his head. "By '*that*' do you mean the ringing in my ears?"

Amanda's boyfriend popped up from his seated position and scanned their surroundings. "No, it's an engine. There."

He stood and followed David's line of sight to a black Jeep barreling down the highway from the south. It was still several miles away but the sight of the vehicle caused him to shiver.

"It's Vargas," David whispered.

"How can you be sure?"

"Because one of those Jeeps shot at Mandy and me." David glanced behind him to the mesquite tree where Amanda slept. "If they don't look too hard, that bush can hide us. Let's go now before they get any closer." He hopped down from the rock landing mostly on his left leg before running in a crouch to the tree.

Josh followed, although much more ungainly due to his off-kilter balance with an arm in a sling and the tingling numbness in his groin.

They made it behind the tree, each man squatted on either side of Amanda.

She never stirred, except for a slight snore.

The Jeep continued its trek down the road.

As it got closer, he could make out men in the driver and passenger seats and a third standing up in the back with a gun across his back. "Yep, Vargas' guys," he whispered.

"Just keep going," David mumbled. "Nothing to see here."

Before the vehicle came in line with their hiding place, the man in the back leaned down to the driver, who nodded and slowed. The man jumped out before it came to a complete stop and walked a few feet toward them before unzipping his pants.

"Lie down. Slowly," David hissed. He shot a protective arm across Amanda as they watched the man relieve himself.

"Of course he'd pick now to stop for a piss," Josh whispered.

The other two men hopped out and joined the third for their own bathroom break. Once the first was done, he lit a cigarette and wandered around the desert floor blowing clouds of smoke in the still air.

"Smoking is bad for you," Josh said.

"Shhh," David admonished.

The man mostly stared up at the blue sky as he puffed on his cigarette, but he looked in their direction and tilted his head.

"Does he see us?" Josh asked, afraid to take his eyes Vargas' goon.

"No, you idiot. He sees your trash." His voice was low and tight with anger.

He let his eyes move down from the man to the rock they'd been sitting on just minutes earlier. His empty soda bottle glistened like a beacon. "Shit."

The man pulled his weapon from his back and shouted over his shoulder with his cigarette dangling from the side of his mouth. As he crept closer to the rock, his companions pulled their own weapons and followed close.

"Give me the gun." David ordered and Josh slid it across the dirt. "Don't make any sound or move a muscle."

The drug lord's henchmen made it to the rock, and one lifted Josh's bottle. He unscrewed the lid, sniffed inside before setting it down.

Thankfully, no sweat rolled off the outside of the bottle, but Josh still feared something would betray the fact it hadn't been sitting out there for ages.

The man with the cigarette gestured to the others to split off while he took three steps toward their left. After every step, he stilled and turned his ear up, as if listening for the sounds of their breath. His eyes scoured the landscape around him.

"You keep an eye on the other two," David said, but Josh couldn't take his eyes off the man with the biggest gun.

The other two men trekked south, moving further away.

His arms went numb as the man took another two steps closer.

Instead of focusing on their hiding place, the man studied a scraggy bush. He tossed his cigarette and took another step toward the bush.

His intent gaze baffled Josh. At barely four feet high and thorny it would provide insufficient coverage for three Americans on the run. But then, he saw it. The bush trembled slightly, moved by a non-existent breeze.

The other two goons now watched.

Amanda's rhythmic snoring stopped and Josh moved his eyes from the men to her face long enough to watch her lick her dry lips. When he looked up, the bush shook with more fury and a small deer burst through the back and made a run for the road.

The animal only managed a few strides before the gunman's shot brought it down. Laughter erupted from the others as the gunman regained his footing from the surprise deer attack.

They crowded around their game, studying it intently before

they dragged the carcass back to the Jeep without a glance behind them.

"Did I just hear a gunshot?" Amanda's voice was quiet, but in the silence, once the blood stopped rushing through his ears, it sounded like she was shouting.

"Stay where you are," David whispered, not looking down at her. "I'll tell you when it's clear."

It took some time before the men were able to haul the deer back to the vehicle and secure it to their liking. Rather than continue on their path north, they made a U-turn and headed back south.

David eased up to a crouch after their turn and made his way back to the rock to watch the vehicle disappear.

Josh stayed on the ground with Amanda, who'd pulled herself in a seated position.

Once the Jeep cleared the horizon, he grabbed Josh's discarded bottle and charged around the tree. "It's illegal to litter." David hurled the bottle and it bounced off his right arm.

"Since you're a former quarterback that should be considered assault with a deadly weapon." He gritted his teeth to ward off the tears that sprung to his eyes.

"What was that about?" Amanda's voice was heavy with sleep and exhaustion.

"Your ex is going to get us killed with his carelessness." David's hands shook as he paced the ground in front of them.

"What did he do?" Amanda stood in front of David, forcing him to stop his incessant movement.

He didn't answer her; instead he glowered at Josh.

"What happened?" Amanda repeated.

"I left a soda bottle on the rock where I was sitting." It was better if he answered her to keep David from blowing it out of proportion. "You need to cut me some slack, Stephens. As hard as it is to believe, this is my first time running for my life."

"But it's not your first time to use common sense," Amanda spat at him. She turned to David. "Do you think they'll be back?"

"Depends on if they see Hank's truck behind that gas station and put two and two together."

She pulled her long hair away from her face and braided it down her back. "If they didn't see the truck coming this way, they may see it as they head back."

Josh watched as a silent conversation passed between Amanda and David. The feeling of being a child at the control of his parents settled over him. He'd always be on the outside looking in as long as they operated as a cohesive unit.

"We can't stay here any longer," she said.

"Did you get enough rest?"

"I'm fine. How's your knee?" Despite her trying to keep the question private, it easily made its way to Josh's ears.

*Knee? Why would she ask about a specific body part?*

Then Josh remembered David's landing from the rock and how he'd made a point of landing on his left leg first.

"Fine," the man answered in a low voice. "Williams, you ready to go?"

Josh bent over and picked up the soda bottle David had chucked at him and tossed it in the air a few times. He trotted over to the rock and placed it back where he'd left it when they'd run for cover.

"What are you doing?" Amanda asked.

"Using common sense. If they come back and find it gone, they'll know we were close by. But if they see it they'll assume we were well on our way."

David crossed his arms in front of his chest and gave him a hard stare. "Good call. From now on, we leave nothing behind. It's like camping, we carry out what we carry in and we bury our waste."

Josh started heading north, leaving them to follow. "Whatever you say, Boy Scout," he tossed over his shoulder. "You're in charge."

## 39

No one spoke during the second night of walking. The moon grew only slightly, but even with its faint light, they used the flashlight in longer intervals to illuminate their way. The glow of a few villages dotted the desert around them, but nobody suggested veering off course to seek shelter there.

There was a silent agreement among them; trust no one.

Josh was beginning to feel like he was cast in that category as well. He fell behind as they trudged forward, studying David's gait in the illuminated intervals. The longer they walked, the more pronounced his limp on his right leg.

"Stephens, what's up with the gimpy walk?"

David glanced over his shoulder. "What's up with your gimpy walk, Williams?"

Josh opened his mouth to respond, but admitting a scorpion sting near the nuts would only prompt laughter at his expense. "So, what did you blow out your ACL chasing kids through a mall?" He went back to his goading.

"Shut up, Josh," Amanda said without looking behind her.

"Why? Look, I'm just trying to get to know Stephens better."

His voice dripped innocence. "Plus, conversation will keep me from thinking about the bleeding blister on my foot."

Three sets of feet shuffling through the desert served as Josh's conversation until David finally answered. "I took a bad hit playing football in college."

"No surprise Amanda would fall for you. Our girl here has always had an eye for the jocks. Isn't that right, babe?" His taunting was met with silence.

"What happened? Coach quit passing you and you were left writing traffic tickets?" Josh didn't see David tense up in preparation for his attack.

One minute, the man was walking forward ignoring his gibes and the next minute he had him by the shirt collar.

"It's called an obligation to your family," David snarled through gritted teeth. "Not that a man who stole a couple of million from his clients *and* his father would understand that."

He exaggerated a pout. "Amanda, you need to be careful with this one. Seems like he'll bite when provoked. By the way, that hurts."

She grabbed David's arm, forcing him to release Josh's shirt. "Relax. He's just trying to get a rise out of you. Let it go."

The former quarterback took a step back and Josh adjusted Amanda's shirt-turned-sling. His shoulder throbbed from the jostling.

David rubbed the stubble on his face. "Let's take a break." He shrugged the backpack off and dropped before unzipping the top. "We've got three sodas and two packets of pork rinds left. Let's split a packet of food and each take a bottle of soda. I know I'm going to sound like a broken record, but we need to conserve the drinks."

They sat in a circle, silently passing the food around. A chill took over the air and Josh felt Amanda shivering next to him. He should offer to give her shirt back; sitting there in a tank top and shorts provided no shelter from the schizophrenic desert temperatures. But his shoulder ached.

"Are you cold, Amanda?" Josh asked.

"Compared to being locked in a cooler, this is quite pleasant."

He sipped on his soda to suppress his smile.

"Here," David said with his mouth full of pork rinds. As he chewed he tugged his T-shirt over his head and handed it to Amanda.

"Won't you get cold?" she asked.

"I run hot at night, remember?"

Josh rolled his eyes to avoid the suggestive smile plastered on the man's face. "I'm surprised you've made it this long without taking something off."

When they finished their snack, no one made any gesture to continue. David's head sagged in exhaustion and Amanda rested her own head on her knees. After a while, the sun lit the eastern horizon and they quietly stood to look for shelter.

David offered to stand guard for the first part of the day.

Josh and Amanda curled up on the hard ground facing each other, his bag serving as a pillow. A gentleman would've offered it to her to use. At least a gentleman without a stolen money would.

"Why are you being that way?" she asked.

"Just being my usual self."

"That's the problem. He saved your life. You could try being a little nicer."

"I actually saved *his* life first by breaking him and Hank out of their shed. And, I risked my own so you could escape. Oh, and let's not forget that this is less than twenty-four hours after you pointed a gun at me."

"There's no reason to keep score."

He studied her face in the budding daylight. Her cheekbones protruded and dark circles colored the skin beneath her hazel eyes. As a poised blonde, he'd loved watching the other men stare when they'd entered a room, but she looked less dazzling with brown hair and guessed that hardly anyone gave her a second glance these days. "There's always a reason to keep score," he said before turning his back and nodding off.

Josh awoke several hours later and rolled over to find David lying next to him with his shirt back in its rightful place.

Amanda stood several feet away, looking off in the distance. The sun was high in the sky, indicating it was well past noon.

Sweat rolled down David's face and discolored the top of his T-shirt. The air was unusually still and stifling. Josh smacked at the cotton filling his mouth, eager for any bit of liquid on his tongue, even if it was the thick syrupy sodas that was their only form of hydration.

Pedro's backpack lay in front of David's chest. Ever since they took off from the old gas station, Amanda's man held tight to the backpack, guarding their supplies, rations and gun.

*Screw it, I'm thirsty.*

Josh pulled the backpack toward him. David probably had an extra soda he was holding for just him and Amanda. Carefully pulling the zipper from the top to the side as to not wake David, he broke open the top, exposing the contents to the bright sun. The flashlight, a bag of pork rinds and two half full bottles of soda sat neatly side by side.

Josh reached in, sure there was a secret hiding place and his palm closed on warm glass. Curious, he brought the bottle out of the bag and turned it over in his hands. Tequila. The same brand Vargas used as his everyday liquor. The seal was still in place, so either the tequila was forgotten, or being saved for a special occasion.

He glanced down at the sleeping man. *Like when they finally get rid of me.* He shoved the bottle back in place and zipped up the backpack.

Josh got to his feet and joined his ex standing guard, the gun hanging idly in her hands.

"Want some company?"

Amanda narrowed her eyes. Her dark circles had lightened after her rest.

Josh held up his right hand. "I come in peace. I was going to apologize first, for the way I acted last night. You're right, we're all exhausted and our nerves are shot. And." Josh swallowed hard and forced his face to contort into a chagrined look. "It's hard seeing you with Stephens. How long have you guys been together?"

Amanda took a deep breath and exhaled slowly, looking out over the vast desert. "We're not." She faced him; exhaustion allowed her emotions to be on full display. "There's nothing left. I broke him. I broke us."

"Maybe you can fix it? If you guys can't feel the attraction between you then something's wrong."

"We can feel it all right. It's just..." She looked to where David lay sleeping. "Complicated."

"Well, it wouldn't be any fun if it wasn't."

"No, with David it's much more fun when it's *not* complicated. When it's just us and not all the other crap."

"Do I fall into the 'other crap' category?" Josh smirked.

She released one of her hypnotic smiles, the kind where her eyes lit up like gold, light radiated from her cheekbones and her teeth glowed like a string of pearls. "You are King Crap."

## 40

Their third day hit hard. David's feet swelled inside his boots, pinching his pinkie toe to the point of numbness. Mandy's shoulders blistered to an angry raspberry and blood stained the heels of her sneakers. Williams was uncharacteristically quiet. Maybe it was because his cracked lips oozed.

They all spoke less, which suited David just fine. The sound of the wind pounded through his head with the roar of a cyclone.

The sun started to slip away when Mandy stood, brushing off the bottom of her shorts, as if it made any difference. They were so filthy that their clothes would have to be burned when they got home.

*If...*

"Come on, let's go," she said.

Neither man moved.

"Thirty more minutes." Josh's voice was flat.

"No, we're going now." Mandy scowled down at him. "You're either coming, or we're leaving you."

David wasn't eager to come to Williams' defense, but neither was he ready to start another night of fruitless walking. "A little more rest won't hurt." He flexed and tightened his hands, hoping to shake off the tremors. Was it dehydration or not having a drink in several days? One nip of tequila was all he needed.

"But—"

"It won't make any difference." The words came out much harsher than intended. He lifted his gaze from a cactus to her sunburned face.

She narrowed her eyes and folded her arms over her chest. Her already red cheeks flushed a shade darker. "So you're on *his* side now."

He pushed off the ground. He wanted to wrap his arms around her, to reassure her no matter what, he was always on her side. Even when it hurt him.

Especially when it hurt her.

David touched her arms, the skin warm, but she didn't flinch. "We're all on the same side. It'll be good for us."

Mandy took a step back, and paced. "Good for what? Good for us to be a little more rested when Vargas finds us? What if that thirty minutes is the only thing between us making it home or dying in this damn desert?" Her last pass took her twenty feet away, where she stood with her back to them, facing the setting sun.

"You need to calm her down," Josh finally spoke.

"Says the man who ran off and left her to clean up his mess." He didn't wait for a snarky comeback. David followed Mandy to where she stood, but at a safe enough distance to allow her precious alone time.

If she turned around, if she needed him, he was there. That was all he'd ever wanted. For her to know he was there, even if he wasn't standing right beside her.

"Alex, Hank, Pedro." She spoke to the sun. "Alex, Hank, Pedro. AlexHankPedro." She turned to look at him. "That's the only thing going through my head right now. I'm scared to death if we don't keep moving I'll add your names to the list of people who have died because of me." Her chest heaved and shoulders trembled.

This wasn't all on her. If he hadn't hesitated, waited a day before taking her to El Paso and turning her over to Fallon, she wouldn't be here.

Sure, Alex would likely still be dead, and possibly Hank, but Pedro would be alive. Josh would be holed up in the hell he'd created, and David would be cracking the seal on a fresh bottle of tequila, telling himself with each shot that he'd made the right decision.

"Come on, Williams. Let's go," he said, not breaking eye contact with Mandy.

"If I have a temper tantrum, too, will you give in to me?"

David opened his mouth to respond, but Josh cut him off.

"I'm going to take a leak, and then we can go."

Josh take off in the opposite direction, but David couldn't bring himself to stop looking at Mandy.

It was then he saw what was in her core. Determination to do the right thing, even if the right thing hurt. That was what had drawn him to her, even though it'd infuriated him sometimes, but only because she was so much stronger than him.

"I'm afraid." Her voice quivered.

"I know."

She closed her eyes and shook her head. "I'm afraid if we don't keep moving, I'm going to just lie down and die."

He pressed his lips together. "We'll head out as soon as Williams gets back."

David reached for the backpack and slung it over his shoulder.

Mandy kicked up dirt, trying to cover up any tracks.

Josh's bag rested against a rock, the first time it'd been alone since they took off on their journey.

He leaned down to grab it, but the bag flopped open, spilling its contents. "What the hell?" Stacks of brightly colored Mexican *pesos* stared up at him.

Mandy peered over his shoulder, cursing under her breath. "Why didn't he tell us he had this?"

He squatted and thumbed through the bundled banknotes. "Because it's stolen." He tossed the money back into the pile. "I'd guess from the very man who wants us dead." At the sound of approaching footsteps, he stood.

Should he hit Williams before he tries to talk his way out of it?

Or, let him speak, just to see what spews from the golden-tongued city boy's mouth.

Josh adjusted his makeshift sling as he walked, not looking up until he nearly ran into them. His gaze darted to the ground. "Shit," he sighed. "I can explain—"

Mandy's palm collided with the side of his face, cutting off his words. "You bastard." She pushed him, causing Josh to take an awkward step back. "This was not some heroic deed. This was just another case of saving your own ass. I should've known." She pounded her fists on his chest. "What were you going to do with the money? Buy your way out of this and leave us stranded?"

Josh retreated again, this time his foot caught on a rock and he fell backward.

Mandy followed his fall, throwing half-hearted punches in his direction.

David should stop her. Hell, he'd wanted to deck the guy since they'd met, but he just didn't have the energy. Mentally or physically.

"Do something." Josh growled as he blocked punches with his good arm.

David wrapped his arms around her waist and pulled her back to him.

Like a wild animal, she strained, pulling against to get back at Williams, her heels slipping in the dry dirt.

Josh sat on the ground, his head hanging. "You're right," he panted. "But you're also wrong. We wouldn't have made it this far if I'd have left it in the room."

Mandy pursed her lips and looked at David.

He didn't believe the guy either, but what choice did they have.

"Why keep it a secret?" David asked.

Josh peered up at him. "I don't need to give you another reason not to trust me." He swayed as he stood. "Admit it, if I'd told you what was in the bag from the beginning, you'd found a way to leave me." He narrowed his eyes. "There's more than enough distrust to go around. Anyway, if we got caught you guys had plausible deniability."

Without waiting for an answer, he pushed through them, stuffed the money in the bag.

David watched until Josh zipped up the bag. "You're not taking that."

"What do you suggest I do with it?"

"Stash it somewhere. Anywhere."

Josh stared him down for several minutes before rolling his eyes and disappearing around some boulders. He returned empty handed and walked past them, ignoring them, setting off toward the north.

"What now?" she asked.

"We walk. And, keep an eye on him."

The sun had disappeared and the gray-blue twilight descended over them. Josh stayed several yards in front of them, never turning back to see if they followed. When the last strains of daylight fell away, David flicked on the flashlight, following the dust in the man's wake.

"He's right you know," Mandy said, breaking up the monotony of their footsteps. "The distrust among us. You don't fully trust me, and it's deserved. But I trust you, completely. No matter what."

He stopped, his legs suddenly refusing his brain's direction to keep moving. The weight of her falsely placed trust was too much to carry. "There's something I need to tell you."

She froze one step in front of him.

Was it best to break her heart one chip at a time, or shatter it all at once?

He opened his mouth, but the words wouldn't come out. Maybe he had to warm up to the real infraction. Admit to his misdemeanor before confessing his felony.

"David?"

"After you left Phoenix—" How could he explain the ridicule? The whispering behind his back that he should've known something was off about her. The people crossing the street rather than walking by him. The silence that descended over a restaurant when he entered.

How people cared less about a killer being locked away than

their little town had gotten dragged through national news? How could he make her understand that the one person who'd stood by him was also the one person Mandy had wronged? And, who'd wronged Mandy in return.

"It must've been awful," she said. "I was so stupid, everything I did there was a mistake." Mandy reached for his hand.

He jumped at her touch and begged himself to not recoil.

"Not everything, but you know what I mean. Thank God I actually found out who killed Katie. Because what I did to you, to Shiloh..."

David's hand went numb at Shiloh's name and fell from Mandy's warm grasp.

Her sharp intake of breath told him she knew. Something at least.

"It was the night I got fired," he said. "Only once."

Josh's footsteps approached, but he couldn't face the man.

"Fired for dating you. I'd been drinking at home most nights until then, but I found myself at Riley's. Shiloh drove me home."

David tried to call up the fuzzy memories, the same images he berated himself with daily. Shiloh steering him down the hall to his room. Helping him into bed. Taking off his boots and pulling a quilt over him. Telling him she was so sorry about everything.

Maybe it was her long hair tickling his face, or her soft flowery scent. Somehow he hadn't seen Shiloh when he'd leaned up, he hadn't felt her lips when he kissed her.

When it was over, when he was trailing kisses down her neck, it wasn't Shiloh's name he cooed.

It was Mandy's.

"It was my fault. Not hers." David flicked the light in her direction. He needed to see what this did to her.

Her face was still. No crinkling eyes holding back tears. No downturned mouth. No spark of temper. "Why are you telling me this?" Mandy's voice was as steady as her expression.

He nodded in Josh's direction. "Because I'm no better than him."

The only response was the sounds of the desert. A light breeze rustled the dry vegetation. Anonymous claws scurried over a rock. The roar of a jet thundered high overhead.

"You're wrong." Mandy's words lifted the mass that sat on his shoulders.

David straightened and lifted his chin. If she was this forgiving of Shiloh, perhaps she'd understand why he called Fallon.

"You're *worse* than him. Josh would never hurt me to make himself feel better. I'm tired. Of walking, of running. Quite frankly, I'm tired of both of you. Let's call it a night."

The weight came crashing back on him.

## 41

The warm tequila burned going down David's throat, but it still managed to quash the firestorm of emotions. Mandy didn't know how right she was.

He was much worse than Josh.

The rest of his confession was perched on his tongue, ready to dive into the deep end, but it got cold feet and climbed back down his throat.

The heat of the day captured in the grains of sand transferred through his jeans roasting the parts of his body that weren't blistered by the sun. He reclined on his left elbow, admiring the thick canopy of stars rising out of the horizon and reaching overhead. The bottle was perched on his lips when footsteps approached behind him.

David didn't bother turning around. He could tell by the weight of vibration they weren't her steps. Not that he'd expect her to come after him.

They sat far enough apart to be alone, but close enough together to not feel lonely.

"I was wondering when you were going to break out that

bottle," Josh said, squatting to sit next to him, holding his injured arm out for balance.

He finished his drink and handed the bottle over. "So you knew I had it?"

The man nodded as he drank.

"Did she know?"

"She does now," Josh said, coughing a bit as he swallowed and offering the tequila back. "That tastes like shit."

"You think I'm drinking it for the flavor?" David took another swig. "I figured you'd be moving in to comfort Mandy, seeing how I'm an ass and all."

"Weepy girls aren't really my thing. Plus, you've got the booze."

"How is she?"

"Pissed. Hurt. Tired." Mandy's ex took another drink. "She'll be fine."

"No, she won't." He held the bottle up to the starlight as he screwed the lid back in place, a quarter of the small contents was already gone. Any more liquor would be deadly with his dehydration.

*Then again...* He twisted the cap off and took one more nip before Josh reached for it.

"Why did you do it?" the guy asked before taking another swig. "You'd won, dude."

David plucked the tequila away from Josh and took another long gulp. The bitter warm liquor mingled with the acid and soda, forcing his stomach muscles to clench. "It's not a competition." He handed it back.

"That's where you're wrong. What's that saying? *All's fair in love and war*?"

The numbing edge of drunkenness barely touched the pain, both on his body and in his conscience. "I have a hard time believing you ever loved her."

The alcohol made several more passes between them. It was a terrible idea. Possibly deadly, but David was tired of making the right decision. After everything they'd been through, he deserved at least one fuck-up.

"I tried to." Josh's words broke the quiet. "Hell, I *wanted* to. Of all the girls, I thought that maybe she could be the one."

He studied the liquor. Only about a third of the tequila was left. He was starting to feel as if his head would float away at any moment. Another sip of bad, warm oblivion and he'd be soaring toward the stars, leaving his decapitated body below. "You want to know why I did it? Because she's *right*. I'm worse than you and she deserves to know that."

The man laughed. "Screwing some chick after you and Amanda split up? I should call you Alter Boy instead of Boy Scout."

"Oh, I'm no Alter Boy. It was far worse than that."

"Hmm, let me guess, let me guess," he slurred.

Was that a sign of dehydration or drunkenness? David's own tongue felt thick in his mouth.

"You ran over her pet rabbit? Or did she catch you checking some girl out? That always pissed her off. Oh I know, I know, you accidentally told her that her butt looked big." Josh laughed so hard he snorted, and then burped.

The smell of second-hand tequila caused David's stomach to spasm.

The dude had no clue. He could wear his devil-may-care attitude like a badge of honor now that it was all in the open. But not David, he still had to hold his betrayal close to his heart.

Like a sacred vow.

Or a sin.

The last of the tequila flowed down his throat, pushing against what was threatening to come up from his stomach. "That day that we were kidnapped, I lied to her." David heard the words coming from his mouth, but didn't know he'd made the decision to say them. "In a messed up way, Vargas saved me from doing something that would've hurt her way more than anything you did."

Josh stilled beside him, so much that he'd thought perhaps he'd passed out. "What was it?" he finally spoke up.

"I told her we were going to El Paso to try to find Hank, and I knew someone who could get us into Mexico from there."

Suddenly the cool night air grew warm. The vast desert closed in around him. Suffocating him.

*Where's Mandy?*

He needed to find her. To make sure she was okay. David rolled onto all fours, and he felt the earth tilt beneath him. He convinced one leg to come forward, but the other ignored him and he ended up in a crocked half-split.

"Hey man, you all right?" Josh appeared beside him.

"I need to check on her. Have you made sure no one got her while we were here?" The words stumbled into each other. David leaned on the man, trying to pull himself to standing.

"She's fine, buddy." Josh gestured over his shoulder with his chin. "Amanda's on that rock back there. I've been keeping an eye on her. I think she's sleeping."

David followed his gaze. The darkness swam around him, so if Mandy was there, he couldn't tell which was her and which was the rock. He tried again to stand, but dizziness overtook him and he landed squarely on his butt.

"Just stay here," Josh said. "I'll watch her for you. What did you lie to her about?"

He couldn't focus on anything. *Mandy. Josh.* The dirt in front of him. The stars bobbed like buoys on the ocean. *Mandy.* He needed to apologize to her. To tell her that if he died, she was better off with Josh. His stomach turned again, like an angry sea.

"What?" Was Josh talking? The words floated by him.

"You said you'd lied to her. That you weren't really taking her to find Hank. Where were you taking her?"

David rolled over and like a wobbly toddler learning to stand, he pushed himself up, butt in the air followed by his torso. Then he saw her. Curled on the stone in the fetal position. Alone.

She'd been alone since that moment she left Chicago. She'd traveled to Texas alone. It was only during her time in Phoenix that she'd found a partner. But he'd tossed her aside when he found out she wasn't as perfect as he'd made her out to be.

Then she'd been alone again, confronting Katie's killer in Foster's bookstore when he'd tried to kill them both. He'd played that tape so many times. The fear in her voice. Foster slapping her. Mocking her. And then she'd left Phoenix. *Alone.* To find Josh.

And now, lying there ten feet away, she was alone again.

"Stephens, stay with me buddy." Josh grabbed an arm, steadying David as he swayed.

"There's this woman, Fallon. A friend of mine. She's FBI." His stomach roiled again and he bit down to wait for the waves of pain to finish, but they were a tsunami, building on each throb in his gut.

He had to get the words out. They might be his last and he couldn't die without Mandy knowing the truth about him.

David took a step toward the rock, but his foot only shuffled forward. "I was going to turn her in. To the FBI." The ground buckled and pitched, a rolling sea of guilt churned beneath his feet before a tidal wave of regret crashed into him, bringing him to his knees.

Josh steadied him, but David felt them both sliding down.

"Amanda," the man shouted. "A little help."

A set of soft hands gripped the sides of David's face, lifting his head up. Even in the darkness and through his inebriated haze, there was the woman he'd fallen in love with. The same one he'd been about to toss aside.

"David?" She knelt beside him. "Are you okay?"

He braced himself on his thighs, trying to slow his breathing to stop the hurricane in his gut. "Do you think you can forgive me?"

She pressed her lips together and stroked his cheeks. "I should be the one apologizing. It wasn't my place to get upset." Mandy wrinkled her nose. "How drunk are you?"

"I'd call him shit-faced," Josh said from behind him.

"Oh, sweetie, this isn't good. You're dehydrated, we don't have any water. Do you know what a bad idea this was?"

"It's becoming extremely clear," he said. "Okay, let's go." He managed to get himself back to standing. After a moment of not feeling the earth turn, David took a tentative step forward.

"Where are you going?" Mandy asked.

"Home."

She crossed her arms and looked down at the ground. "Let's rest tonight. Maybe we can cover some ground before the heat of the day tomorrow."

"But I thought this is what you wanted."

"None of this is what I wanted. What I wanted was to get us all home safe and sound, but you're in no shape to walk. You're going to hurt yourself."

David looked at them, standing together, forming a barrier between him and Texas. "Oh, I get it, now you've teamed up against me. This is just one big game, isn't it?"

"That's not it at all," Josh said, reaching for him. "I'm pretty buzzed myself. Let's sleep it off and get moving tomorrow."

He shrugged him off. "Screw you both. Y'all can play whatever mind games you want without me. If I don't see you in Texas, I'll see you in Hell." He spun on his heel, but the ground bucked like a bronc. David managed to lift one leg, but instead of hitting solid earth, it felt as if his foot broke through a frozen lake, pulling him under the minute his body hit the dirt.

## 42

"I'm not leaving him." Amanda crossed her arms.

"I didn't suggest we leave him."

"I could feel you thinking it."

Josh sighed. After Stephens had passed out the evening before, it'd taken all he could muster with one arm to help Amanda drag him under a mesquite tree.

"Don't tell me you found some mushrooms to nibble on."

She ignored him again, like she'd done since David had taken ill.

Josh suppressed a smile as he recalled David's confession. *Who knew the Boy Scout could do something so...devious.*

"I'm not suggesting we leave him, but he'd want us to continue on."

Amanda finally turned her head, her red-rimmed eyes flared at him. "He's not dead," she hissed. "Don't talk about him in the past tense. He can hear you."

"We're all going to be in the past tense if we don't do something." He climbed out from under the shade.

Sometime during the night, high clouds had moved in to canopy the sky. Instead of offering relief from the heat, moisture clung to the air, making Josh feel as though he was trying to move through a sauna. "Listen, we have nothing to eat, nothing to drink. Put your feelings aside for a minute and be realistic. It's a miracle we've lasted as long as we have, but it's survival of the fittest. And sweetheart, *he's* not the fittest."

She led him further away from the tree.

"Do you really think he's conscious enough to hear us?" Josh asked as her fingernails dug into his good arm.

"I don't know, but just in case, I don't want him to hear us giving up. Or, talking about leaving him. I know how abandonment feels." She narrowed her eyes. "It sucks."

"Will you quit being pissed with everyone?"

Amanda took two steps toward the tree.

It was his turn to grab her arm. "Stop, for just a minute. Can we have a conversation without you getting mad? Stephens has been in charge since we left, and he's done fine, aside from getting plastered and passing out. But even if he wakes up in a couple of hours he's in no frame of mind to lead us. We need to take charge and we need a plan."

She looked off into the desert. A hot wind blew her tangled hair across her face.

"Once upon a time we made a really good team." He licked his dry lips as he stared at her profile. Beneath the three-day-old sweat and dirt, she was still the beautiful woman who'd captivated him when she'd strode into his office with a well-tailored suit and high heels. "You shouldn't have trusted me then, and you have absolutely no reason to now. But, until we cross that border, we have to rely on each other to stay alive." Josh looked back at the body lying under the tree. "To keep him alive."

Amanda's face contorted and her eyes blinked. "Dammit. All I want to do is cry, but I'm so dehydrated I can't." She covered her face with her hands.

*This* was a new side to Amanda Martin.

Her vulnerability softened his face and his shoulders sank, even the one held in a splint made of her shirt. Maybe this was the Mandy David saw. If she'd showed this side of herself when they were together in Chicago, would he have felt different about her?

Was it because she wore her ice queen shell to bed that caused him to stray? In all likelihood, no, he would've just crushed her much worse if she allowed him to see it.

"There'll be time for that later, but right now I need you to put it all away, all the hurt and fear. Be the Amanda Martin I hired. Be smart, be calm." Josh pulled her to him, wincing as she rested her forehead on his sore shoulder, but not flinching or offering any indication of discomfort.

As she sobbed dry tears into his shirt, he rubbed her back and convinced the tingling below his waist he was too tired and thirsty to think about *that*.

When her sobs subsided, she pulled away and rubbed her face, smearing dirt across her cheeks.

"Let's go back in the shade where we can keep an eye on Stephens and figure out what to do next." He fought the urge to clear the messy strands of hair from her face.

Amanda checked David when they returned, but there was no change.

His skin had an eerie paleness about it, despite the red blister of sunburn. Shallow breaths escaped his lungs and his eyes jerked wildly beneath his lids. It didn't take a doctor to know this man was close to death.

"So, what do you think we should do?" she asked, hugging her knees to her chest.

"I'm no scientist, but my guess is that a tree like this needs more water than what falls from the sky."

"Do you think there's a river nearby?"

"That or an underground spring." Josh grabbed the backpack and pulled out two empty soda bottles. "You stay here. I'll see if I can find some water."

"How far will you go?"

"As far as it takes."

Amanda pursed her lips. "Promise me you won't go too far."

"Are you going to miss me?" The raise of his eyebrow punctuated his question.

She answered with the roll of her eyes. "I—I'm afraid to be

alone," she whispered, her eyes darting down to her worn, bloodied sneakers.

"You've never been afraid of anything before." Her gaze slapped him as it shot from the ground to his own. Her hazel eyes told him she was a completely different person than the woman he'd last seen in Chicago.

"How bad was it?" Josh didn't need to clarify; she knew exactly what the '*it*' was.

"Diane didn't even see the gun. She was busy answering the phone." Her voice was steady, flat with numbness. "Liz was in my office, waiting for me. He thought she was me. Neither of us had a chance to tell him otherwise before he shot her. After that, it was a blur between people screaming and gunfire. He kept tossing grenades like toys. He didn't care about any of us. I mean sure, at least three of us probably deserved it, but not Liz or Diane or any of the others." Her words faded as a light breeze rustled the leaves above them.

While he'd been flying first class to El Paso with a fake passport, his colleagues and the woman he'd spent the past three years with were being shot at. Josh had sipped bad chardonnay while they'd feared for their lives.

"I'm sorry." It was a weak thing for him to say, but it felt appropriate.

Amanda nodded. "I still see him. Not as much as I used to, but sometimes if I get really scared."

Josh looked at her, a question poised on his dry lips.

"The man. From the office," she added. "I saw him a lot right after it happened. David probably thought I was nuts." She laughed and Josh realized she wasn't speaking to him so much as to herself. "I thought I was crazy because I knew he wasn't there. He couldn't have survived that explosion, and if he did there was no rational way he could have followed me." She took a deep breath. "I see him when I'm afraid, and I'm really scared right now. If I'm alone for too long I might see him. Even though I know he's not there, I may run and I don't want David to wake up alone and assume we left him."

He swallowed the lump in his throat. "Every fifteen or twenty minutes, I'll check in with you. I shouldn't have to go too far away, but if you get scared, just say my name and I'll be right back." Josh hesitated. "Amanda, whether it's Stephens or someone you haven't met yet, you'll never be alone."

"What about you?"

"What about me?" he repeated.

"Why didn't you take me with you?"

The truth was he'd thought about taking her, and being on the run with her. Then he'd remembered how Bonnie and Clyde ended and hadn't wanted to meet the same fate. "Leaving you was the kindest thing I could've done for you." Josh walked away from the tree, kicking at the dry rocks hoping to find mud somewhere to indicate water below, but all he was successful in finding was more dust.

He looked over his shoulder and saw Amanda sitting next to David. From this distance she looked like a scared little girl, complete with a crusty scab on her knee.

It'd been four days since they'd left and three days since they'd seen any sign of Vargas' men. Where were they?

He expected them to parachute in at any moment and carry him off to receive the most severe and cruelest punishment the drug lord could administer. It was quiet. Too quiet. *Calm down or you're going to start seeing Vargas' shadow.*

The Mexican desert was huge and there was no way for his former boss to know which part of the vast Texas-Mexico border they planned to cross. Regardless, Josh couldn't help but feel that with each step closer to Texas they were walking closer to Vargas. The man knew where they were headed. It'd be so much easier to sit and wait for them than to spend time chasing them through the desert. And if they didn't make it to the border...

"We just saved him some bullets," he muttered to the dirt.

With nothing indicating water in his area, he went back toward the tree. A few feet in, Amanda waved him away and he veered off to the right, searching for any signs.

"A tree grows in the desert."

How would his newly acquired habit of talking to himself be

received in prison? Would the other prisoners stay far away from the crazy man who told himself jokes?

"Amanda, you okay?" he shouted, not feeling like turning back.

"Yeah."

"I'm going to walk around to the back side. I'll be right back." Josh circled farther to the right and finally he saw it. A dry creek bed cut a shallow path through the desert floor just five feet from the tree.

He dropped to his knees and dug through the dirt. Nothing bubbled up except more dry dirt. The creek bed had a slight rise to the north. If he walked upstream maybe he'd find the main source of water.

"Hey, Amanda, I'm going to follow this creek bed upstream a bit. You doing okay?"

She paused so long in her answer he was afraid he'd have to run back to the tree to check on her. "I'm fine. Be careful."

Every few feet he'd kick at the dirt, but the cracked ground was hard. The farther he walked, the higher the side of the creek bed rose until he could barely look over the banks. Using his good arm, he tried to heave himself out of the banks of the creek bed, but a pain flashed through his temple and dry cough erupted from his chest, causing him to slide back down on his knees.

Josh rubbed his eyes and tried again, this time using his knees to keep him steady. It felt like it took him hours to climb the six feet out of the creek bed, and when he finally made it to the banks, the tree looked like a small sapling in the distance.

He wiped the bottom of his shirt across his forehead, but no moisture stared back at him. He'd stopped sweating. "Son of a bitch," he muttered. Josh slowly stood, afraid any sudden movement would cause him to black out. His eyes followed the creek bed north. Dry as far as he could see. He sat back down so hard pain shot up from his tailbone.

*I need to go back to Amanda. David may have finally gone to that big foot-ball field in the sky.*

There was something going on under the tree that he couldn't face. Even if it was nothing. Would it be better to stay where he was?

Maybe Amanda would look for him and come up on his bleached bones. Of course, his bones wouldn't be bleached that soon, but from the heat bearing down on him he was in a microwave cooking from both the outside and inside.

If he died looking for water, he'd be a notch higher than Stephens who'd died because he got drunk off a bottle of contraband tequila. At least he would die doing something for her.

"How do I know Stephens is going to die first? He's in the shade and I'm out here baking."

Josh stood up faster this time, but the sudden movement clouded his vision with pixilated, fuzzy black squares, like an old video game. When the pieces finally cleared away, his eyes focused on a figure to his left. From fifty yards away, someone in a wide-brimmed hat applied paint to a canvas.

The person reached out, made two swooping marks and took a step back. Then again. Reach out, two swooping marks and step back.

He became entranced by the repetitive motion and felt himself sway.

When the person put the paintbrush down and reached inside a cooler at its feet, Josh was no longer in charge of his body.

"Trust no one. Except the person with the bottle of water."

His feet were heavy and he shuffled through the dirt toward the painter.

Reach out, swoop, step back and drink. The painter never looked in his direction.

Ten yards closer and he could tell it was a woman, white hair curled at her shoulders and pale hands sprouted from the sleeves of a white shirt.

Reach out, swoop, step back, drink and look in his direction.

The bottle froze just inches from her lips. Her eyes narrowed from under her hat and she took a step away from him. Josh stopped; afraid the woman would vanish and be another sign of his impending insanity. "I'm sorry to bother you," he shouted, his voice sounding harsh in his ears. "I'm lost, actually we, I'm with two, uh, friends. We're thirsty."

The woman bent down and reached into her cooler. When she stood another bottle of water was in her hand. She moved toward him, her wide-legged pants dancing in the breeze and her hat struggling against the tie under her chin.

His eyes focused on the water bottle as she offered it to him with a smile. Condensation already dripped down the side and he was tempted to lick it, not wanting to sacrifice any of the precious liquid.

The cap came off with an "ah" and he took a long swallow, closing his eyes so all of his senses could focus on the feeling of the cold, wet liquid coursing down his throat.

When he finished draining every drop, he looked back at the woman. Were she and the water were a mirage? Was Josh actually dying?

Instead, she simply smiled with the warmth of a grandmother baking cookies. "It's good to see you, Josh," she finally said. "I've been expecting you."

## 43

D avid choked on the deluge of liquid rushing toward his stomach. His throat closed up and the water dribbled out of the side of his mouth, his dry T-shirt greedily soaking it in.

"David. It's time to wake up."

A female voice floated over him, sounding happy, relieved, scared, worried.

"Wake up. Please. I need you to drink this." Her voice was pleading, urgent.

He commanded his eyes to open, and when they did, he was standing on his driveway at home in Phoenix. The hum of cicadas filled the air as she ran to him in the waning daylight.

Just like the first time he'd seen her, she was lost in thought, jogging in shorts and a tank top, her long brown hair pulled back in a ponytail.

"Why won't he wake up? He's breathing. What's wrong?"

Mandy halted her jog. He smiled at the memory—how embarrassed she was, how she turned and ran from him, and how he'd enjoyed the back view as much as the front.

"An ear for an ear," a voice hissed beside him. Vargas' white linen suit flowed in the wind. A heavy gust lifted the man's shoulder length hair, revealing a bloody stump where his ear should have been.

Vargas' hand lifted and aimed a gun where Mandy stood.

David opened his mouth to tell her to run, but only water poured out. He rolled to his side, the choking cough forcing his eyes to flutter open.

"I told you that was too much," Mandy hissed. "Here, sit up."

He felt her hands under his arms and he pushed himself off the ground, looking up at her as she sat behind him so he could lean against her.

"We've been saved. We're going to be okay." She tucked her hair behind her ear. "We have water. Can you try to drink some for me?"

He nodded, but as he did, agony thrashed back and forth in his brain. His neck was stiff, but he was able to lift his head slightly and let the cool liquid burst through his lips.

"You'll want to drink slowly," a female voice said from behind him.

David rolled his eyes up and studied the plump, soft face of a woman he'd never seen before. "Who's that?" he croaked, his mouth instantly dry again.

"Lois," Mandy whispered behind him. "Josh went out looking for water and found her painting in the desert. We're going home." Excitement fueled her dry voice.

"Guess that makes you the hero, Williams." David pulled his legs up and draped his arms over his knees, turning so he could face her along with the other two people peering at him.

Josh looked over his shoulder at the graying sky that covered the sun.

"Figured you'd be gloating. How long have I been out?"

"Since last night," Mandy said, sitting back on her heels. "Josh and I pulled you over here to the shade."

His brain throbbed at the memories of the previous night. The revelation to Mandy about his night with Shiloh, and the tequila he kept hidden. The worse confession he couldn't bring himself to mutter. Or did he?

Much after that was a hazy cloud of broken scenes and confusing images, but he felt as if he'd breathed life to his greatest betrayal.

David took another sip of the water and studied the older woman's soft face. White hair flowed from underneath a wide hat, hanging in loose waves down to her elbows. Blue eyes, with the lightest frosting of cataracts, smiled down at him.

"You kids are lucky I was out here," she said. "The clouds cooled it down so I could get some painting done. Another day and I might've found three bodies instead of three lost souls."

Silence descended on the group as he took another drink.

Josh looked distracted, almost jittery as his eyes darted around the empty plane, like he was waiting for someone to come jumping out from behind even the smallest cacti.

"What's crawled up you?" David asked, seeing the man cringed at his question.

"Nothing," he mumbled. "Let's get the hell out of here."

Josh turned and started walking.

David narrowed his eyes toward the man's path. There was a white SUV parked in a short distance. He looked back to Lois, the woman's gaze never left his face.

"He's right, we should get going. Do you think you can walk?" she asked, her eyes suddenly hard.

"Yeah, Mandy, can you give me a hand?"

She nodded and helped him stand. Once a wave of dizziness passed, he felt stronger, but still leaned on Mandy, wanting to keep her close by.

Lois started in the direction of the car, while he shuffled his feet, keeping them intentionally several paces behind.

"You don't really need any help," Mandy whispered, looking down at their moving feet.

"What's up with Williams?" David said through gritted teeth. His brain rattled around his skull with each step.

"He's been acting weird since he got back." She shrugged beneath his shoulder. "Maybe it's sinking in that he's really going to jail."

He pondered her words as their rescuer continued several paces ahead of them. "What do you know so far about her?"

"Lois Graham, says she's from Houston, has a home just ten miles from here. Retired teacher, lives here full time now."

"What does she know?"

"I've been following Josh's lead, but from what I gathered we're lost and that's it."

David took another sip of water as they walked. The nausea from earlier subsided and his thoughts felt clearer with each sip he took. His instincts told him to question why an elderly woman alone in the Mexican desert was so eager to take three stranded Americans home.

He looked at Mandy. Her long hair hung in tangled clumps and her arms glowed like rubies. Dried blood crusted on her knee and her gray tank top was soiled with sweat rings and dirt.

"Do you trust her?" he asked. He'd always had good instincts, something he'd honed in the police academy, but he'd been off his game.

Before Mandy could answer him, Lois stopped and waited for them to catch up to her. Rather than halt their hushed conversation, she switched gears. "I don't know what I want more, a cold shower or a hot meal."

"I can help with both," Lois answered, confirming his suspicions that the woman's hearing was intact. "I'm glad to see you moving on your own. I wasn't sure how we were going to get you to the car when I found you." She lifted her chin to size him up under her wide hat.

They were a mile and a half from a one-lane desert highway, and compared to all the other walking they'd done, it was a stroll through the park. Lois made idle comments about the various plants as they passed them. Josh should've strutted like a bird with a broken wing, but instead he simply walked fast with his head down.

"Mandy said you're a retired teacher. What did you teach?"

They walked side by side, Mandy on his left side, helping him take pressure off his throbbing knee, and the older woman on his right, cutting glances from under her hat.

"Texas history, college-level. Where did you play football?"

David stopped walking and studied her with his mouth open, nearly causing Mandy to trip over her own feet with the shift of momentum.

Lois barely glanced over her shoulder, but kept walking.

Had Mandy or Josh said something about him?

"I tutored a bunch of football players. Your size gave it away," she answered his silent question. "And that limp tells me something stopped you from playing."

He started walking again, focused on keeping his left leg in line with his right. "Texas. I was knocked out my junior year."

Heat radiated from her car as they opened the doors.

Josh reached for the passenger side door handle, but Lois chastised him into letting David ride shotgun so he could stretch out his legs.

Before she started the ignition, she turned to face them in her seat. Her furrowed brow and downturned mouth filled in the lines on her face. "I'm going to need your weapons before we go," she said. "I'm sure you can appreciate that as an old woman out in these parts, I can't be too careful. Even if you kids do look like you come from nice families."

He glanced back to the backseat. Josh looked out the window, refusing to meet his gaze, and Mandy sat with the backpack between her feet. He nodded and she pulled the gun out of the bag and handed it over. He intercepted to unload the magazine before handing both to Lois.

"Just one?"

"Yeah," Mandy answered.

The older woman put the gun in her lap and pulled out on the highway. The car was silent except for the air whooshing from the vents, first hot but quickly cooling, causing his sunburned skin to break out into painful goose bumps.

David took a deep breath and peered out of the corner of his eyes. Josh sat behind Lois, staring out his window as the desert flew by. Mandy was behind him and appeared to have nodded off with her head resting against the window.

"How long have you kids been out in the desert?"

"Few days," Josh answered.

"Hard to tell," he spoke over him, cutting his eyes to the backseat.

Lois tightened her grip on the steering wheel and her already thin lips disappeared from her face as the car surged forward a little faster.

Ten minutes later they turned off the road and pulled into a quaint, yet sprawling stucco house.

Mandy stirred when the retired teacher shifted the car into park and Josh turned his attention to the house.

"Well, let's get you inside so you can get cleaned up, rest a little and put some food in your bellies."

"Actually, if we can just borrow your phone, I can call a friend to come get us and we'll be out of your way before sundown," David said, staring into Lois' icy blue eyes.

"I get terrible reception out here."

"Well, then, if we can trouble you to just drive us a little farther to the border."

"I've got night blindness. You don't want an old lady driving home late by herself out here, do you? Why don't you kids rest up overnight and I'll drive you in bright and early tomorrow morning."

He looked back at Mandy and Josh. Dark circles discolored the skin under their eyes. Mandy's collarbone poked out beneath her tank top, and her arms were so thin he was afraid the simplest fall would cause one to break.

David swallowed back his discomfort. They needed a break. One night wouldn't hurt.

*The sirens going off in my head are nothing more than this hangover.*

He nodded. "We appreciate the hospitality."

Inside the house, the living room was spacious yet cozy and large windows looked out at a courtyard enclosed by the rest of the house. A cool tile floor was covered with a thin, worn bearskin rug that curled on the edges.

David watched as Mandy instantly relaxed, but Josh seemed coiled tight. Like a snake ready to strike. She perused the woman's built-in bookshelves, but held her body away from the books like she was afraid she'd get them dirty.

Lois watched from David's side and then joined her at the bookcase. "Honey, when was the last time you took a shower?"

Mandy bit her lip and crossed her arms in front of her chest, as if to hide some of the dirt. "I don't know," she whispered. "What's today?"

David looked down at his boots. Her clean freak nature must be cringing at the thought of the layers of dirt and sweat covering her body and clothes.

"Come on," Lois grabbed her hand. "Let's find the pretty girl under all that dirt. You can use my bathroom. I'll wash your clothes, too."

The older woman led Mandy away, leaving him and Josh alone in the living room. Their eyes met at the same time and held each other's gaze, neither willing to be the first to look away.

"Thank you," David said. "You saved our lives. Her life." He nodded down the hallway that'd swallowed the ladies.

The sound of running water washed over the silence.

Amanda's ex shrugged his acknowledgement but didn't speak nor break his intense stare.

David cocked his head slightly.

*He should be rubbing my face in it. He hasn't said two words since we got in the car.*

"Williams, you okay?"

Josh broke his stare and looked down the hall. His face was blank, but it was a mask covering something real.

"I wouldn't be thanking me yet, Boy Scout."

He stepped in closer, blocking Josh's view of the hallway. "What happened while I was out?" David took another step, a question perched on his lips, but footsteps on the tile tore his attention away.

"Well, that'll be one happy young woman in a bit." Lois emerged and Josh moved away from him. "I've only got one other bathroom so you boys will have to take turns. I'll wash your clothes with Mandy's, but I'm afraid you'll have to make do with bathrobes while you wait. My husband's long gone. Josh, why don't you follow me."

David exhaled a deep breath when Lois led Josh down the opposite hallway, far away from Mandy.

She rejoined him minutes later and led him to the kitchen. "Here, you need more water." Lois pushed a tall glass of water across the counter.

He drained half the glass in two gulps and sat it down before answering.

"You're lucky I found you when I did. A few more hours and I'd only brought two home with me."

"I appreciate it."

She smiled and refilled his glass. "We've also got some rains moving in," she said, handing the glass back to him.

"After three days of wandering in the hot sun, a little rain would've felt nice."

"You don't want to be caught out in the desert in heavy rains. You're Border Patrol. You should know that."

David slowed his gulping and looked at her over the rim of the glass. Either Mandy or Josh must've divulged his profession while he was out. Rather than confirm, he finished drinking and sat the glass back on the counter.

*Did dehydration turn my instincts into paranoia?*

Lois pulled a Mexican beer out of the fridge and his mouth filled with saliva for the first time in a week. She caught him fondling the bottle with his eyes and slid it across to him and grabbed another one for herself.

"I guess you deserve a beer after all you've been through. Cheers." She took a long drink, her eyes studying him over the bottom of the bottle. "Why were you in the desert?"

"That has to be the most memorable shower of my life." Josh came into the kitchen in a bathrobe and towel drying his hair with his right hand while holding his injured left arm close to his body.

"Josh, dear, I meant for you to use the shorter bathrobe and to save the long one for David."

He draped the towel across his shoulders. "Oops. I did save you some hot water."

He put his empty beer bottle on the counter and started walking to the doorway for his shower.

"David, you can trust me," she said.

He glanced over his shoulder. He never believed *anyone* who said they could be trusted.

## 44

Amanda had expected to pass out the minute her head hit the pillow. The combination of sheer exhaustion and a filling dinner should've added up to a blissful slumber, but she felt trapped by the crisp sheets.

Three a.m. mocked her from the digital clock and shadows teased her from outside the window as she flung the covers off and slipped out of bed. Lois' white cotton nightgown swallowed her thin frame, but it felt soft against her sunburned skin.

The house was dark and silent. The center courtyard of the Spanish-style home beckoned and she gently opened the door leading outside. She tilted her face up to her old friend, the night sky. No stars shone down on her, thicker clouds had moved in late in the day.

Light from two dim lamps cast enough glow for her to find a seating area surrounding a silent fire pit. Amanda abandoned her borrowed house slippers, tucked her feet under her and watched lightning dance in the distance.

This was her final night in Mexico. Her journey to find Josh would come to a close in less than a day. A chapter in her life that'd started with being wrapped up in his crimes would conclude with them both going to jail.

When the Chicago chapter of her life had closed, she'd fought it, unwilling to accept that she'd changed, that her life was never going to be the same. This time, Amanda allowed the sensation of closure to permeate every pore. She'd feared change before, but now, even though she'd be handcuffed and put in jail, she anticipated it like a child waiting for Christmas morning.

*Will I get a phone call like the movies?* If so, the call would be to her parents.

Her eyes closed to power her ears listening for her dad's voice in the distance. She stroked her head, pretending the hand to be her mom's. Her arms hugged her too-thin body tight; feeling the rib cage her brother would mock for protruding. In the dark distance beyond where her eyes could take her, she could feel her family.

*Do they feel me? Can they tell I'm coming home?*

She let her head rest against the back of the wooden bench.

*You did it, kiddo.* She could almost hear Hank speak to her from above. Her second call would be to El. It'd be a tough conversation, but she had to be the one to tell him.

"Thank you, Hank," she whispered, a single tear slipped down her cheek. She'd tried to cry many times over the past three days, but dehydration had called attention to the drought in her tear ducts with only a meager trickle making its way through after David had admitted to sleeping with Shiloh.

*David.*

At this point in their lives, everyone had some baggage. It was just a matter of if one's baggage was neatly packed away, folded on the creases, sweaters rolled to prevent wrinkles; or if it was a hurriedly packed mess bursting at the seams.

Some people's baggage fits perfectly into an overhead bin, but hers and David's would have to be checked. Then they'd have to pay the overweight fee on top of that.

It wasn't having baggage that bothered her. It was the thought that once one of them opened the suitcase; the contents would spill out and never be tucked back inside. Could she shove Shiloh back into the bag, especially after knowing David had slept with her? But, what about David? He'd spent the past several days with her and Josh. How often did he think of her and Josh together? There was no reason for her to be upset, yet she felt like there was every reason to be.

"I'm quite the catch," she sighed up to the stars.

"I always thought so."

Amanda jumped at David's voice. She hadn't heard him walk up behind her.

"Don't tell me the bed is too soft."

"Four walls make me claustrophobic. What about you?" she whispered.

"Too tired to sleep." His knees jutted from under the short bathrobe as he sat next to her. "I have the strangest urge to cross my legs when I sit."

The laughter erupting from her throat felt foreign. "At least you have the legs for it," she teased.

"I got up for a glass of water and saw you sitting out here. I'm glad I found you. I've been trying to work up the courage all night to knock on your door."

David had shaved. Without his beard, she could study the lines and colors painted on from just the few days in the sun. What was going to happen to them tomorrow? Would he stand by while she was arrested, pretend she was nothing more than any other criminal?

"I'm sorry I got so angry last night," she said. "What you told me just knocked the wind out of me. But, I had no reason to get mad at you. We broke up. I left town. There isn't a reason in the world that we would've waited for each other."

David tilted his head. "You're so full of shit." His voice was gentle even though the words were scolding and accusatory. "Yes, we weren't together, but there's no one else in the world I'd rather be with than you, no matter who you were or what you did before we met. I, on the other hand, owe you an apology. I was cruel and I..." His voice cracked and he averted his eyes. "I only told you because I couldn't stand being a fraud. I wouldn't blame you if you hated me right now."

"I don't hate you." Amanda willed him to look at her, but he met her unspoken plea with silent stubbornness. She took his chin in her fingers and turned his face to hers. "I don't hate you," she repeated. "Quite the opposite. I love you. So much that I want to push you away and pull you to me at the same time. My selfish side wants you, but then logic tells me you deserve better."

"I agree with your selfish side." His dimples sliced into his chiseled cheeks when he smiled. He laced his fingers with hers and warmth radiated up her bare arms. "What's next for us?"

She glanced back out into the darkness, staring into what she guessed to be the direction of Chicago. "If I ask you a question, will you promise to tell me the truth, even if you think it might hurt me?"

David's smile faded into a scowl.

"Did that night with Shiloh mean anything to you? Really. Any emotion at all?"

His fingers went cold in her hand. "Yes and no."

Amanda's heart slowed but she forced her face not to react.

"I was drunk. And, for that little bit of time that I thought it was you, it meant the world to me. I was so happy to have you back, but when I realized what I'd done, it felt like you left me all over again. As for Shiloh, all I feel for her is remorse for hurting her, the same remorse I feel for hurting you. But that's where the similarities end. I wouldn't follow her into Mexico."

She shifted her gaze back to him. When his eyes met hers, they were warm and wet.

In *his* eyes was her next chapter. The exact plot wasn't outlined, but there was no doubt in her mind that he'd be the main character.

In one move, she lifted herself from the bench and straddled David's lap. His hand grasped the back of her head as he pulled her mouth to his, their teeth collided in a painful, awkward moment that reminded her of junior high and locked braces.

It only took a second for them to get their rhythm back as they took turns reacquainting themselves with each other. With one hand on her back holding her in place, his other traced her body along the outside of Lois' gown, down her back, around her hip, her stomach danced as his fingers passed by on the way to her breasts.

"I love you." David breathed into her ear when she finally let his mouth leave hers. His teeth playfully tugged on her earlobe.

Amanda shifted in his lap and felt his body respond to hers. Desire lapped at her, building like a gathering storm.

His mouth moved down her neck and her hands pulled apart his bathrobe and began their descent.

"No, not here." David broke their kiss.

"Yes. Here. Now." It's been too long and she wasn't going to settle with waiting another minute.

He pulled his head back to meet her eyes. "I don't want a quickie on a bench. I want to do this right. Your room."

She pouted in his direction as she climbed off his lap. "Fine, you win."

"Trust me, sweetheart, you'll win in the end."

They were broken, bloodied and bruised but that didn't take away from the intense lovemaking for which they were long overdue.

Thunder from the approaching storm rumbled outside, intensifying her quivering skin at his touch. Lightning flickered through the windows, illuminating the bruises on his chest from the beating she'd witnessed in Vargas' courtyard.

Rain pelted the glass, drowning out the sounds of Amanda's ecstasy. When the storm passed, they lay facing each other as the room lightened in shades of gray.

"Did it hurt?" she asked as her fingers passed over his bruised ribs.

"Maybe, but all my blood was elsewhere so I didn't notice," David answered behind heavy eyelids.

She leaned up and kissed the smile on his lips.

"What about you?" he asked as he pulled her too-thin frame closer. "You okay?"

Amanda stared into his dark eyes. At that moment, she was more than okay, but before she could answer, her gaze fell to the digital green numbers demanding her attention even more than him.

Six-thirty a.m. She could already hear Lois moving around in the kitchen. In just a couple of hours, they were going to leave Mexico behind and she was going to turn herself in.

Her peace with her fate was replaced by sorrow. *This* was the pinnacle of their relationship. Everything to follow would be long distances and time apart.

David might promise to wait for her while she served her prison sentence, but in reality, it would only make them resent each other. She tried to push the future aside, but not before it forced a tear down her cheek.

"Oh, Mandy, baby, I'm sorry." He pulled her close at the appearance of that lone tear. "It was a bad idea. We're both so dehydrated. I should've stopped us until we're back to normal."

Amanda shook her head. "No, that's not it. It's just..." If she told him her fear, he'd say that he'd be there with her every step of the way; nothing could pull them apart; it didn't matter if they went broke with legal fees.

She knew that when he would open his mouth, the words from a love song would tumble out. And, despite the post-orgasmic bliss she enjoyed, anything sentimental would make her vomit.

"I'm really tired and need to get some sleep."

David tugged her head down to his chest and cradled it with one arm while he stroked her back with the other. "I'll wake you when I smell coffee brewing."

She gave herself over to the warmth radiating from his chest and the rhythmic rise and fall of his breath. Something stirred within her, the part of her that wanted to take advantage of the closeness one more time, but she tamped it down. It would only make the inevitable that much worse. Instead, she succumbed to the relaxed drowsiness and let sleep pull her under.

A sudden shift beneath her jolted her awake.

"Williams, what the hell do you think you're doing?" David growled as he sat up in bed. Even though the sheet covered Amanda's chest, he yanked it up to her chin.

"Josh," she said, pushing herself upright. "Not a good time."

"Shhh," he hissed as he closed the bedroom door. His jeans were unbuttoned and he fumbled with turning his shirt right side out while still babying his injured shoulder. "I'm glad you guys fucked and made up, but play time is over. You need to get dressed *now*." He punctuated his command by tossing their newly cleaned clothes at them.

"Hey, man, how about some privacy here." David grabbed his briefs and put them on under the covers.

Amanda tried to push the fog of sleep out of her brain. *Why is Josh here?*

"Do I need to remind you that I've seen it all before?" He narrowed his eyes at her. "From various angles."

David shot out of the bed.

"Vargas is coming," Josh blurted.

## 45

Agony radiated from Josh's shoulder as he tried to tie his boot laces. He could hear Amanda dressing behind him, but didn't dare peek over his shoulder.

"How can you be sure?" David stared down at him with his arms crossed, a stance they must teach in the police academy.

He'd lain awake all night listening to the clock ticking in his room. When Lois had greeted him in the desert, he'd imagined it was some sort of auditory mirage; that there couldn't possibly be a way she knew his name.

With Stephens close to death, he guessed they'd all died and the old lady was an angel judging which afterlife they deserved. If he was the faithful type, he believed they deserved to wander the desert for eternity.

He straightened when he felt the bed shift behind him as Amanda sat to put on her shoes.

"How's your shoulder?" she asked. She hadn't put on her long-sleeved shirt, instead it rested on the bed between them. "Do you want me to fix a sling again?"

Josh nodded, not because he needed it, but because he could feel David's rage deepen at her show of tenderness.

"I asked you a question," David growled. Even with the kitchen on the other side of the house, they could hear dishes clanging.

He sighed as Amanda knotted the sleeves of her shirt around his neck. "I don't think it was an accident that Lois found us."

Her fingers froze and her face whitened beneath her sunburn.

David cursed under his breath.

"How do you know this?" Her weak voice shook.

"I thought it was dehydration at first," Josh spoke to his feet. "When Lois greeted me in the desert by my name. There was no possible way she could've known that, but we were all out of our minds with thirst and exhaustion."

Amanda collapsed on the bed next to him, her face slack from shock. "You didn't tell her anything about us, did you?"

He shook his head and ran his good hand through his hair. With each tick of the clock, his desire to survive grew to the point that he needed them on his side long enough to get back across the border. "She already knew it all. Last night I started replaying everything in my head and I realized what was going on." He glanced into David's angry eyes, hoping he'd believe him enough to not want to kill him. "You have to know I wouldn't have put you guys at risk after all we've been through together." His voice broke, a strange feeling blocking his throat, making him wonder if he was choking on a lie. Or, the truth.

"Don't make it sound like we're going to grab beers one day to reminisce," David leaned down, his face just inches from Josh's. "This is *your* mess, so you're going to stay to clean it up. Mandy, come on, we're going."

He shot up from the bed and blocked the door. *David had the balls to make this play?* While he had a meager chance of surviving Vargas' wrath with Amanda and David, he had *no* chance of making it to the end of the day if the drug lord arrived to only one of them. Especially the one who stole his money.

"Whoa, whoa, whoa." Josh tried to keep his voice down, but it struggled against true fear. "You can't do that. He's going to kill me."

"Tell me why I should give a damn," the man barked.

"How are you two getting out of here? You going to ask Lois to borrow her car? Call a cab? If you remember, she has our gun. The woman thinks I'm on her side. You're going to need me to get out of here, and that pisses you off."

David took a menacing step in his direction, his nostrils flared and his jaw muscles tight. "You know what I've been trying to figure out this whole time, Williams? Whose team you're on."

Even though no space stood between them, Josh took a step toward him, bumping his sore arm into the man's chest. "Never been one for team sports."

"Somehow that doesn't surprise me." David glanced over his shoulder. "Let's go."

Amanda sat on the edge of the bed, staring at the floor with her long hair pushed behind her ears.

David reached past him for the doorknob, but her voice filled the room before he could open the door.

"We're not leaving him." She kept her eyes down to the floor.

Josh leaned against the door to get a better view of the shock on the man's face.

"What?" A mixture of hurt and accusation coated his voice.

She pushed off the bed and reached for David's hand.

He tried to recoil, but she held tight.

Josh bit the inside of his cheek to suppress his smile. *Storm clouds building over paradise.*

"I—we—didn't go through hell to leave him here." She spoke calmly. "It's not what Hank died for, or Alex or Pedro, or any of the other people lying in the ground because of him."

*Playing up to his hero complex. Score one for Amanda.*

"I'll let you be the one to put the handcuffs on him," she added, soft and seductive.

*Bitch.*

David's shoulders heaved as he sighed. "Fine," he turned to face Josh. "How are we going to get out of here?"

He motioned for them to move away from the door and they stood in the corner, all three heads huddled. "I got up in the middle of the night to help myself to granny's medicine cabinet, looking for something to take the edge off the pain. Seems Lois has a problem falling asleep." He pulled a full bottle of sleeping pills from his pocket. "I've been crushing them all night."

David crossed his arms in front of his chest and nodded. "How?"

Josh could almost see the wheels turning in the jock's head.

"She's making breakfast. If Amanda can pull her away from the kitchen long enough, I can sprinkle this in her juice and then we just wait for the meds to kick in."

"Why Mandy? I can get her out of the kitchen just fine."

He smiled, ready to let loose of one of the bombs in his arsenal. "I'm so glad you asked, Stephens. Before I came into this love nest, I wandered past the kitchen, where I overhead Lois on the phone, telling Rafi that she'd have lunch waiting for him. I've been agreeable, and Amanda seems to buy her story without question, but you, my friend, don't trust her. And, *she* doesn't trust you."

Amanda leaned into David.

Josh had to look away when she smiled up at him.

"I've got this." She glanced around the room, her eyes darting to the night table next to the bed, the bureau across the room before she sat on the bed, staring down at the three-inch long and two inch wide scab on her knee.

Gritting her teeth, she pulled off the scab in one quick motion. The wound glared at them for a moment before blood rushed to the surface, spilling over the edge and running down her leg."I cut myself shaving." Without another glance at either of them, she walked out of the room.

Josh could hear her calling for Lois, and voices in the kitchen.

A minute later, the women passed back by the closed door.

Lois clucked at Amanda like a mother hen, saying she needed to get hydrogen peroxide on the wound to make sure it was all cleaned out.

"Don't come out until you're called for breakfast," he hissed at David and closed the door quietly behind him.

The beautiful aroma of breakfast danced with the smell of fresh-brewed coffee. Lois had set the table for them, three set with plates and orange juice, and one setting with a coffee cup with bright pink lipstick on the rim.

*Bingo.*

With his good hand, Josh flicked the top of the lid off the bottle and poured half of the crushed sleeping pills into Lois' cup. When he was sure there was enough to knock out an elephant, he looked into the container. White powder stared up at him, begging to not go to waste.

Amanda's voice carried back into the kitchen, profusely thanking the older woman for her kindness.

Josh slipped the nearly empty bottle back into his pocket just as the women rounded the corner.

## 46

"I will always remember this cup of coffee," Amanda said, setting the steaming mug back on the table. After wandering the desert, coffee took on a richness she'd never tasted before. No longer was it simply sustenance to start the day.

It'd taken everything she had to hold back a shout of excitement when she'd seen Josh in the kitchen, hovering over the breakfast table like a naughty child stealing bites before being invited to eat.

David squeezed her knee, and she reached down to hold his hand. Exhaustion enveloped her, but it was a small price to pay for the closeness they'd shared just hours earlier.

"When should we leave?" he asked, his voice lighter than what she'd heard in days.

Rivulets ran down the dirty glass. It'd been raining for hours, and even though their savior had turned out to be a devil in disguise, a tiny part of her was thankful the woman had found them when she did.

"Oh, I'm not so good at driving in the rain." Lois lifted her cup of coffee to her lips, her voice was sluggish, the words fusing together. "Why don't we just rest some more this morning until it stops?" She stifled a yawn with the back of her hand. "I don't know about you guys, but this weather makes me exhausted."

Amanda smiled. *Sleep, Lois. Sleep.* How long would it take before the pills kicked in? Would it battle for dominance with the caffeine? Would they be less effective crushed?

Food and anticipation tangoed in her stomach. All they had to do was act like nothing was wrong, that they were three very appreciative people, tired, sore and sunburned, but not much worse for the wear. They didn't suspect that the kind old lady who'd taken them in, washed their clothes and fed them was about to turn them over to a drug lord.

David played the part well. A biscuit in one hand, fork in the other, he shoveled food so fast she hoped it wouldn't make him sick. He only dropped his fork to drain his glass of orange juice.

"Want mine?" She smiled at him. Would they ever have this? Rainy mornings. Breakfast. Sharing OJ.

"I'll get him some more." Josh jumped up from his place, knocking his knee on the underside of the table, jostling their plates and sloshing some of her juice over the side.

"He can have mine," she said. "I'd rather have coffee anyway."

Her ex sulked in his chair.

Was it because this was his final morning of freedom? That in just a few hours, it'd all be over for him. For her too, but she was ready. Ready to end the running. Eager to meet whatever came next. No matter how hard prison would be, she'd survived the desert. It couldn't get much worse.

Amanda stared at Josh over the rim of her coffee mug. He swallowed and looked away. She kicked him under the table. He ignored her. She kicked him again, harder.

This time he pulled his eyes away from whatever had interested him in the corner.

"What?" she mouthed.

He shook his head and averted his eyes again.

"How close are we to a border crossing?" David punctuated his question with a big bite of biscuit.

Despite the fact that this woman was working for the enemy, Amanda had to hand it to her, she could cook.

Lois was slow to respond, her upper eyelashes flirting with the lower. "Oh, about an hour or so."

Josh pushed his plate out of the way to put his elbows on the table. "How long until Rafael gets here?"

The woman yawned and rested her chin on her hands, her lashes finally joining together.

Her ex reached over and shook her, the woman jolted awake. "Come on, Lois. How long do we have?"

"I'm just so tired. You kids help yourself to whatever you want in the kitchen. I'm going to..."

"Lois!" Josh shouted and the woman's eyes shot open. "How much longer until Rafi is here?"

"Oh, you know my Rafi? My favorite pupil. I always thought he'd be president one day. Wake me when he gets here, would you, dear? He should be here..." Her forehead bounced as it hit the table.

Amanda gasped, thinking the woman died, but a soft snore reverberated off the wood and her rounded back rose and fell in a slow rhythm. "Really, Josh," she snapped. "Did you have to give her so much? We don't know how much time we have or really where we're going."

"It did the job," he barked back. "It doesn't matter if we have ten minutes or two hours. Grab her keys."

David swayed when he stood. "We need her phone, too."

"What do you need the phone for anyway?" Josh asked. "You heard her, no cell service."

He rummaged around the kitchen, pulling open drawers and tossing sheets of paper around. "We're going to need someone to get us through the checkpoint."

"Or, have them waiting there to arrest me," her ex said, flatly.

She sighed. "What did you think was going to happen? We might not be going home to a parade, but we've got to get home."

Josh rolled his eyes and left them alone in the kitchen.

David slowed his frantic searching. He took a step toward the table, but his leg buckled and he stumbled into her.

She guided him to a chair. "You okay?" she asked. Had he overdone it? Was he still dehydrated?

He grabbed her arm. His face was slack and eyelids closed in long, lazy blinks. "Mandy." Her name was garbled, unsure. "I think he did it to me, too."

"What?"

David shook his head, but the movement was uncoordinated. "It just hit me."

Amanda let the *it* sink in. She grabbed his half full coffee cup, bringing it to his lips. "Drink."

David complied but some of the liquid dribbled out of the corner of his mouth. When that cup was empty, she pushed hers in front of him.

"Fight it. Keep drinking coffee. We should never have trusted him."

As he finished her coffee, she refilled his cup and sat it in front of him.

Footsteps echoed off the tile as Josh jogged back into the kitchen.

Amanda stood, blocking David. Protecting him.

Her ex skidded to a stop when he rounded the corner.

"You just couldn't help yourself," she spat. Awareness traveled throughout her body, checking for parts that felt loose, as if she could float away to slumber like Lois and David. "Am I going to pass out in a minute as well?"

"I know you hate me, but I did this for both of us."

"Do not project your narcissism onto me," she snarled.

"Oh, cut the I-deserve-to-go-to-jail bullshit, will you?" he shouted. "You don't deserve *any* of this. I brought you into this. I made you who you are. You've been doing nothing but telling me how I screwed up your life. And, you're right."

David shifted behind her. "You're a dead man, Williams," he slurred.

"I've been dead for years. It's not really that bad once you get used to it." The words might have been an answer to David's threat, but Josh's transfixed gaze told her a different story.

It was the same intense stare as when they'd first met at his investment firm. His green eyes so clear, so hypnotic that it'd felt more like foreplay than an interview. Amanda would've done anything for those eyes. And, she had. Many times over.

When he'd handed her trumped up numbers, explaining that their firm was smarter than the rest. When he'd left her waiting at a restaurant, making it up to her with lies, vacations and jewelry. When he'd given her an envelope full of money, and left town. Left her.

"We can slip away." His voice was softer. "We can go further south, Belize or Costa Rica. We can start over. No drug dealers, no jail. Just us." Josh took a step toward her. "I can be better this time."

David sprung up behind her, but she held him back. She didn't need him, not for this fight. This time, it wasn't for Liz, or Hank, or Alex. This time, the fight was for *her*. It was for her past.

It was for her future.

"Go. To. Hell." Amanda lifted her chin and squared her shoulders. "You're right. You made me, but I'm nothing like you. I'm not going to do to David what *you* did to me. He's nothing but honesty and integrity. You couldn't be better, not even if you tried, because you're never going to be him."

His face hardened and his eyes narrowed.

She wouldn't look away. She wasn't going to flinch. Even if they didn't have time for this. Even if what Lois told them was true, Vargas was on his way and they were wasting precious minutes. She wouldn't give him the luxury of winning.

A phone ringing broke his stare. The trilling sound was beside her.

Amanda knelt down next to Lois, reaching a hand in the pocket of her pants first on the right side and then the left. The chiming started again, and this time she could feel the accompanying vibration.

She pulled her hands out of the pockets, and reached into the apron pouch, a spot that would normally hold a whisk or spoon, not the direct line to the man hunting them.

"Well, you found your cell phone," Josh said.

The phone silenced once her palm closed around it. She brought it out of the pocket and flipped open the massive clamshell. Her hands froze, the blood draining from her fingers faster than the water pouring down outside.

The sight of his name in her hand awakened every nerve in her body, every synapse begging to get as far away from this house as she could. The blood continued its flood down her body, pooling in her stomach, churning the food, coffee and juice, turning it into something that made her sick with fear.

"Vargas found us," she said, holding out the screen for them to see.

Missed Call. Rafi.

## 47

W hen the phone dinged the arrival of a voicemail, Amanda dropped it and jumped. She was too afraid to listen to it, afraid to hear that he was just outside, waiting for his favorite teacher to greet him with lunch and three fugitives. "We have to go, now. David." She shook his shoulder. He was awake, but she could see him fighting the effects of the drugs. "Can you find our gun?"

He nodded and trotted out of the kitchen. Giving him a mission would get him moving around, to fight off the sleepiness.

"Last chance, Amanda." Josh's words were low. "We can walk out right now. Take Lois' car. Vargas will go easy on him. After all, it was never about Stephens, it was about me. And, you."

Before she could answer, David jogged back, popping the magazine into the gun. "Okay, let's go."

The older woman's SUV sat in the front of her house. The rain hadn't let up since it'd started. Rather than hurdle over the puddles, Amanda ran straight through them. Water flooded her sneakers, flowing over blisters worn so deep that just the sensation was a million tiny pinpricks.

They were soaked and shivering inside the car. Josh hopped into the front and David climbed into the back, keeping the gun in his lap.

She prayed there would be enough gas to get them to the nearest crossing. The needle shot skyward once she cranked the car, climbing until just above the three-quarters of a tank mark. She exhaled and threw the car into reverse.

The back end of the car skidded when she pulled onto the two-lane road. Frantic windshield wipers barely kept up with the desert monsoon. Gun-metal gray clouds clung close to the ground, making it look more like twilight than mid-morning.

*Drive. Fast. North. Now.*

The speedometer approached eighty, but the tires kept losing their grip on the road.

"Amanda, please don't kill us," Josh mumbled, bracing against the dash. "Do you even know where you're going?"

*Home.* That's all she could think about, but he was right. She slowed to a more manageable speed. For all they knew Vargas could be just leaving his compound, making the drive at a leisurely pace.

"Where's the closest crossing?" She glanced up in the rearview mirror.

His expression was wiped clean by exhaustion. "If we can make it to Presidio there's a crossing. Give me the phone. I'll see if I can call someone to meet us."

Lightning forked across the sky and thunder boomed in its wake. Amanda took a deep breath. This was no time to panic. Except for the fact that a pissed-off drug dealer was likely not too far behind them, David was fighting off God knows how many sleeping pills and it was all she could do to not reach over and strangle Josh.

*Put it that way and it's the perfect time to panic.*

She handed the phone back. "Are you calling Border Patrol?" She met his eyes in the rearview mirror. Was Lloyd the only agent working for Vargas?

He nodded. "You've got a point. I've got a friend in the FBI. Someone I trust. I'll call Weatherby. She'll get us in."

Josh shuffled in the seat next to her and she cut her gaze to him.

The car crested a hill. That was when she saw it, far behind them, two sets of headlights followed. The cold explosion of fear in her heart realized that only one other person would be out on a day like this.

"Dammit," David said. "No signal."

Amanda pressed harder on the accelerator, but the car balked at the next hill. A scream clawed its ways up in her throat. Primal. Angry. This wasn't going to happen. Not this close to the border.

*Hold it together. Get us home.*

"Stephens, is this the same FBI agent you were going to turn Amanda in to?" Josh's smug voice clashed with the crackle of thunder.

She was so focused on the road that his words almost didn't sink in until she heard David curse in the backseat. "What?"

Josh stared straight ahead, his face mostly hidden by his wavy, loose hair.

"David?" The top of his head stared back at her from the rearview mirror. "What's he talking about?" The car flew down the next hill and Amanda had no choice but to focus back on the road. The orange needle crawled closer to ninety. The steering wheel jerked in her hands as they hit puddles and ruts.

"We should've run, Amanda," her ex murmured. "No matter which way we go, we're walking into a trap."

She eased off the gas and forced herself to take deep breaths. This was just another one of his mind games. Josh's last ditch attempt to not go to jail. In just a couple of hours this would all be over. Amanda swallowed the metallic tang of betrayal. "You just can't accept it, can you? You lost and I won."

"He's right." David's words were nearly drowned out by the rain and road noise, but they boomed in her ears.

Two words.

That was all it took to crush her. Everything she'd built in her mind about the future. All she'd held in her heart about David, about the type of man he was. He would be. Their new foundation hadn't been constructed on a bedrock of truth and trust. It was fabricated on quicksand.

"You're lying." The words were desperate, pleading. Her hands shook on the steering wheel and she could feel the car rocking. "Please tell me you're lying."

"I'm sorry, baby. That day we were kidnapped, we weren't going to look for Hank. I only did it because I was worried you'd get killed."

Amanda's foot fell off the gas pedal. The world slowed down. Darkness clouded the edges of her vision, whittling the road in front of them down to a tunnel. For a moment, she was completely alone in the car. She was always alone. The idea that she'd have David gave her false hope. False courage.

False meaning.

An explosion to her left snapped her back to the car. The driver's side mirror was gone. A black Jeep crept up behind them. A man hung out the passenger window, aiming a gun at them.

"Down!" David shouted.

She ducked and floored the gas. The road pitched to the left. A gap in the landscape followed the highway.

The Rio Grande. Texas.

They were close. All she had to do was get them across the river. Whatever happened after that didn't matter now.

Another gunshot took out the other mirror. Josh cursed and ducked even further. A pop followed an even louder bang. The car tugged to the right.

David shouted instructions at her, but his words were lost in her screams and more gunfire.

"Hold on," Amanda screamed, jerking the car to the side of the road. It came to a rest twenty feet from a drop-off. The two cars flew past them, but the red taillights told them it was only temporary.

"We have to cross here," David said.

She looked past Josh. A gaping maw stared back at her. "There's no bridge."

Her ex grunted. "I think I'd rather take my chance with the psychopath."

Headlights crested the road in front of them. Vargas' men were heading back.

"Go," Amanda pushed Josh out the passenger side and followed him.

David got out of the back and held the gun up.

Tires crunched on the other side of the car.

"Congratulations, my friends," Vargas shouted over the roar of the rain and the rushing river. "You managed to survive much longer than I expected."

David lifted his head, but glass rained down as gunfire shattered a window.

"Sadly, your little adventure must come to an end." The drug lord almost sounded whimsical.

"The river won't be too much of a drop," David said. "We just need to get in the water, ride it downstream a bit and then climb out."

"You make it sound so easy," Josh mumbled.

"Come out, and I promise to make it a swift end," Vargas shouted. "Relatively speaking."

Josh tried to look nonchalant, but fear crawled all over his face.

David's jaw was tight with determination, as if it could overwrite his betrayal.

Just as her ex said that he made her, she'd made David. *Before* her, he'd been an amazing, uncomplicated man living the life he chose in the town he loved. He was impeccable. People trusted him; he trusted people.

Now he was broken, like an old windmill that's weathered too many storms. Tangled, bent into an unnatural shape. No longer recognizable.

It didn't have to be her to turn Josh in. David could make that happen. That was what mattered most. Making Josh stand up in front of the people he wronged, to look them in the eye and see the hurt, the damage.

She grabbed the gun from David.

"Mandy, what—"

"You're still fighting the drugs and Josh is down an arm. I got this. You two run, I'll be right behind." She hoped he wouldn't hear the lie woven through her words. "Besides, I hit him once, bet I can do it again."

"I don't like this."

Amanda quirked her mouth into a tight smile. "I think you owe me one."

He cupped the side of her face and kissed her hard. If it wasn't their final kiss, she would've pulled away. Slapped him. Instead, she focused on the feel of his lips, wiped away the memory of Josh's words and rewound back to her room, when it was just them.

Mandy and David.

She broke away. "Run. I'll be right behind."

"I'm sorry," he said. David reached across her and grabbed Josh's shirt, pulling him forward in a low run.

She let them get several feet in front of her before she held her hands up. "I'm coming out," she shouted.

## 48

Amanda kept her eyes on the ground in front of her. She stood, turning her back on the river. On David and Josh. On freedom.

A line of men protected Vargas. The pants of his beige linen suit were soaked. He held a black umbrella over his head. A blast of thunder stifled shouts of her name.

"I'm coming out," she repeated.

"I've never doubted your courage," he said. "Or, your intelligence. But your compatriots..."

She walked to the front of the car, the clicking, gurgling hood serving as the only barrier between them. The gun dangled from her fingers. Rain sliced into her face. "I wanted Josh, that's all. David didn't ask for any of this."

"I'm in no mood for bargaining."

"I've nothing to offer you." She cocked her head slightly, hoping to hear two distinct splashes. "Kill me now. Take me back. Torture me. Whatever you want. I'm yours. Let them go."

The drug lord paced behind his men. Six heavily armed men stood between them, but he clearly feared her. An average woman, one who chased ex-boyfriends relentlessly, stubborn to the point of it becoming a clinical diagnosis, somehow held sway over a man like Vargas.

Who knew.

"What're you waiting for?" she shouted. This is the moment she should've had in Chicago. Standing up to an aggressor intent on bringing everyone down. She should've stood there and looked the man in the eye while he'd pulled the trigger. Life wouldn't rewind her back to then, but she had *now*. "Come on, Rafael."

Amanda was about to step around the car when she was tackled from behind.

Josh flipped her over and pinned her arms to the ground. "What are you doing?" he growled at her.

"Let me go." She squirmed, trying to wiggle out from under him but he held tight. "It's the only way to get you both home."

For the first time ever, she read his face.

So much flashed across in seconds; regret, resignation, remorse, respect. In between the flickering emotion, she saw what he'd worked so hard to hide. It was always there, shoved so deep down into his soul that it never got the nourishment it needed to grow and thrive.

"Only a man who loves you would risk having you hate him." His words were spoken with a lover's tenderness. Misplaced in so many ways.

Boots splashed in puddles. David kneeled beside them.

No words passed, but Amanda saw the exchange, the affirmation.

Josh plucked the gun from her hand. "Tell my mother I love her."

Firm hands pulled her to her feet and dragged her away.

"You bastard." She fought against David, but her feet slipped in the mud, forcing him to drag her before she could get her feet under her. "No, we're not leaving him."

"We are. Mandy, this is what he wanted." A single gunshot exploded and he grunted next to her, pitching forward a bit. "Shit. Go."

The edge of the cliff rushed toward them. Another shot and this time Amanda could feel it whiz past her head. She wrapped her arms tight around his waist as the ground gave way to air.

And, then they were falling.

The collision with the rushing water was like slamming into an undulating wall of concrete. The impact was everywhere. Her feet, legs, torso. Water rushed up her nose and into her throat, causing her to gag and more water poured into her mouth. She opened her eyes, trying to get her bearings, but was assaulted by churning dirt.

Her arms were empty. Somewhere in the fall, she'd lost David. She bobbed up, her head breaking the surface. All she could see was angry waves.

"David!" she shouted. The current sprinted her downstream, but she fought against it.

Something dropped into the water in front of her. One of Vargas' men stood at the cliff, his rifle staring at her.

Another bullet hit, this time she could feel the heat of it by her arm. Amanda took a breath and sank, letting the water overtake her.

She dove deeper. Blindly feeling around, begging her fingers to find David's T-shirt. When did she let go of him? Was it when they hit the water?

He had to be nearby. Her fingertips brushed the rocky bottom of the Rio Grande. Nothing. No David.

Her lungs burned. Panic flooded her heart. Fire burned behind her eyes.

Just when her body was about to take over, about to force her upwards for air, a galaxy exploded, jolting Amanda back, sucking her deeper into the abyss.

---

## 49

He couldn't take his eyes off the water. The flurry of bubbles breaking the surface gave way to a masked diver, surfacing long enough to shake his head and go back under.

Dogs brayed and yelped in the distance, eager to please their handlers with some sign of Mandy.

Three days later, this area of the Rio Grande was practically unrecognizable. Gone was the angry rapids. Gone was the thunderous rain. Gone was the sharpshooter on the ridge across the river firing into the water.

David's eyes went back to a spot nestled among the reeds. That was where the shooter had aimed. Had he been throwing bullets to the wind, or had he seen Mandy surface?

A coffee cup appeared in front of him with Fallon's worried face hovering behind it.

"Thanks," he said. The bitter drink pummeled his empty stomach with the punch of a prize fighter.

"They find anything?" She'd practically stalked him since he'd walked out of the hospital, refusing any treatment except for stitching up the bullet graze to his side. He didn't have time to be coddled by doctors.

Mandy was out here, alone.

He had to find her before Vargas did.

"No." One-word answers was all he could muster since he'd given his statement. He'd spent so many words saying nothing important. Somehow he couldn't bring himself to breathe life into the only words that mattered.

That he never got a chance to make it right. That the last thing Mandy had heard was that he'd betrayed her.

*If she died thinking...* David cleared his throat. Cleared the treacherous thoughts.

"Her parents are here." His friend craned her head over her shoulder.

He followed her gaze to the couple speaking with a team of investigators, all donning jackets with the various agencies blazoned across the back. He'd met them before. When they'd come to Phoenix hoping to learn something about their daughter.

Mandy was a younger replica of her mom but with her dad's eyes. It was hard enough facing them then, this time would be worse than a firing squad.

"They probably think I'm good for nothing but losing their daughter." David went back to watching the river. But he wasn't seeing the placid river, he was watching them fall, replaying the moment when he'd lost track of her, trying to mentally pause the movie in his head to figure out where she was. How he'd lost her.

"Look, there's a chance she could've gotten picked up on the Mexico side," Fallon said. "I've called some contacts over there. To see if they'll look for her..."

He glanced in her direction, waiting for her to finish that thought. Look for her where? The hospitals? Morgue? Riverbank?

For all he knew her body could've been carried all the way down to the Gulf, caught up in the flotsam and jetsam of the ocean.

David tried to read Fallon's eyes through her sunglasses. Was she wanting to find Mandy to make an arrest? Was she hoping her body would appear, bloated beyond recognition leaving him with a grotesque final memory of the woman he loved?

Just a week ago he was ready to start a new chapter of his life with a tiny first step of going out with Fallon. Would he be ready for that step again? Could he?

The pitch in the dogs' barking changed and a single, long whistle cut through the air.

They'd found something.

He sprinted down the sandy bank, ignoring the screaming pain in his side. Heavy breaths followed close behind him. Likely Fallon. Maybe Mandy's dad even.

A handler pulled a mud-caked sneaker from the riverbank. Even smeared in dingy brown silt, two distinctive bloodstains stood out; one at the heel from a furious blister and another from when she'd lost a toenail.

His stomach rose and fell in one motion. Did this mean she got out? Could she have kicked off the shoes to swim better?

David walked to the river's edge, the water lapping at the toe of his boots. How could something so serene and calm cause so much destruction?

Before he knew it the water was at his knees. Just like that day, when he'd kept diving in and diving in. Refusing to give up until he found her.

"David," Fallon shouted. "What are you doing?"

He didn't answer. Instead he made a silent pledge to Mandy.

The river might have stolen her, but it couldn't have her. Not forever.

Not as long as he loved her.

Not as long as he remembered her.

## 50

H er gasp unleashed a cacophony of coughing. It felt like the painful first breath of an infant emerging from the womb. Only, she was already breathing, and the womb was her own mind.

A throbbing sensation in her head competed with the dull pain radiating from the center of her body. Amanda opened her eyes, but the blinding white walls forced them closed again.

She licked her cracked lips. Her eyes tried to open again, slowly. First a slit of the right, then a crack on the left.

A machine beeped next to her. She tried to sit up, but pain sliced through her abdomen and she cried out.

At the sound of her scream, a nurse ran into her room, clucking in Spanish as she forced Amanda's shoulders back on the pillow.

She thrashed under her hands, trying to free herself, but she choked on more painful, dry air. *"Habla Ingles?"* Amanda rasped. She tried to remember basic words, but they floated around her brain with little meaning. *"Donde? Donde estoy?"*

*"Un hospital en Mexico,"* the nurse answered.

*A hospital.* That much she'd already figured out. *Mexico.* She closed her eyes and tried to bring forth memories.

Rain. Water. Gunfire. Haze hung over her thoughts, like she didn't live through her last memories but rather simply viewed them.

Running. Betrayal. David pulling her forward. Jumping with David. Vargas. She was ready to sacrifice herself. But, Josh. Water, everywhere.

Amanda had David. Then she lost him.

That was it. She broke the surface but any other recollections were buried deep in her bandaged head.

Had Josh jumped? Where was David?

"*Dos hombres,*" she said, searching for the words to finish her question. "*Conmigo. Dos hombres conmigo?*"

The nurse smiled as she stroked the top of Amanda's head, her hand caressing the bandages. "*No, no hombres. Lo siento, niña. Habo mucha muerte.*"

No men. *Lo siento.* Sorry. *Muerte.* Death.

She turned her head toward the window and gazed out the spotless blue sky.

They were gone. Her chest heaved as more pain radiated from the center of her body, but it was nothing compared to the pain at the center of her soul.

David was gone.

*Muerte.*

Dead.

No matter the language, it meant the same. He'd never be back. And Josh. She'd wanted him dead more than anything, but the actual feeling was so empty.

David. *Muerte.*

Dead.

He'd died for her.

Her soul felt heavy, like it would sink to the bottom of a river. The cuts on her cheeks burned as her tears flowed over them.

**The End**

# SNEAK PREVIEW OF PROSPERA PASS
## CHAPTER 1
### PHOENIX BOOK 3

The exhale of her opening door jolted Amanda awake. The Mexican faded desert her mind, taking David and Josh with it.

The cruelness of reality confronted her with white-washed walls, air conditioning and the constant beep of a machine that told her, unfortunately, she was still alive.

The slow click of heels announced her guest. Doctors and nurses rushed in with short steps, the sound of their footfalls smothered by sneakers. Father Joaquin's steps were always deliberate, always steady and, most days, welcomed.

"*Mija*, are you sleeping?" He dragged the chair across the linoleum.

"If I was, I'm not now." She pushed herself upright, wincing as pain sliced through her hips. That happened when she daydreamed about before. She'd forget about the rock tumbler of a river that'd fractured her pelvis and left her with a splotchy scar kissing her temple.

Joaquin laughed as he folded himself into the chair. "I spoke with the doctor. He's happy with your progress. Mostly..."

"Well, tell him I'm sorry I'm not quite ready to do the splits,"

Amanda said, shifting in her hospital bed. The *'mostly'* was what the doctors couldn't see happening in her mind. "What's in the bag?" She gestured toward the plastic bag sitting between his feet.

"They say that some senses bring you back to a memory. A whiff of salty air can remind you of a family vacation. Or, car exhaust can take you back to living in a big city."

"Do you have jars of smog in there?" She swallowed an apology, hoping it would pick up the bitterness that coated her every word on the way down.

He chuckled again. "I think when we find out who you are, we'll discover you're a famous comedian." The priest brought the bag up to his lap. *"Fresca o chocolate?"*

Condensation clung to the side of the ice cream containers. Amanda couldn't help but smile. During one of his first visits, he'd asked if there was anything he could do for her. The words *'ice cream'* had tumbled from her mouth and he'd been sneaking it in ever since. Although, she suspected it was with the doctor's blessing.

"Chocolate, although I doubt that'll bring up any useful memories."

Joaquin pulled the lid off the pint and passed it to her. "Oh no," he said, digging through the bag for a moment before producing two wooden spoons along with a book of baby names. "That's just a snack for us. This, *mija*, is what I'm hoping will help."

Amanda shoved a large spoonful of ice cream into her mouth. The cold headache punished her at once, squeezing her brain in a vise that promised a migraine if she didn't slow down. At least she'd had that grimace to hide what was truly going through her mind.

How long could she keep up the charade of amnesia?

"What's a priest doing with a baby name book?" The ice cream rendered her tongue cold and heavy, the words came out in a lisp.

"Oh, the great lengths we go to for our flock." He sighed as he cracked the spine. "I ordered it online two days ago."

"So, how's this supposed to work?" She stabbed the frozen dessert with her spoon rather than look at the man. Growing up Catholic, she was at a serious disadvantage when it came to lying to priests. "You say my name, and I wait for the trumpets and angels singing?"

"Yes, definitely a comedian. Maybe it'll be that obvious, or maybe it will be more subtle, the desire to tilt your head toward me, or a pull in your heart." Joaquin licked his fingers and thumbed through the pages. "Or, maybe this is a huge waste of time and you'll feel nothing. In which case, you got a visitor and some free ice cream. Let's start at the beginning. Abigail." He glanced over the top of the book. "Abra, Ada, Adalyn, Adelaide, Adele..."

His accent, mixed with the melodic cadence of names, lulled her to the valley between being asleep and awake. Amanda had spent much of her days here, visiting the time in the desert, back when David and Josh were still alive.

Back when *she* was still alive in some sense.

"Adrianna, Adrienne, Agatha, Aggie..."

Faking amnesia had been an impulse lie. Not one she'd crafted and molded. Not like the falsehoods that'd spewed from Josh's mouth.

Lies so well-nurtured they thrived on more than the truth. Hers was a baby fib, born of the child-like need to stick her fingers in her ears and *la-la-la* everything they said to her.

Ranchers had found her caked in mud and bleeding. She'd stirred, so they knew she was alive, but when they tried to move her, she'd passed out in pain. Amanda didn't remember any of it; that was what Father Joaquin had told her on his first visit.

"Agnes, Ainsley, Aja, Alaina..."

When she'd finally woken up, the little Mexican hospital had hummed with jubilance. During her slumber, she'd managed to become the underdog, the long shot horse that everyone bet on. Somehow, she'd pulled ahead and crossed the finish line into consciousness. But what was her prize?

"Alecia, Aletha, Alexa, Alexandra..."

Time lost all meaning.

It didn't matter if it'd been three weeks or three months. Day after day was the same. Doctors and nurses came in, speaking to her in a language she barely understood. Staring at her with mournful eyes. Amanda could never tell if they were sad she was hurt or sad she was alive.

"Alexis, Alison, Alisha, Alissa…"

It was only when Joaquin showed up that she'd fully understood her situation. They knew she was American, but her injuries were so severe, they couldn't send her home. Not that she could tell them *where* home was. No ID, mixed with claiming no memory of who she was or where she came from, meant she'd stay with them until it was time for discharge or she got her memory back.

Why would she want her memory back? It was filled with nothing but loss, betrayal and heartbreak. Sure, Amanda had plenty of happy memories, but those were tucked so far away they were practically out of reach.

"Allegra, Ally, Alora, Amalie…"

The closer Joaquin got to her name, the more she wanted to take her broken body and run.

Her legs twitched, remembering her evening runs.

*Will I ever be able to run again?*

The ice cream churned in her stomach. A ringing in her ears grew louder, as if attempting to drown out the word that was coming.

"Amanda." The priest paused for a bite of ice cream.

Her name hung in the air. It floated over her, looking for a place it could sink in. A word she'd heard every day since she came into this world hadn't fallen on her ears in weeks.

Did she hear the trumpets? Were the angels singing?

Instead, a cold numbness chilled her through the thin hospital gown and scratchy blankets. It felt different than the other names he'd said to her. As if she was standing in a bedroom full of pink lace, rainbows and kittens while she wore a nose ring, mohawk and thick black eye makeup. The name was hers, but it didn't belong to her.

"Azabeth, Azul, Azure." He closed the book and held it in his lap.

Her new friend studied her, but she fought to avoid his stare.

Was he looking for any changes in her posture? Checking her face for tears?

Amanda scraped the bottom of her ice cream container before bringing it to her mouth and slurping the last of the chocolate from inside. Good manners be damned, it gave her a reason to avoid eye contact.

"So, that's the *A's*," he said. "Anything, *mija?*"

She shrugged. "The angels and trumpeters were silent." Were they going to go through the entire alphabet of names? What would happen the day he started on the M's? Would her heart shatter when he said Mandy?

Would the name David called her be too much to cover up?

Joaquin leaned toward her, resting his elbows on his knees and took her hand. His thumb gently caressed the tape holding down the needle poking into her skin. It was a much more intimate gesture than a priest should allow. "How are you? I mean really, no comebacks, no, what do you call it, snark."

On most days she existed, a living being that breathes. On other days, Amanda felt only physical pain, something that she'd built her tolerance to and didn't need to hit the button for pain meds.

It was on those rare days when the emotional hurt was so all-encompassing and everything was clouded black that she'd allow herself to waft into a blissful, drug-filled haze.

"Do you believe in Purgatory, Father?"

"Some in the Church do believe in it."

Amanda glanced at him from the corner of her eye. "I'm there, and I know I should fight to pull myself up, toward Heaven, but really at this point, I just want to let go and fall."

Joaquin squeezed her hand, firm enough to show disdain at her answer, but not so much to hurt. "If God thought you were done on Earth, you would've died in that river. But you didn't. I might not know what you are called, *mija*, but I know *you*. You're a fighter, a survivor. You're here for a higher calling."

"Please don't give me the '*part of His plan*' speech." Her words fought against the growing lump in her throat. She wasn't ready to cry, not in front of Father Joaquin when an accidental confession would be picked up in the debris of tears.

He smiled, transforming his face from serious handsome to relaxed, charismatic attractive.

How many *señoritas* cried when he'd gone to the Seminary?

"His plan was never to cause you hurt. Maybe to truly find your calling you have to shed your former life."

*Like a snake shedding its skin.*

Joaquin stood and planted a kiss on top of her head. "Rest up, *mija*. I'll be back soon and we'll start on the B's. We've got a lot of names to cover."

She kept her eyes focused on the opposite wall. After the door snapped shut and after his footsteps receded, Amanda allowed herself a deep gasping breath, as if surfacing from a long dive.

# ACKNOWLEDGMENTS

Writing a novel is a long road. Some parts of the journey can only be taken alone, but I've been fortunate to have many friends and family along for the ride. To my husband, Colby, thank you for always being patient and supportive. My parents for instilling the love of reading in me at an early age, and realizing those tall tales I came up with as a kid were just my budding storytelling skills. My sister Angie and brother-in-law Mike Madrid for their love and support. To Carol Barreyre, C.A. Szarek, Susan Sheehey, Chris Crawford, Ted Rork and Sarah Hamilton, my poor, beleaguered writing buddies, who had to suffer through eleventy billion versions before I got it right. And to Christine Broderson, who basically told me to get out of the way of the story. To Jayna Wallach for being psychic and always seeming to know when I need to hear a kind word. New Zealand awaits! To my awesome early readers - Gail Cooksey, Chris Blain and Misty Sunday. Thank you for giving me that boost of confidence when I needed it. And to you - all of you who shared a kind word or cheered me on as I tried to get this next part of Amanda's story right. For you I will be eternally grateful.

# ABOUT THE AUTHOR

Kimberly Packard is an award-winning author of women's fiction. She began visiting her spot on the shelves at libraries and bookstores at a young age, gazing between the Os and the Qs.

When she isn't writing, she can be found running, doing a poor imitation of yoga or curled up with a book. She resides in Texas with her husband Colby, a clever cat named Oliver and a yellow lab named Charlie.

Her debut novel, *Phoenix*, was awarded as Best General Fiction of 2013 by the Texas Association of Authors.

*For more information:*

www.kimberlypackard.com
kimberly@kimberlypackard.com

# ALSO BY KIMBERLY PACKARD

Phoenix | Phoenix Book 1

Prospera Pass | Phoenix Book 3

The Crazy Yates | A Christmas Novella

.

CPSIA information can be obtained
at www.ICGtesting.com
Printed in the USA
LVOW12s0910080118

562205LV00001B/135/P